BRET EASTON ELLIS

THE INFORMERS

Bret Easton Ellis is the author of *Less Than Zero*, *The Rules of Attraction* and *American Psycho*. He was born in 1964 and raised in Los Angeles. He is a graduate of Bennington College and lives in New York City and Richmond, Virginia.

Acclaim for BRET EASTON ELLIS's

THE INFORMERS

"*The Informers* cuts a more sweeping swath through *Less Than Zero*'s dazzling, decadent California lifestyle. . . . [It] is clearly the work of a wiser, more self-assured writer." —*Miami Herald*

"I can't think of Ellis without recalling Orwell and Jack Kerouac: social observers who used documentary realism in novels that cast a keen eye on the times in which they lived. The journalistic approaches of Orwell, Kerouac, and Ellis take wildly different forms, but their passages of real life are similar in effect. . . . Ellis's descriptive powers in defining time and place are precise and horrifying." —*Seattle Weekly*

"[With] a canny journalist's eye for detail and dialogue, Ellis' storytelling carries the complete lack of sentiment and empathy of a seasoned nihilistic novelist." —*Los Angeles Times*

"Sparkles with a disturbing mix of humor and ultraviolence." —*Detroit Free Press*

"A profoundly moral writer [with a] characteristically spare and hypnotic prose style which beats out these lives of quiet desperation with a slow pulse as gentle as it is compelling. . . . Ellis has been compared to Fitzgerald and here we see why." —*Modern Review*

"*The Informers* is full of morbid Gothic sensibility, sick jokes and outrageous detail . . . hilarious . . . ambitious. . . . It [has] sharp observations and impeccably controlled prose." —*Newsday*

"*The Informers* shows the work of a writer at the peak of his powers, deeply concerned with the moral decline of our society. The book takes us from the first to the seventh circles of hell, from Salinger to de Sade." —Will Self

THE INFORMERS

BRET EASTON ELLIS

The Informers

Vintage Contemporaries

Vintage Books

A Division of Random House, Inc.

New York

FIRST VINTAGE CONTEMPORARIES EDITION, AUGUST 1995

The Library of Congress has cataloged the Knopf edition
as follows:
  Ellis, Bret Easton.
  The informers / Bret Easton Ellis.—1st ed.
  p. cm.
  ISBN 0-679-43587-5
  I. Title.
  PS3555.L5937I54 1994
  813'.54—dc20
  94-4012
  CIP
  Vintage ISBN: 679-74324-3

Design by Peter A. Andersen
Author photograph © Quintana Roo Dunne

Manufactured in the United States of America
10 9 8 7 6 5 4 3 2 1

One night I was sitting on the bed in my hotel room on Bunker Hill, down in the middle of Los Angeles. It was an important night in my life, because I had to make a decision about the hotel. Either I paid up or I got out: that was what the note said, the note the landlady had put under my door. A great problem, deserving acute attention. I solved it by turning out the lights and going to bed.

JOHN FANTE
Ask the Dust

CONTENTS

THE INFORMERS

1

BRUCE CALLS FROM MULHOLLAND

Bruce calls, stoned and sunburned, from Los Angeles and tells me that he's sorry. He tells me he's sorry for not being here, at campus with me. He tells me that I was right, that he should have flown to the workshop this summer, and he tells me that he's sorry he's not in New Hampshire and that he's sorry he hasn't called me in a week and I ask him what he's doing in Los Angeles and don't mention that it has been two months.

Bruce tells me that things went bad ever since Robert left the apartment they were sharing on Fifty-sixth and Park and went on a white-water-rafting trip with his stepfather down the Colorado River, leaving his girlfriend, Lauren, who also lives in the apartment on Fifty-sixth and Park, and Bruce alone, together, for four weeks. I have never met Lauren but I know what kind of girl Robert is attracted to and I can picture what she must look like clearly in my mind and then I'm thinking of the girls who are attracted to Robert, beautiful and pretending to ignore the fact that Robert, at twenty-two, is worth about three hundred million dollars, and I picture this girl, Lauren, lying on Robert's futon, head thrown back, Bruce moving slowly on top of her, his eyes shut tightly.

* * *

Bruce tells me that the affair started a week after Robert left. Bruce and Lauren had gone to Café Central and after they sent back the food and decided just to have drinks, they agreed it would be sex only. It would happen only because Robert had gone out West. They told each other that there really was no mutual attraction beyond the physical and then they went back to Robert's apartment and went to bed. This went on, Bruce tells me, for one week, until Lauren started dating a twenty-three-year-old real estate tycoon who is worth about two billion dollars.

Bruce tells me that he was not upset by that. But he was "slightly bothered" the weekend Lauren's brother, Marshall, who just graduated from RISD, came down and stayed at Robert's apartment on Fifty-sixth and Park. Bruce tells me that the affair between him and Marshall lasted longer simply because Marshall stayed longer. Marshall stayed a week and a half. And then Marshall went back to his ex-boyfriend's loft in SoHo when his ex-boyfriend, a young art dealer who is worth about two to three million, said he wanted Marshall to paint three functionless columns in the loft they used to share on Grand Street. Marshall is worth about four thousand dollars and some change.

This was during the period that Lauren moved all of her furniture (and some of Robert's) to the twenty-three-year-old real estate tycoon's place at the Trump Tower. It was also during this period that Robert's two expensive Egyptian lizards apparently ate some poisoned cockroaches and were found dead, one under the couch in the living room, its tail missing, the other sprawled across Robert's Betamax—the big one cost five thousand dollars, the smaller one was a gift. But since Robert is somewhere in the Grand Canyon there is no way to get in touch with him. Bruce tells me that this is why he left the apartment on Fifty-sixth and Park and went to Reynolds' house, in Los Angeles, on top of Mulholland, while Reynolds, who is worth, according to Bruce, a couple of falafels at PitaHut and no beverage, is in Las Cruces.

Lighting a joint, Bruce asks me what I have been doing, what has been happening here, that he's sorry again. I tell him about readings, receptions, that Sam slept with an editor from the *Paris Review* who came up from New York on Publishers' Weekend, that Madison shaved her head and Cloris thought she was having chemotherapy and sent all her stories to editors she knew at *Esquire, The New Yorker, Harper's,* and that it just made everyone very blah. Bruce tells me to tell Craig that he wants his guitar case back. He asks if I'm going to East Hampton to see my parents. I tell him that since the workshop is just about over and it's almost September, I don't see the point.

Last summer Bruce stayed with me at Camden and we took the workshop together and it was the summer Bruce and I would swim in Lake Parrin at night and the summer he wrote the lyrics to the theme song from "Petticoat Junction" all over my door because I would laugh whenever he sang the song not because the song was funny—it was just the way he sang it: face stern yet utterly blank. That was the summer we went to Saratoga and saw the Cars and, later that August, Bryan Metro. The summer was drunk and night and warm and the lake. An image I never saw: my cold hands running over his smooth, wet back.

* * *

Bruce tells me to touch myself, right now, in the phone booth. The house I'm in is silent. I wave away a mosquito. "I can't touch myself," I say. I slowly sink to the floor still holding the phone.

"Being rich is cool," Bruce says.

"Bruce," I'm saying. "Bruce."

He asks me about last summer. He mentions Saratoga, the lake, a night I don't remember at a bar in Pittsfield.

I don't say anything.

"Can you hear me?" he's asking.

"Yeah," I whisper.

"Is, like, the connection clear?" he asks.

I'm staring at a drawing: a cup of cappuccino overloaded with foam and beneath that two words scrawled in black: *the future*.

"Mellow out," Bruce sighs, finally.

After we hang up I walk back to my room and change. Reynolds picks me up at seven and as we drive to a small Chinese restaurant on the outskirts of Camden, he turns the radio down after I say Bruce called and Reynolds asks, "Did you tell him?" I don't say anything. I found out over lunch today that Reynolds is currently involved with a townie named Brandy. All I can think about is Robert on a raft, still somewhere in Arizona, looking at a small photograph of Lauren but probably not. Reynolds turns the radio up after I shake my head. I stare out the window. It's the end of summer, 1982.

2

AT THE STILL POINT

"It's been a year," Raymond says. "Exactly."

I have been hoping that no one was going to mention it but I knew as the evening went on that someone would say something. I just didn't think it was going to be Raymond. The four of us are at Mario's, a small Italian restaurant in Westwood Village, and it's a Thursday and late in August. Even though school doesn't start until early October everyone can tell that summer is ending, has ended. There is really not a lot to do. A party in Bel Air that no one expresses too much interest in going to. No concerts. None of us has a date. In fact, except for Raymond, I don't think any of us sees anyone. So the four of us—Raymond, Graham, Dirk and myself—decide to go out to dinner. I don't even realize that it has been a year "exactly" until I'm in the parking lot next door to the restaurant and almost hit a tumbleweed that blows in front of me too quickly. I park and sit in my car, realizing what the date is, and I walk very slowly, very carefully, to the door of the restaurant and pause a minute before I go in, staring at a menu encased in glass. I am the last to arrive. No one is saying a whole lot to anyone else. I try to keep what little conversation there is on other topics: new Fixx video, Vanessa Williams, how much *Ghostbusters* is grossing, maybe what classes we're going to take, making plans for surfing maybe the next day. Dirk resorts to telling bad jokes we all know and don't think are funny. We order. The waiter leaves. Raymond speaks.

"It's been a year. Exactly," Raymond says.

"Since what?" Dirk asks uninterestedly.

Graham looks over at me, then down.

No one says anything, not even Raymond, for a long time.

"You know," he finally says.

"No," Dirk says. "I don't."

"Yeah, you do," Graham and Raymond say at the same time.

"No, I really don't," Dirk says.

"Come on, Raymond," I say.

"No, not 'come on, Raymond.' What about 'come on, Dirk'?" Raymond says, looking at Dirk, who isn't looking at any of us. He just sits there staring at a glass of water, which has a lot of ice in it.

"Don't be a jerk," he says softly.

Raymond sits back, looking satisfied in a sad sort of way. Graham looks over at me again. I look away.

"It hasn't seemed that long," Raymond murmurs. "Has it, Tim?"

"Come on, Raymond," I say again.

"Since *what*?" Dirk says, finally looking at Raymond.

"You know," Raymond says. "You know, Dirk."

"No, I don't," Dirk says. "Why don't you just tell us. Just say it."

"I don't have to say it," Raymond mutters.

"You guys are being total dicks," Graham says, playing with a bread stick. He offers it to Dirk, who waves it away.

"No, come on, Raymond," Dirk says. "You brought this up. Now say it, pussy."

"Tell them to shut up or something," Graham says to me.

"You know," Raymond says weakly.

"Shut up," I sigh.

"Say it, Raymond," Dirk dares.

"Since Jamie . . ." Raymond's voice breaks. He grits his teeth, then turns away from us.

"Since Jamie what?" Dirk asks, his voice rising, getting higher. "Since Jamie what, Raymond?"

"You guys are being total dicks." Graham laughs. "Why don't you just shut up or something."

Raymond whispers something that none of us can hear.

"What?" Dirk asks. "What did you say?"

"Since Jamie died," Raymond finally admits, mumbling.

For some reason this shuts Dirk up and he sits back, smiling, as the waiter places food on the table. I don't want garbanzo beans in my salad and I had warned the waiter about this when we ordered but it seems inappropriate to say anything. The waiter places a plate of mozzarella marinara in front of Raymond. Raymond stares at it. The waiter leaves, returns with our drinks. Raymond keeps staring at his mozzarella marinara. The waiter asks if everything is all right. Graham is the only one of us who nods.

"He always ordered this," Raymond says.

"For Christ sakes, mellow out," Dirk says. "Then order something else. Order the abalone."

"The abalone is very good," the waiter says, before leaving. "So are the grapes."

"I can't believe you're acting this way," Raymond says.

"What way? That I'm not acting like you?" Dirk picks up his fork, then puts it back down for the third time.

Raymond says, "That you seem like you just don't give a shit."

"Maybe I don't. Jamie was a jerk. A nice guy but he was a jerk too, okay?" Dirk says. "It's all over. Don't fucking dwell on it."

"He was one of your best friends," Raymond says accusingly.

"He was a jerk and he was *not* one of my best friends," Dirk says, laughing.

"You were his best friend, Dirk," Raymond says. "Don't act now like you weren't."

"He mentioned me on his yearbook page—big deal." Dirk shrugs. "That's about it." Pause. "He was a little jerk."

"You don't care."

"That he's dead?" Dirk asks. "He's been dead a year, Raymond."

"I can't believe you don't give a shit is all."

"If giving a shit means sitting around here crying like some fag about it . . ." Dirk sighs, then says, "Look, Raymond. It was a long time ago."

"It's only been a year," Raymond says.

Things I remember about Jamie: getting high with him at an Oingo Boingo concert in eleventh grade. Drunk on the beach in Malibu at a party at an Iranian classmate's house. A lame trick he played on some frat guys from USC at a party in Palm Springs, which actually injured Tad Williams pretty badly. I don't remember the joke but I remember Raymond, Jamie and myself stumbling down one of the corridors of the Hilton Riviera, all three of us stoned, Christmas decorations, someone losing an eyeball, a fire truck arriving too late, a sign above a door that said "DO NOT ENTER." Doing okay coke on a yacht with him on prom night and him telling me that I was easily his best friend. Doing another line off a black enamel table, I had asked about Dirk, about Graham, Raymond, a couple of movie stars. Jamie said he liked Dirk and Graham and that he didn't like Raymond a whole lot. "Dude is bogus" were his exact words. Another line and he said that he understood me or something like that and I did another line and believed him because it is easier to move through the motions than not to.

* * *

One night late in August, on the way to Palm Springs, Jamie tried to light a joint and either lost control of the car because he was speeding or had a blowout and the BMW flew off the freeway and he was killed instantly. Dirk had been following him. They were going to spend the weekend before Labor Day at Jeffrey's parents' place in Rancho Mirage and they had left a party we had all been at in Studio City and it was Dirk who had pulled Jamie's crushed, bloody body from the car and who had waved down some guy who was on his way to Las Vegas to build a tennis court and the guy drove to the nearest hospital and an ambulance arrived seventy minutes later and Dirk had sat there in the desert staring at the dead body. Dirk never spoke about it a lot, just little details he gave us the week after it happened: the way the BMW tumbled, rolled across sand, a smashed cactus, how the upper part of Jamie's body burst through the windshield, the way Dirk pulled him out, laid him down, looked through Jamie's pockets for another joint. I have been tempted a lot of times to go out to where it happened and check it out but I don't go out to Palm Springs anymore because whenever I'm there I feel very wasted and it's a drag.

"I just can't believe you guys don't care," Raymond is saying.

"Raymond," Dirk and I say in unison.

"It's just that there's nothing we can do," I finish.

"Yeah." Dirk shrugs. "What can we do?"

"They're right, Raymond," Graham says. "Things are blurry."

"In fact I feel like a big smudge," Dirk says.

I look over at Raymond and then back at Dirk.

"He's dead and all but that doesn't mean he wasn't a jerk," Dirk says, pushing his plate away.

"He wasn't a jerk, Dirk," I tell him, suddenly laughing. "Jerk Dirk, Dirk jerk."

"What do you mean, Tim?" Dirk asks, looking straight at me. "After that shit he pulled with Carol Banks?"

"Oh Christ," Graham says.

"What shit did he pull with Carol Banks?" I ask, after a moment of silence. Carol and I had been seeing each other off and on throughout our junior and senior years. She went to Camden a week before Jamie died. I haven't spoken to her for a year. I don't think she even came back this summer.

"He was fucking her behind your back," Dirk says, and he gets pleasure out of telling me this.

"He screwed her ten, twelve times, Dirk," Graham says. "Don't make it seem like it was some hot affair or anything."

I had never really liked Carol Banks anyway. I lost my virginity to her a year before we actually started dating. Cute, blond, cheerleader, good SATs, nothing too great. Carol had always called me nonchalant, a word I never understood the meaning of, a word I looked up in a number of French dictionaries and could never find. I always suspected that Jamie and Carol had done something but since I never really liked Carol that much (only in bed and even there I was unsure) I sit at the table, uncaring, not moved by what everyone but me knew.

"You, like, all knew this?" I ask.

"You always told me you never really liked Carol," Graham says.

"But you all knew?" I ask again. "Raymond—did you know?"

Raymond squints for a moment, his eyes fixed on a point that he can't see, and he nods, doesn't say anything.

"So what, big deal, right?" Graham says more than asks.

"Are we gonna go to a movie or what?" Dirk asks, sighing.

"I can't believe you guys don't care," Raymond says loudly, suddenly.

"Do you wanna go to a movie?" Graham asks me.

"I can't believe you guys don't care," Raymond says again, softer.

"I was there, you asshole," Dirk says, grabbing Raymond's arm.

"Oh shit, this is so embarrassing," Graham says, shifting lower into his chair. "Shut up, Dirk."

"I was there," Dirk says, ignoring Graham, his hand still wrapped around Raymond's wrist. "I am the one who stayed and pulled him out of the fucking car. I'm the one who watched him fucking bleed to death out there. So don't give me any shit about how I don't care. Right, Raymond. I don't care."

Raymond has already started crying and pulls away from Dirk and gets up from the table, heading toward the back of the restaurant, to the men's room. What few people are left in the restaurant are now looking over at our table. Dirk's cool posing cracks a little. Graham looks somewhat anguished. I stare back at a young couple two tables away from us until they look away.

"Someone should go talk to him," I say.

"And say what?" Dirk asks. "And say fucking what?"

"Just, um, talk to him?" I shrug feebly.

"I'm not going to." Dirk crosses his arms and looks everywhere but at me or Graham.

I stand up.

Dirk says, "Jamie thought Raymond was an asshole. Do you understand? He fucking *loathed* him. He was friends with him just because we were, Tim."

After a beat, Graham says, "He's right, dude."

"I thought Jamie was killed instantly," I say, standing there.

"He was." Dirk shrugs. "What? Why?"

"You told Raymond he, um, bled to death."

"Christ—what's the difference? I mean, really," Dirk says. "Jesus, his parents had the fucking wake at Spago for Christ sakes. I mean, come on, guy."

"No, really, Dirk," I'm saying. "Why did you tell Raymond that?" Pause. "Is that the truth?"

Dirk looks up. "I hope it made him feel worse."

"Yeah?" I ask, trying not to grin.

Dirk stares at me hard, then stops, losing interest. "You never grasp anything, Tim. You look okay, but nothing works."

I leave the table and go to the men's room. The door is locked and above the sound of the toilet being flushed repeatedly I can hear Raymond's sobs. I knock. "Raymond—let me in."

The toilet stops flushing. I can hear him sniffling, then blowing his nose.

"I'll be okay," he calls back.

"Let me in." I'm twisting the knob. "Come on. Open the door."

The door opens. It's a small bathroom and Raymond is sitting on the toilet, the lid closed, beginning to cry again, his face and eyes red and wet. I am so surprised by Raymond's emotion that I lean against the door and just stare, watching him bunch his hands into fists.

"He was my friend," he says between intakes of breath, not looking up at me.

I'm looking at a yellowed tile on the wall for a long time, wondering how the waiter, who I am positive I had asked not to put garbanzo beans in my salad, actually had. Where was the waiter born, why had he come to Mario's, hadn't he looked at the salad, didn't he understand?

"He liked you . . . too," I say finally.

"He was my best friend." Raymond tries to stop crying by hitting the wall.

I try to lean down, pay attention and say "Uh-huh."

"Really, he was." Raymond keeps sobbing.

"Come on, get up," I say. "It'll be all right. We're going to the movies."

Raymond looks up and asks, "Will it?"

"Jamie really liked you too." I take Raymond by the arm. "He wouldn't want you to act like this."

"He really liked me," he says to himself or asks.

"Yeah, he really did." I can't help but smile when I say this.

Raymond coughs and takes some toilet paper and blows his nose, then he washes his face and says that he needs some pot.

We both go back to the table and try to eat a little but everything's cold, my salad already gone. Raymond orders a good bottle of wine and the waiter brings it, along with four glasses, and Raymond proposes a toast. And after the glasses are filled he urges us to lift them and Dirk looks at us like we're insane and refuses to, draining his glass before Raymond says something like "Here's to you, buddy, miss you a lot." I lift my glass, feeling stupid, and Raymond looks over at me, his face swollen, puffy, smiling, looking stoned, and at this still point, when Raymond raises his glass and Graham gets up to make a phone call, I remember Jamie so suddenly and with such clarity that it doesn't seem as if the car had flown off the highway in the desert that night. It almost seems as if the asshole is right here, with us, and that if I turn around he will be sitting there, his glass raised also, smirking, shaking his head and mouthing the word "fools."

I take a sip, cautiously at first, afraid the sip is sealing something.

"I'm sorry," Dirk says. "I just . . . can't."

3

THE UP ESCALATOR

I'm standing on the balcony of Martin's apartment in West-wood, holding a drink in one hand and a cigarette in the other, and Martin comes toward me, rushes at me, and with both hands pushes me off the balcony. Martin's apartment in Westwood is only two stories high and so the fall is not that long. As I'm falling I hope I will wake up before hitting the ground. I hit the asphalt, hard, and lying there, on my stomach, my neck twisted completely around, I look up and focus on Martin's handsome face staring down at me with a benign smile. It's the serenity in that smile—not the fall really or the imagined image of my cracked, bleeding body—that wakes me up.

I stare at the ceiling, then over at the digital alarm clock on the nightstand next to the bed, which tells me it is almost noon, and I uselessly hope that I have misread the time, shutting my eyes tightly, but when I open them again the clock still reads that it is almost noon. I raise my head slightly and look over at the small, flickering red numbers glowing from the Betamax and they tell me the same thing the hands on the melon-colored alarm clock do: almost noon. I try to fall back asleep but the Librium I took at dawn has worn off and my mouth feels thick and dry and I am thirsty. I get up, slowly, and walk into the bathroom and as I turn on the faucet I look into the mirror for a long time until I am forced to notice the new lines beginning around the eyes. I avert my gaze and concentrate on the cold water rushing out of the faucet and filling the cup my hands have made.

I open a mirrored cabinet and take out a bottle. I take its top off and count only four Libriums left. I pour one green-and-black capsule into my hand, staring at it, then place it carefully next to the sink and close the bottle and put it back into the medicine cabinet and take out another bottle and place two Valiums from it on the counter next to the green-and-black capsule. I put the bottle back and take out another. I open it, looking in cautiously. I notice there is not too much Thorazine left and I make a mental note to refill the prescription of Librium and Valium and I take a Librium and one of the two Valiums and turn the shower on.

I step into the big white-and-black tile shower stall and stand there. The water, cool at first, then warmer, hits me in the face hard and it weakens me and as I slowly drop to my knees, the black-and-green capsule somehow lodged in the back of my throat, I imagine, for an instant, that the water is a deep and cool aquamarine, and I'm parting my lips, tilting my head to get some water down my throat to help swallow the pill. When I open my eyes I start moaning when I see that the water coming down at me is not blue but clear and light and warm and making the skin on my breasts and stomach red.

After dressing I walk downstairs, and it distresses me to think of how long it takes to get ready for a day. At how many minutes pass as I wander listlessly through a large walk-in closet, at how long it seems to take to find the shoes I want, at the effort it takes to lift myself from the shower. You can forget this if you walk downstairs carefully, methodically, concentrating on each footstep. I reach the bottom landing and I can hear voices coming from the kitchen and I move toward them. From where I stand I can see my son and another boy standing in the kitchen looking for something to eat and the maid sitting at the large, wood-block table staring at photographs in yesterday's *Herald-Examiner,* her sandals kicked off, blue nail polish on her toenails. The stereo in the den is on and someone, a woman, is singing "I found a picture of you." I walk into the kitchen. Graham looks up from the refrigerator and says, unsmiling, "Up early?"

"Why aren't you at school?" I ask, trying to sound like I care, reaching past him into the refrigerator for a Tab.

"Seniors get out early on Mondays."

"Oh." I believe him but don't know why. I open the Tab and take a swallow. I have a feeling that the pill I took earlier is still lodged in my throat, stuck, melting. I take another swallow of Tab.

Graham reaches past me and pulls an orange out of the refrigerator. The other boy, tall and blond, like Graham, stands by the sink and stares out the window and into the pool. Graham and the other boy have their school uniforms on and they look very much alike: Graham peeling an orange, the other boy staring out into water. I'm having a hard time not finding either one of their stances unnerving, so I turn away, but the sight of the maid sitting at the table, sandals by her feet, the unmistakable smell of marijuana coming from the maid's purse and sweater, somehow seems worse and I take another swallow of the Tab, then pour the rest of it down the sink. I begin to leave the kitchen.

Graham turns to the boy. "Do you want to watch MTV?"

"I don't . . . think so," the boy says, staring into the pool.

I pick up my purse, which is sitting in an alcove next to the refrigerator, and make sure my wallet is in it because the last time I was in Robinson's it was not. I am about to walk out the door. The maid folds the paper. Graham takes off his burgundy letterman's sweater. The other boy wants to know if Graham has *Alien* on cassette. From the den the woman is singing "circumstance beyond our control." I find myself staring at my son, blond and tall and tan, with blank green eyes, opening the refrigerator, taking out another orange. He studies it, then lifts his head when he notices me standing by the door.

"Are you going somewhere?" he asks.

"Yes."

He waits for a moment and when I don't say anything he shrugs and turns away and begins to peel the orange and somewhere on the way to Le Dôme to meet Martin for lunch I realize that Graham is only one year younger than Martin and I have to pull the Jaguar over to a curb on Sunset and turn the volume down and unroll a window, then the sun-roof, and let the heat from today's sun warm the inside of the car, as I concentrate on a tumbleweed that the wind is pushing slowly across an empty boulevard.

Martin is sitting at the round bar in Le Dôme. He is wear-ing a suit and a tie and he is tapping his foot impatiently to the music that is playing through the restaurant's sound sys-tem. He watches me as I make my way over to him.

"You're late," he says, showing me the time on a gold Rolex.

"Yes. I am," I say, and then, "Let's sit down."

Martin looks at his watch and then at his empty glass and then back at me and I am clutching my purse tightly against my side. Martin sighs, then nods. The maître d' shows us to a table and we sit down and Martin starts to talk about his classes at UCLA and then about how his parents are irritating him, about how they came over to his apartment in Westwood unannounced, about how his stepfather wanted him to come to a dinner party he was throwing at Chasen's, about how Martin did not want to go to a dinner party his stepfather was throwing at Chasen's, about how tiredly words were ex-changed.

I'm looking out a window, at a Spanish valet standing in front of a Rolls-Royce, staring into it, muttering. When Martin begins to complain about his BMW and how much the insurance is, I interrupt.

"Why did you call the house?"

"I wanted to talk to you," he says. "I was going to cancel."

"Don't call the house."

"Why?" he asks. "There's someone there who cares?"

I light a cigarette.

He puts his fork down next to his plate and then looks away. "We're eating at Le Dôme," Martin says. "I mean, Jesus."

"Okay?" I ask.

"Yeah. Okay."

I ask for the check and pay it and follow Martin back to his apartment in Westwood where we have sex and I give Martin a pith helmet as a gift.

I am lying on a chaise longue by the pool. Issues of *Vogue* and *Los Angeles* magazine and the Calendar section from the *Times* are stacked next to where I am lying but I can't read them because the color of the pool takes my eyes away from the words and I stare longingly into thin aquamarine water. I want to go swimming but the heat of the sun has made the water too warm and Dr. Nova has warned about the dangers of taking Librium and swimming laps.

A poolboy is cleaning the pool. The poolboy is very young and tan and has blond hair and he is not wearing a shirt and he is wearing very tight white jeans and when he leans down to check the temperature of the water, muscles in his back ripple gently beneath smooth clean brown skin. The poolboy has brought a portable cassette player that sits by the edge of the Jacuzzi and someone is singing "Our love's in jeopardy" and I'm hoping the sound of palm fronds moving in warm wind will carry the music into the Suttons' yard. I'm intrigued by how deep the poolboy's concentration seems to be, at how gently the water moves when he skims a net across it, at how he empties the net, which catches leaves and multicolored dragonflies that seem to litter the water's gleaming surface. He opens a drain, the muscles in his arm flexing, lightly, only for a moment. And I keep watching, transfixed, as he reaches into the round hole and his arm begins to lift something out of the hole, muscles momentarily flexing again, and his hair is blond and windblown, streaked by sun, and I shift my body in the lounge chair, not moving my eyes.

The poolboy begins to raise his arm out of the drain and he lifts two large gray rags up and drops them, dripping, onto concrete and stares at them. He stares at the rags for a long time. And then he makes his way toward me. I panic for a moment, adjusting my sunglasses, reaching for tanning oil. The poolboy is walking toward me slowly and the sun is beating down and I'm spreading my legs and rubbing oil on the inside of my thighs and then across my legs, knees, ankles. He is standing over me. Valium, taken earlier, disorients everything, makes backgrounds move in wavy slow motion. A shadow covers my face and it allows me to look up at the poolboy and I can hear from the portable stereo "Our love's in jeopardy" and the poolboy opens his mouth, the lips full, the teeth white and clean and even, and I overwhelmingly need him to ask me to get into the white pickup truck parked at the bottom of the driveway and have him instruct me to go out to the desert with him. His hands, perfumed by chlorine, would rub oil over my back, across my stomach, my neck, and as he looks down at me with the rock music coming from the cassette deck and the palm trees shifting in a hot desert wind and the glare of the sun shining up off the surface of the blue water in the pool, I tense and wait for him to say something, anything, a sigh, a moan. I breathe in, stare up through my sunglasses, into the poolboy's eyes, trembling.

"You have two dead rats in your drain."

I don't say anything.

"Rats. Two dead ones. They got caught in the drain or maybe they fell in, who knows." He looks at me blankly.

"Why . . . are you . . . telling me this?" I ask.

He stands there, expecting me to say something else. I lower my sunglasses and look over at the gray bundles near the Jacuzzi.

"Take . . . them, away?" I manage to say, looking down.

"Yeah. Okay," the poolboy says, hands in his pockets. "I just don't know how they got trapped in there?"

The statement, really a question, is phrased in such a languid way that though it doesn't warrant an answer I tell him, "I guess . . . we'll never know?"

I am looking at the cover of an issue of *Los Angeles* magazine. A huge arc of water reaches for the sky, a fountain, blue and green and white, spraying upward.

"Rats are afraid of water," the poolboy is telling me.

"Yes," I say. "I've heard. I know."

The poolboy walks back to the two drowned rats and picks them up by their tails which should be pink but even from where I sit I can see are now pale blue and he puts them into what I thought was his toolbox and then to erase the notion of the poolboy keeping the rats I open the *Los Angeles* magazine and search for the article about the fountain on the cover.

I am sitting in a restaurant on Melrose with Anne and Eve and Faith. I am drinking my second Bloody Mary and Anne and Eve have had too many kirs and Faith orders what I believe to be a fourth vodka gimlet. I light a cigarette. Faith is talking about how her son, Dirk, had his driver's license revoked for speeding down Pacific Coast Highway, drunk. Faith is driving his Porsche now. I wonder if Faith knows that Dirk sells cocaine to tenth graders at Beverly Hills High. Graham told me this one afternoon last week in the kitchen even though I had asked for no information about Dirk. Faith's Audi is in the shop for the third time this year. She wants to sell it, yet she's confused about which kind of car to buy. Anne tells her that ever since the new engine replaced the old engine in the XJ6, it has been running well. Anne turns to me and asks me about my car, about William's. On the verge of weeping, I tell her that it is running smoothly.

Eve does not say too much. Her daughter is in a psychiatric hospital in Camarillo. Eve's daughter tried to kill herself with a gun by shooting herself in the stomach. I cannot understand why Eve's daughter did not shoot herself in the head. I cannot understand why she lay down on the floor of her mother's walk-in closet and pointed her stepfather's gun at her stomach. I try to imagine the sequence of events that afternoon leading up to the shooting. But Faith begins to talk about how her daughter's therapy is progressing. Sheila is an anorexic. My own daughter has met Sheila and may also be an anorexic.

Finally, an uneasy silence falls across the table in the restaurant on Melrose and I stare at Anne, who has forgotten to cover the outline of scars from the face-lift she had in Palm Springs three months ago by the same surgeon who did mine and William's. I consider telling them about the rats in the drain or the way the poolboy floated into my eyes before turning away but instead I light another cigarette and the sound of Anne's voice breaking the silence startles me and I burn a finger.

On Wednesday morning, after William gets out of bed and asks where the Valium is and after I stumble out of bed to retrieve it from my purse and after he reminds me that the family has reservations at Spago at eight and after I hear the wheels on the Mercedes screech out of the driveway and after Susan tells me that she is going to Westwood with Alana and Blair after school and will meet us at Spago and after I fall back asleep and dream of rats drowning, crawling desperately over each other in a steaming, bubbling Jacuzzi, and dozens of poolboys, nude, standing over the Jacuzzi, laughing, pointing at the drowning rats, their heads nodding in unison to the beat of the music coming from portable stereos they hold in golden arms, I wake up and walk downstairs and take a Tab out of the refrigerator and find twenty milligrams of Valium in a pillbox in another purse in the alcove by the refrigerator and take ten milligrams. From the kitchen I can hear the maid vacuuming in the living room and it moves me to get dressed and I drive to a Thrifty drugstore in Beverly Hills and walk toward the pharmacy, the empty bottle that used to be filled with black-and-green capsules clenched tightly in my fist. But the store is air conditioned and cool and the glare from the fluorescent lighting and the Muzak playing somewhere above me as background noise have a pronounced anesthetic effect and my grip on the brown plastic bottle relaxes, loosens.

At the counter I hand the empty bottle to the pharmacist. He puts glasses on and looks at the plastic container. I study my fingernails and uselessly try to remember the name of the song that is floating through the store's sound system.

"Miss?" the pharmacist begins awkwardly.

"Yes?" I lower my sunglasses.

"It says here 'no refills.' "

"What?" I ask, startled. "Where?"

The pharmacist points to two typed words at the bottom of the piece of paper taped to the bottle, next to my psychiatrist's name and, next to that, the date 10/10/83.

"I think Dr. Nova made some kind of . . . mistake," I say slowly, lamely, glancing at the bottle again.

"Well." The pharmacist sighs. "There's nothing I can do."

I look at my fingernails again and try to think of something to say, which, finally, is "But I . . . need it refilled."

"I'm sorry," the pharmacist says, clearly uncomfortable, shifting from one foot to the other nervously. He hands me the bottle and when I try to hand it back to him he shrugs.

"There are reasons why your doctor did not want the prescription refilled," he offers kindly, as if speaking to a child.

I try to laugh, wipe my face and gaily say, "Oh, he's always playing jokes on me."

I think about the way the pharmacist looked at me after I said this as I drive home, and I walk past the maid, the smell of marijuana drifting past me for an instant, and up in the bedroom I lock the door and close the shades and take off my clothes and put a movie in the Betamax and get into washed, cool sheets and cry for an hour and try to watch the movie and I take some more Valium and then I ransack the bathroom looking for an old prescription of Nembutal and then I rearrange my shoes in the closet and then I put another movie in the Betamax and then I open the windows and the smell of bougainvillea drifts through the partially closed shades and I smoke a cigarette and wash my face.

I call Martin.

"Hello?" another boy answers.

"Martin?" I ask anyway.

"Uh, no."

I pause. "Is Martin there?"

"Uh, let me check."

I can hear the phone being set down and I want to laugh at the idea of someone, some boy, probably tan, young, blond, like Martin, standing in Martin's apartment, putting the phone down and going to look for him, for anyone, in the small three-room studio but it does not seem that funny after a while. The boy comes back on the line.

"I think he's at the, um, beach." The boy doesn't seem too sure.

I say nothing.

"Would you like to leave a message?" he asks, slyly for some reason, and then, after a pause, "Wait a minute, is this Julie? The girl Mike and I met at 385 North? With the Rabbit?"

I don't say anything.

"You guys had about three grams on you and a white VW Rabbit."

I do not say anything.

"Like, hello?"

"No."

"You don't have a VW Rabbit?"

"I'll call back."

"Whatever."

I hang up, wondering who the boy is and if he knows about me and Martin, and I wonder if Martin is lying on the sand, drinking a beer, smoking a clove cigarette beneath a striped umbrella at the beach club, wearing Wayfarer sunglasses, his hair slicked back, staring out into where the land ends and merges with water, or if he instead is actually on his bed in his room, lying beneath a poster of the Go-Go's, studying for a chemistry exam and at the same time looking through the car advertisements for a new BMW. I'm sleeping until the tape in the Betamax ends and there's static.

I am sitting with my son and daughter at a table in a restaurant on Sunset. Susan is wearing a miniskirt that she bought at a store called Flip on Melrose, a store situated not too far from where I burned my finger at lunch with Eve and Faith and Anne. Susan is also wearing a white T-shirt with the words LOS ANGELES written on it in red handwriting that looks like blood that hasn't quite dried, dripping. Susan is also wearing an old Levi's jacket with a Stray Cats button pinned to one of the faded lapels and Wayfarer sunglasses. She takes the slice of lemon from her glass of water and chews on it, biting at the rind. I cannot even remember if we have ordered or not. I wonder what a Stray Cat is.

Graham is sitting next to Susan and I am fairly sure that he is stoned. He gazes out past the windows and into the headlights of passing cars. William is making a phone call to the studio. He is in the process of tying up a deal, which is not a bad thing. William has not been specific about the movie or the people in it or who is financing it. Through the trades I have heard rumors that it is a sequel to a very successful movie that came out during the summer of 1982, about a wisecracking Martian who looks like a big, sad grape. William has been to the phone in the back of the restaurant four times since we arrived and I have the feeling that William leaves the table and just stands in the back of the restaurant, because at the table next to ours is an actress who is sitting with a very young surfer and the actress keeps glaring at William whenever William is at the table and I know that the actress has slept with William and the actress knows I know and when our eyes meet for a moment, an accident, we both turn away abruptly.

Susan begins to hum some song to herself, as she drums her fingers on the table. Graham lights a cigarette, not caring if we say anything about it, and his eyes, red and half closed, water for a moment.

"There's this, like, funny sound in my car," Susan says. "I think I better take it in." She fingers the rim of her sunglasses.

"If it's making a funny noise, you should," I say.

"Well, like, I need it. I'm seeing the Psychedelic Furs at the

Civic on Friday and I totally have to take my car." Susan looks at Graham. "That's if Graham got my tickets."

"Yeah, I got your tickets," Graham says with what sounds like great effort. "And stop saying 'totally.'"

"Who did you get them from?" Susan asks, fingers drumming.

"Julian."

"Not Julian."

"Yeah. Why?" Graham tries to sound annoyed but seems tired.

"He's such a stoner. Probably got crappy seats. He's such a stoner," Susan says again. She stops drumming, looks at Graham straight on. "Just like you."

Graham nods his head slowly and does not say anything. Before I can ask him to dispute his sister, he says, "Yeah, just like me."

"He sells heroin," Susan says casually.

I glance over at the actress, whose hand is gripping the surfer's thigh while the surfer eats pizza.

"He's also a male prostitute," Susan adds.

A long pause. "Was that . . . statement directed at me?" I ask softly.

"That is, like, such a total lie," Graham manages to say. "Who told you that? That Valley bitch Sharon Wheeler?"

"Not quite. I know that the owner of the Seven Seas slept with him and now Julian has a free pass and all the coke he wants." Susan sighs mock-wearily. "Besides, it's just too ironic that they both have herpes."

This makes Graham laugh for some reason and he takes a drag off his cigarette and says, "Julian does not have herpes and he did not get them from the owner of the Seven Seas." Pause, exhale, then, "He got VD from Dominique Dentrel."

William sits down. "Christ, my own kids are talking about quaaludes and faggots—Jesus. Oh, take your goddamned sunglasses off, Susan. We're at Spago, not the goddamned beach club." William gulps down half of a white-wine spritzer, which I watched go flat twenty minutes ago. He glances over at the actress and then at me and says, "We're going to the Schrawtzes' party Friday night."

I am fingering my napkin, then I'm lighting a cigarette. "I don't want to go to the Schrawtzes' party Friday night," I say softly, exhaling.

William looks at me and lights a cigarette and says, just as softly, looking directly at me, "What do you want to do instead? Sleep? Lay out by the pool? Count your shoes?"

Graham looks down, giggling.

Susan sips her water, glances at the surfer.

After a while I ask Susan and Graham how school is.

Graham doesn't answer.

Susan says, "Okay. Belinda Laurel has herpes."

I'm wondering if Belinda Laurel got them from Julian or the owner of the Seven Seas. I am also having a hard time restraining myself from asking Susan what a Stray Cat is.

Graham speaks up, barely, says, "She got them from Vince Parker, whose parents bought him a 928 even though they know he is completely into animal tranquilizers."

"That is really . . ." Susan pauses, searches for the right word.

I close my eyes and think about the boy who answered the phone at Martin's apartment.

"Grody . . . ," Susan finishes.

Graham says, "Yeah, totally grody."

William looks over at the actress groping the surfer and, grimacing, says, "Jesus, you kids are sick. I've gotta make another call."

Graham, looking wary and hungover, stares out the windows and over at Tower Records across the street with a longing that surprises me and then I'm closing my eyes and thinking about the color of water, a lemon tree, a scar.

* * *

On Thursday morning my mother calls. The maid comes into my room at eleven and wakes me by saying, "Telephone, su madre, su madre, señora," and I say, "No estoy aquí, Rosa, no estoy aquí . . ." and drift back to sleep. After I wake up at one and wander out by the pool, smoking a cigarette and drinking a Perrier, the phone rings in the poolhouse and I realize that I will have to talk to my mother in order to get it over with. Rosa answers the phone so the phone stops ringing, which is my cue to move back up to the main house.

"Yes, it's me." My mother sounds lonely, irritated. "Were you out? I called earlier."

"Yes." I sigh. "Shopping."

"Oh." Pause. "For what?"

"Well, for . . . dogs," I say, then, "Shopping," and then, "for dogs," and then, "How do you feel?"

"How do you think?"

I sigh, lie back on the bed. "I don't know. The same?" and then, after a minute, "Don't cry," I'm saying. "Please. Please don't cry."

"It's all so useless. I still see Dr. Scott every day and there's the therapy and he keeps saying, 'It's coming along, it's coming along,' and I keep asking, 'What's coming along, what is coming along?' and then . . ." My mother stops, out of breath.

"Does he still have you on the Demerol?"

"Yes." She sighs. "I'm still on the Demerol."

"Well, this is . . . good."

My mother's voice breaks again. "I don't know if I can take this anymore. My skin, it's all . . . my skin . . ."

"Please."

". . . is yellow. It's all yellow."

I light a cigarette.

"Please." I close my eyes. "Everything is all right."

"Where are Graham and Susan?"

"They're at . . . school," I say, trying not to sound too doubtful.

"I would have liked to talk to them," she says. "I miss them sometimes, you know."

I put the cigarette out. "Yes. Well. They . . . miss you too, you know. Yes . . ."

"I know."

Trying to make a conversation, I ask, "So, what have you been doing with yourself?"

"I just got back from the clinic and I'm in the process of cleaning out the attic and I found those photographs we took that Christmas in New York. The ones I've been looking for. When you were twelve. When we stayed at the Carlyle."

For the past two weeks now my mother always seems to be cleaning out the attic and finding the same photographs from that Christmas in New York. I remember the Christmas vaguely. The hours that passed as she chose a dress for me on the day before Christmas, then brushing my hair in long, light strokes. A Christmas show at Radio City Music Hall and the candy cane I ate during the show, which resembled a thin, scared-looking Santa Claus. There was the night my father got drunk at the Plaza and the fight between my parents in the taxi on the way back to the Carlyle and later that night I could hear them arguing, the predictable sound of glass breaking in the room next to mine. A Christmas dinner at La Grenouille, where my father tried to kiss my mother and she turned away. But the thing I remember most, the thing I remember with a clarity that makes me cringe, is that there were no photographs taken on that trip.

"How's William?" my mother asks when she gets no reply from me about the pictures.

"What?" I ask, startled, slipping back into the conversation.

"William. Your husband," and then, with an edge, "My son-in-law. William."

"He's fine. Fine. He's fine." The actress at the table next to ours last night in Spago kissed the surfer on the mouth as he scraped caviar off a pizza, and when I got up to leave she smiled at me. My mother, her skin yellow, her body thin and frail from lack of food, is dying in a large, empty house that overlooks a bay in San Francisco. The poolboy has set traps smudged with peanut butter around the edges of the pool. Randomness, surrender.

"That's good."

Nothing is said for close to two minutes. I keep count and I can hear a clock ticking and the maid humming to herself while cleaning the windows in Susan's room down the hall, and I light another cigarette and hope that my mother will hang up soon. My mother finally clears her throat and says something.

"My hair is falling out."

I have to hang up.

The psychiatrist I see, Dr. Nova, is young and tan and drives a Peugeot and wears Giorgio Armani suits and has a house in Malibu and often complains about the service at Trumps. His practice lies off Wilshire and it's in a large white stucco complex across from Neiman Marcus and on the days I see him I usually park my car at Neiman Marcus and wander around the store until I buy something and then walk across the street. Today, high in his office on the tenth floor, Dr. Nova is telling me that at a party out in the Colony last night someone "tried to drown." I ask him if it was one of his patients. Dr. Nova says it was the wife of a rock star whose single has been number two on the *Billboard* charts for the past three weeks. He begins to tell me who else was at the party, when I have to interrupt him.

"I need the Librium refilled."

He lights a thin Italian cigarette and asks, "Why?"

"Don't ask me why." I yawn. "Just do it."

Dr. Nova exhales, then asks, "Why shouldn't I ask you?"

I'm looking out the window. "Because I asked you not to?" I say softly. "Because I pay you one hundred and thirty-five dollars an hour?"

Dr. Nova takes a drag from his cigarette, then looks out the window. After a while he asks, tiredly, "What are you thinking?"

I keep staring out the window, stupefied, transfixed by palm trees swaying in a hot wind highlighted against an orange sky and, below that, a billboard for Forest Lawn.

Dr. Nova is clearing his throat.

Slightly irritated, I say, "Just refill the prescription and . . ." I sigh. "All right?"

"I'm only looking out for your best interests."

I smile gratefully, incredulous. He looks at the smile weirdly, uncertain, not understanding where it comes from.

I spot Graham's small old Porsche on Wilshire Boulevard and follow him, surprised at how careful a driver he seems to be, at how he flashes his lights when he wants to change lanes, at how he slows and begins to brake at yellow lights and then comes to a complete stop at red lights, at how cautiously he seems to move the car across the road. I assume that Graham is driving home but when he passes Robertson I follow him.

Graham drives along Wilshire until he makes a right onto a side street after crossing Santa Monica. I pull into a Mobil station and watch as he pulls into the driveway of a large white apartment complex. He parks the Porsche behind a red Ferrari and gets out, looks around. I put on my sunglasses, roll up my window. Graham knocks on the door of one of the apartments facing the street and the boy who was over earlier in the week, in the kitchen, staring out into the pool, opens the door and Graham walks in and the door closes. Graham walks out of the house twenty minutes later with the boy, who is wearing only shorts, and they shake hands. Graham stumbles back to his car, dropping his keys. He stoops down to pick them up and after three tries finally grabs them. He gets into the Porsche, closes the door and looks down at his lap. Then he brings his finger to his mouth and tastes it, lightly. Satisfied, he looks back down at his lap, puts something in the glove compartment and pulls out from behind the red Ferrari and drives back onto Wilshire.

There is a sudden rapping on the passenger window and I look up, startled. A handsome gas station attendant asks me to move my car, and as I start the car up an image that I'm uneasy about the validity of comes into my line of vision: Graham at his sixth-birthday party, wearing gray shorts, an expensive tie-dyed shirt, penny loafers, blowing out all the candles on a Flintstones birthday cake and William brings a Big Wheel tricycle out of the trunk of a silver Cadillac and a photographer takes pictures of Graham riding the Big Wheel around the driveway, on the lawn and eventually into the pool. Driving onto Wilshire, I lose track of the memory, and when I get back home Graham's car is not there.

I am lying in bed in Martin's apartment in Westwood. Martin has turned on MTV and he is lip-synching to Prince and he has his sunglasses on and is nude and pretends to be playing the guitar. The air conditioner is on and I can almost hear its hum which I try to focus on instead of Martin who begins to dance in front of the bed, an unlit cigarette hanging from his mouth. I turn over on my side. Martin turns off the television sound and puts on an old Beach Boys album. He lights the cigarette. I pull the covers up over my body. Martin jumps on the bed, lies next to me, doing leg lifts. I can feel him raising his legs slowly up, then bringing them down again, even more slowly. He stops doing this and then looks at me. He reaches down below the covers and grins.

"Your legs are really smooth."

"I had them waxed."

"Awesome."

"I had to drink a small bottle of Absolut to endure the process."

Martin jumps up suddenly, straddling me, growling, imitating a tiger or a lion or actually just a very large cat. The Beach Boys are singing "Wouldn't It Be Nice." I take a drag off his cigarette and look up at Martin, who is very tan and strong and young, with blue eyes that are so vague and blank they are impossible not to fall into. On the television screen there is a piece of popcorn in black and white and beneath the popcorn are the words "Very Important."

"Were you at the beach yesterday?" I ask.

"No." He grins. "Why? Thought you saw me there?"

"No. Just wondered."

"I'm the tannest one in my family."

He has half an erection and he takes my hand and places it around the shaft, winking at me sarcastically. I take my hand from it and run my fingers up his stomach and chest and then touch his lips and he flinches.

"I wonder what your parents would think if they knew a friend of theirs was sleeping with their son," I murmur.

"You're not friends with my parents," Martin says, his grin faltering slightly.

"No, I only play tennis with your mother twice a week."

"Boy, I wonder who wins those matches." He rolls his eyes. "I don't want to talk about my mother." He tries to kiss me. I push him off and he lies there and touches himself and mumbles the lyrics to another Beach Boys song. I interrupt him.

"Do you know that I have a hairdresser named Lance and Lance is a homosexual? I believe you would use the term 'a total homosexual.' He wears makeup and jewelry and has a very bad, affected lisp and he is constantly telling me about his young boyfriends and he is just extremely effeminate. Anyway, I went to his salon today because I have to go to the Schrawtzes' party tonight and so I walk into the salon and I tell Lillian, the woman who takes the appointments down, that I have an appointment with Lance and Lillian said that Lance had to take the week off and I was very upset and I said, 'Well, no one told me about this,' and then, 'Where is he? On a cruise somewhere?' and Lillian looked at me and said, 'No, he's not on a cruise somewhere. His son died in a car accident near Las Vegas last night,' and I rescheduled my appointment and walked out of the salon." I look over at Martin. "Don't you find that remarkable?"

Martin is looking up at the ceiling and then he looks over at me and says, "Yeah, totally remarkable." He gets up off the bed.

"Where are you going?" I ask.

He pulls on his underwear. "I have a class at four."

"One you actually go to?"

Martin zips up faded jeans and throws on a Polo pullover and slips his Top-Siders on and as I sit on the edge of the bed, brushing my hair, he sits next to me and with a boyish smile spread wide across his face asks, "Baby, could I please borrow sixty bucks? I gotta pay this guy for these Billy Idol tickets and I forgot to go to the Instateller and it's just really a hassle. . . ." His voice trails off.

"Yeah." I reach into my purse and hand Martin four twenties and he kisses my neck and says perfunctorily, "Thanks, baby, I'll pay you back."

"Yes, you will. Don't call me baby."

"You can let yourself out," he calls as he opens the door.

*　*　*

The Jaguar breaks down on Wilshire. I am driving and the sunroof is open and the radio is on and suddenly the car jerks and begins to pull to the right. I step on the gas pedal and press it to the floor and the car jerks again and pulls to the right. I park the car, crookedly, next to the curb, near the corner of Wilshire and La Cienega, and after a couple of minutes of trying to start it again I pull the keys out of the ignition and sit in the stalled Jaguar on Wilshire with the sunroof open and listen to traffic passing. I finally get out of the car and find a phone booth at the Mobil station on the corner of La Cienega and I call Martin, but another voice, this time a girl's, answers and tells me that Martin is at the beach and I hang up and call the studio but I am told by an assistant that William is at the Polo Lounge with the director of his next film and even though I know the number of the Polo Lounge I don't call. I try the house but Graham and Susan are not there either and the maid doesn't even seem to recognize my voice when I ask her where they are and I hang the phone up before Rosa can say anything else. I stand in the phone booth for close to twenty minutes and think about Martin pushing me off the balcony of his apartment in Westwood. I finally leave the phone booth and I have someone at the gas station call the auto club and they arrive and tow the Jaguar to a Jaguar dealership on Santa Monica where I have a humbling conversation with a Persian named Normandie and they drive me back to my house where I lie on the bed and try to sleep but William comes home and wakes me up and I tell him what happened and he mutters "Typical" and says that we have a party to go to and that things will be bad if I don't start getting ready.

I am brushing my hair. William is standing at the sink, shaving. He has only a pair of white slacks on, unzipped. I am wearing a skirt and a bra and I stop brushing my hair and put on a blouse and then resume brushing my hair. William washes his face, then towels it dry.

"I got a call at the studio yesterday," he says. "A very interesting call." Pause. "It was from your mother, which is a strange thing. First of all because your mother has never called the studio before and second of all because your mother doesn't particularly like me."

"That's not true," I say, then burst out laughing.

"You know what she told me?"

I don't say anything.

"Oh come on, guess," he says, smiling. "Can't you guess?"

I do not say anything.

"She told me that you hung up on her." William pauses. "Could this be true?"

"What if it could?" I put the brush down and put more lipstick on but my hands are shaking and I stop trying and then I pick up the brush and begin brushing my hair again. Finally, I look up at William, who is staring at me in the mirror across from mine, and say, simply, "Yes."

William walks to the closet and picks out a shirt. "I really thought you hadn't. I thought maybe the Demerol was getting to her or something," he says dryly. I start to brush my hair in fast short strokes.

"Why?" he asks, curious.

"I don't know," I say. "I don't think I can talk about that."

"You hung up on your own fucking mother?" He laughs.

"Yes." I put the brush down. "Why are you concerned?" I ask, suddenly depressed by the fact that the Jaguar might be in the shop for close to a week. William just stands there.

"Don't you love your mother?" he asks, zipping his pants, then buckling a Gucci belt. "I mean, my God, she's dying of cancer for Christ sakes."

"I'm tired. Please. William. Don't," I say.

"What about me?" he asks.

He moves to the closet again and finds a jacket.

"No. I don't think so." These words come out clearly and I shrug. "Not anymore."

"What about your goddamned children?" He sighs.

"Our goddamned children."

"Our goddamned children. Don't be so boring."

"I don't think so," I say. "I'm . . . undecided."

"Why not?" he asks, sitting on the bed, slipping on loafers.

"Because I . . ." I look over at William. "I don't know . . . them."

"Come on, baby, that's a cop-out," he says derisively. "I thought you were the one who said strangers are easy to like."

"No," I say. "You were and it was in reference to fucking."

"Well, since you don't seem to be too attached to anyone you're not fucking, I'd think we'd be in accord on that score." He knots a tie.

"I'm shaking," I say, confused by William's last comment, wondering if I missed a phrase, part of a sentence.

"Oh Christ, I need a shot," he says. "Could you get the syringe—the insulin's over there." He points, removes the jacket, unbuttons his shirt.

As I fill a plastic syringe with insulin, I have to fight off the impulse to fill it with air and then plunge it into a vein and watch his face contort, his body fall to the floor. He bares his upper arm. I stick the needle in and I say, "You fucker," and William looks at the floor and says, "I don't want to talk anymore," and we finish dressing, in silence, then leave for the party.

And driving on Sunset with William at the wheel, a glass of vodka nestled between his legs and the top down and a warm wind blowing and an orange sun setting in the distance, I touch his hand on the wheel and he moves it to lift the glass of vodka to his mouth and as I turn away and we pass West-wood, up, above it, I can actually see Martin's apartment flash by.

After we drive up through the hills and find the house and after William gives the car to the valet and before we walk toward the front entrance, with a crowded bank of photographers lined up behind a rope, William tells me to smile.

"Smile," he hisses. "Or at least try to. I don't want another picture like that last one in the *Hollywood Reporter,* where you just stared off somewhere else with this moronic gaze on your face."

"I'm tired, William. I'm tired of you. I'm tired of these parties. I'm tired."

"The tone of your voice could have fooled me," he says, taking my arm roughly. "Just smile, okay? Just until we get past the photographers, then I don't give a fuck what you do."

"You . . . are . . . awful," I say.

"You're not much better," he says, pulling me along.

William talks to an actor who has a new movie opening next week and we are standing next to a pool and there is a very young tan boy with the actor and he's not listening to the conversation. He stares into the pool, his hands in his pockets. A warm black wind comes down through the canyons and the blond boy's hair stays perfectly still. From where I'm standing I can see the billboards, tiny lit rectangles, on Sunset, illuminated by neon streetlights. I sip my drink and look back at the boy, who is still staring into the lit water. There is a band playing and the soft, lilting music and the light coming from the pool, tendrils of steam rising from it, and the beautiful blond boy and the yellow-and-white-striped tents that stand on a long, spacious lawn and the warm winds cooling and the palm trees, the moon outlining their fronds, act as an anesthetic. William and the actor are talking about the rock star's wife who tried to drown herself in Malibu and the blond boy I'm staring at turns his head away from the pool and finally begins to listen.

4

IN THE ISLANDS

I am watching my son through a mirrored window from the fifth floor of the office building I own. He is standing in line with someone to see *Terms of Endearment* which is playing across the plaza from where I work. He keeps looking up at the window I am standing behind. I'm on the phone with Lynch and he's talking about the finalities of a deal we worked on last week in New York even though I'm not listening to him. I stare through the glass, relieved that Tim can't see me, that we can't share a wave. He and his friend just stand there waiting for the line to be let in. His friend—I think his name is Sam or Graham or something—looks a lot like Tim: tall and blond and tan, both wearing faded jeans and red USC sweatshirts. Tim raises his eyes to the window again. I put my hand up to surprisingly cool glass and hold it there. Lynch says that since it's Thanksgiving maybe I would like to join O'Brien, Davies and him down in Las Cruces and do some fishing this weekend. I tell Lynch that I'm taking Tim to Hawaii for four days. Graham whispers something in Tim's ear and Graham's movement and subsequent grin seem almost lascivious to me and the idea that they are sleeping together passes and Lynch says maybe he'll talk to me after I get back from Hawaii. I hang up, taking my hand off the window. Tim lights a cigarette and looks up at my window again. I stand there, staring down at him, wishing he wouldn't smoke. Kay calls from her desk,

"Les? Fitzhugh's on line three," and I tell her I'm not here and I stand at the window until the line goes in and Tim disappears through the lobby doors and when I leave the office early, around four, and I'm in the underground parking garage, I lean against a silver Ferrari and loosen my tie, my hands trembling with the effort it takes to unlock the car's door, and then I'm driving away from Century City.

I have repacked the one major piece of luggage I'm taking many times, uncertain of what to bring even though I have been to the Mauna Kea often, but tonight, right now, I'm having trouble. I should have something to eat—it's after nine—but I'm not too hungry due to Valium I took earlier this evening. In the kitchen I find a box of Triscuits and tiredly eat three. The phone rings while I'm rearranging the suitcase, refolding a couple of dress shirts.

"Tim doesn't want to go," Elena says.

"What do you mean, Tim doesn't want to go?" I ask.

"He doesn't want to go, Les."

"Let me talk to him," I ask.

"He's not here."

"Let me talk to him, Elena," I say, relieved.

"He's not here."

"I've made reservations. You know how goddamned hard it is to get reservations at the fucking Mauna Kea during Thanksgiving?"

"Yes. I do."

"He's going, Elena, whether he wants to or not."

"Oh, Les, for God's sake—"

"Why doesn't he want to go?" I ask.

Elena pauses. "He just doesn't think he'll have a good time."

"He doesn't want to go because he doesn't like me."

"Oh damn it, Les, stop feeling sorry for yourself," she says, bored. "That's . . . not true."

"Then what is it?"

"It's just that—"

"It's just *what*? It's just *what*, Elena?"

"It's just that . . . he's probably uncomfortable about . . ." Elena phrases the rest of this sentence carefully: "the two of you going away together, since you've never been away together. Alone."

"I want to take my son to Hawaii for a couple of days, without his sisters, without his mother," I say, then, "Jesus, Elena, we never see each other."

"I understand that, Les, but he's nineteen, for God's sake," she says. "If he doesn't want to go with you I can't force him—"

"He doesn't want to go because he doesn't like me," I say loudly, cutting her off. "You know that. I know that. And I know damn well he put you up to this call."

"If you really think this, then why are you taking him anyway?" Elena asks. "Do you think three days are going to change anything?"

I refold another shirt and put it back in the suitcase, then I sit on the bed, hard.

"I hate to be put in the middle like this," she finally says, admits.

"Damn it," I scream. "He shouldn't put you there."

"Don't yell."

"I don't give a shit. I'm picking him up tomorrow at ten-thirty whether the little bastard wants to go or not."

"Les, don't yell."

"Well, it pisses me off."

"I don't"—she stammers—"I don't want to do this now. I'm getting off. I hate to be put in the middle."

"Elena," I warn. "You tell him he's going. I know he's there. You tell him he's going."

"Les, what are you going to do if he really decides not to go?" she asks. "Kill him?"

In the background, in their house, in her bedroom, a door slams. I hear Elena sigh, heavily. "I don't want to do this. I don't want to be put in the middle. Do you want to talk to the girls?"

"No," I mutter.

I hang up the phone, then walk out onto the balcony of the penthouse with the box of Triscuits and stand next to an orange tree. Cars move along a freeway, one line of red, another moving strip of white, and after the anger brushes past, I'm left with a feeling of caring that seems strangely, hopelessly artificial. I call Lynch to tell him that I'll join him and O'Brien and Davies in Las Cruces but Lynch's girlfriend answers and I hang up.

The limousine picks me up from my office in Century City at ten o'clock. The chauffeur, Chuck, puts my two bags in the trunk after opening the door for me. On the way to Encino to pick up Tim, I pour myself a Stoli, straight, on the rocks and am embarrassed by how quickly I drink it. I pour myself another half glass with a lot of ice and slip a Sondheim tape into the stereo and then I sit back and look out the tinted windows of the limousine as it crawls up through Beverly Glen toward the house in Encino where Tim stays while off from school at USC.

The limousine pulls up in front of the large stone house and I spot Tim's black Porsche, which I bought him for barely graduating from Buckley, sitting by the garage. Tim opens the front door of the house, followed by Elena, who waves uncertainly at the darkened windows of the limo and then walks hurriedly back into the house and closes the door.

Tim, wearing a plaid sports jacket, jeans and a white Polo shirt, holding two pieces of luggage, walks up to Chuck, who takes the suitcases and opens the door for him. Tim smiles nervously as he gets in.

"Hey," he says.

"Hi, Tim, how ya doin'?" I ask, slapping his knee.

He jerks, keeps smiling, looking tired, trying not to look tired, which makes him look even more tired.

"Um, good, I'm fine." He stops for a moment, then asks, somewhat clumsily, "Um, how are, um, you?"

"Oh, I'm okay." I'm smelling something strange, almost herbal, coming off his jacket and I picture Tim in his room, sitting on his bed, this morning, smoking marijuana from a pipe, gathering blind courage. I hope he has not brought any with him.

"This is . . . great," he says, looking around the limousine.

I don't know what to say so I ask him if he wants a drink.

"No, that's all right," he says.

"Aw come on, have a drink." I'm pouring myself another vodka on the rocks.

"It's okay," he says, this time less steadily.

"I'll pour you one anyway."

Without asking him what he wants I pour him a Stoli on the rocks. "Thanks," he says, taking the glass, sipping from it cautiously as if it were poisoned.

I turn the stereo up and sit back and put my feet on the seat across from me.

"Sooo, what are you up to?" I ask.

"Not too much."

"Yeah?"

"Um, when does the plane leave?"

"Twelve sharp," I say casually.

"Oh," he says.

"How's the Porsche running?" I ask after a while.

"Um, good. It's running good," he offers, shrugging.

"That's good."

"How's . . . the Ferrari?"

"Good, though you know, jeez, Tim, it seems like kind of a waste having it in the city," I say, shaking my glass, rattling the ice. "I can't drive it that fast."

"Yeah." He considers this, nodding.

The limousine pulls onto the freeway and begins to pick up speed. The Sondheim tape ends.

"Do you wanna hear something?" I ask.

"What is it?" he asks nervously.

"No. Do you want to play some music?"

"Oh." He thinks about this, flustered. "Um, no. Whatever you want to, um, hear is fine."

I know he wants to hear something so I turn on the radio and find a hard-rock station.

"Wanna hear this?" I ask, smiling, turning the volume up.

"Whatever," he says, looking out the window. "Sure."

I do not like this music at all and it takes a lot of effort and another glass of vodka not to put in the Sondheim tape. The vodka is not working as I hoped.

"Who is this?" I ask, gesturing toward the radio.

"Um, I think it's Devo," Tim says.

"Who?" I heard him.

"A group called Devo."

"Devo?"

"Yeah."

"Devo."

"Right," he says, looking at me like I'm some kind of idiot.

"Okay." I sit back. "I just wanna get that straight."

Devo ends. A new song comes on that's even more annoying.

"Who is this?" I ask.

He looks at me, puts his sunglasses on and says, "Missing Persons."

"Missing Persons?" I ask.

"Yeah." He laughs a little.

I nod and roll down a tinted window.

Tim sips his drink and then brings it back to his lap.

"Were you in Century City yesterday?" I ask him.

"No. I wasn't," he says evenly, without emotion.

"Oh," I say, finishing my drink.

Finally, the song by Missing Persons ends. The DJ comes on, makes a joke, droning about free tickets to a New Year's Eve concert that will be held in Anaheim.

"Did you bring your racket?" I ask, knowing that he did, having seen Chuck place it in the trunk.

"Yeah. I brought my racket," Tim says, bringing the glass to his mouth, pretending to drink.

Once on the plane, in first class, me on the aisle, Tim by the window, I'm a little less tense. I drink some champagne, Tim has a glass of orange juice. He puts his Walkman on, reads a *GQ* he bought at the airport. I begin to read the copy of James Michener's *Hawaii* that I bring to the Mauna Kea whenever I go and I set my headset to "Hawaiian Medley" and listen to Don Ho sing "Tiny Bubbles" again and again and again as we fly toward the islands.

After lunch I ask the stewardess for a deck of cards and Tim and I play a few hands of gin and I win all four games. He stares out the window until the movie starts. He watches the movie and I read *Hawaii* and drink rum and Coke and after the movie Tim flips through the *GQ*, looks out the window at the expanse of sea below us. I get up and walk a little drunkenly upstairs and wander around the lounge and take a Valium and walk back downstairs for the descent into Hilo and as we land Tim clutches the *GQ* tightly until it's permanently curled and the plane pulls up to the gate.

* * *

When we get off the plane, a pretty, sweet-faced Hawaiian girl puts purple leis around our necks and we meet the chauffeur at the gate and he gets our luggage and we sit in the limousine, not saying a lot, barely even looking at each other, and as we drive through the humid midafternoon along the coast, Tim fiddles with the radio and can only get a local station from Hilo playing old sixties songs. I look over at Tim as Mary Wells begins to sing "My Guy" and he just sits there, the purple frangipani lei already starting to brown, hanging limply around his neck, his blank eyes staring sadly out the tinted windows, looking over the sweeps of green land, the *GQ* still clutched in his hands, and I ask myself if this is the right thing to do. Tim glances over at me and I avert my gaze and an imagined sense of imposed peace washes calmly over the two of us, answering my question.

Tim and I are sitting in the main dining room at the Mauna Kea. The dining room has one wall that is open and I can hear the far-off sounds of waves breaking along the beach. A breeze enters the darkened room, the flame of the candle at our table flickering for a moment. The wind chimes hanging from beams below the ceiling whisper softly. The young Hawaiian boy at the piano on a small, semilit stage next to the dance floor plays "Mack the Knife" while two elderly couples dance awkwardly in the darkness. Tim tries, inconspicuously, to light a cigarette. A woman's laughter drifts through the large dining room, leaving me, for some reason, clueless.

"Oh, Tim, don't smoke," I say, sipping my second Mai Tai. "We're in Hawaii for Christ sakes."

Without saying a word or making any sign of protest, without even glancing at me, he puts the cigarette out in the ashtray, then folds his arms.

"Listen," I begin, then, stuck, pause.

Tim looks at me. "Uh-huh. Go on."

"Who"—my mind flops around, falls on something—"do you think is gonna win the Super Bowl this year?"

"I'm not too sure." He starts to bite his nails.

"You think the Raiders will make it?"

"Raiders have a chance." He shrugs, looks around the room.

"How's school?" I ask.

"It's great. School's great," he says, slowly losing his patience.

"How's Graham?" I ask.

"Graham?" He stares at me.

"Yeah. Graham."

"Who is Graham?"

"Don't you have a friend named Graham?"

"No. I don't."

"Oh. I thought you did." I take a large swallow of Mai Tai.

"Graham?" he asks, looking directly at me. "I don't know anybody named Graham."

I shrug this time, looking away. There are four fags sitting at the table across from us, one of them a well-known TV actor, and they are all drunk and two of them keep staring admiringly at Tim, who is oblivious. Tim recrosses his legs, bites at another nail.

"How's your mother?" I ask.

"She's great," he says, his foot beginning to shake up and down so fast it's blurry.

"And Darcy and Melanie?" I ask, grasping at anything. I've almost finished the Mai Tai.

"They get kind of irritating," he says, looking behind me, in a monotone, his face a mask. "All they seem to do is drive down to Häagen-Dazs and flirt with this total geek who works there."

I chuckle for a moment, unsure if I was supposed to. I get the waiter's attention and order a third Mai Tai. The waiter brings it quickly and once he lays it down, our silence ends.

"Remember when we used to come here, during the summer?" I ask, trying to ingratiate myself with him.

"Kind of," he says plainly.

"When was the last time we were all here together?" I wonder out loud.

"I don't really remember," he says without thinking.

"I think it was two years ago. In August?" I'm guessing.

"July," he says.

"That's right," I say. "That's right. It was the weekend of the Fourth." I laugh. "Remember the time we all went scuba diving and your mother dropped the camera overboard?" I ask, still chuckling.

"All I remember are the fights," he says dispassionately, staring at me. I stare back for as long as I can, then I have to turn away.

One of the fags whispers something to another fag and they both look over at Tim and laugh.

"Let's go to the bar," I suggest, signing the check the waiter must have set down when he brought the third Mai Tai.

"Whatever," he says, getting up quickly.

I'm pretty drunk now and I'm weaving through a courtyard unevenly, Tim at my side. In the bar, an old Hawaiian woman dressed in a flowered robe, her neck thick with leis, plays "Hawaiian Wedding Song" on a ukelele. There are a few couples sitting at some of the tables and two well-dressed women, maybe in their early thirties, sitting alone at the bar. I motion for Tim to follow me. We take the two stools next to the women in their early thirties. I lean toward Tim.

"Whaddya think?" I whisper, nudging him.

"About what?" he asks.

"Whaddya think I mean?" I ask.

"About what?" He looks at me irritably.

"Next to us. Them."

Tim looks over at the two women, flinches.

"What about them?"

Pausing, I stare at him, dumbfounded.

"Don't you go out with girls? What is this?" I'm still whispering.

"What?"

"Shhh. Don't you date? Go dating?" I ask.

"Sorority girls and stuff, but . . ." He shudders. "What are you asking me?"

The bartender comes over to us.

"I'll have a Mai Tai," I say, hoping I'm not slurring words. "What about you, Tim?" I ask, slapping him on the back.

"What about me?" Tim asks back.

"What-do-you-want-to-drink?"

"I don't know. A Mai Tai, I guess. Whatever," he says, confused.

One of the women, the taller one, with auburn hair, smiles at us.

"Odds look good," I say, nudging him. "The odds look pretty good."

"What odds? What are you talking about?" Tim asks.

"Watch this." Leaning against the bar, I turn toward the two women.

"Well, ladies—what are you drinking tonight?" I ask.

The taller woman smiles at us and holds up a frosty pink glass and says, "Pahoehoes."

"Pahoehoes?" I ask, grinning.

"Yes," she says. "They're delicious."

"I don't believe this," I hear Tim mutter behind me.

"Bartender, sorry, er . . ." I peer at the smiling gray-haired Hawaiian as he brings over our Mai Tais, until his name tag comes into my line of vision, "Hiki, why don't you bring these two gorgeous ladies another round of . . ." I look at her, still grinning.

"Pahoehoes," she says, smiling lewdly.

"Pahoehoes," I tell Hiki.

"Yes sir, very good," Hiki says, moving off.

"Well, you two—you both look like you were on the beach today, catching some rays. Where are you from?" I ask one of them.

The one who responds takes a sip from her drink.

"I'm Patty and this is Darlene and we're from Chicago."

"Chicago?" I ask, leaning closer. "Is that right?"

"That's right," Patty says. "Where are you both from?"

"We're from L.A.," I tell her, the sound of a blender almost drowning me out.

"Oh, Los Angeles?" Darlene asks, looking us over.

"That's right," I say. "I'm Les Price and this is my son, Tim." I gesture toward Tim as if he's on display, his head bowed down. "He's, er, a little shy."

"Hi, Tim," Patty says carefully.

"Say hello, Tim," I urge.

Tim smiles politely.

"He goes to USC," I add, as if offering an explanation.

The woman playing the ukelele begins to sing "It Had to Be You" and I find myself swaying to the music.

"I have a niece out in L.A.," Darlene says, mildly excited. "She goes to Pepperdine. Ever hear of Pepperdine?" she asks Tim.

"Yes." He nods, looking into his Mai Tai.

"Her name is Norma Perry. Ever hear of Norma Perry? She's a sophomore?" Darlene asks Tim, sipping her Pahoehoe. "At Pepperdine?"

I look over at Tim, who is shaking his head, still looking into his drink, glassy-eyed. "No, I'm, um, afraid, um, not. . . ."

The three of us stare at Tim like he's some kind of blank, exotic creature, more stunned than we should be by how inarticulate he actually is. He keeps shaking his head slowly and it takes massive will on my part to turn away from him.

"Well, how long are you two ladies here?" I ask, taking a large gulp of Mai Tai.

"Until Sunday," Patty says. She has so much jade on her wrist that I'm surprised she can lift her drink. "How about you two?"

"Until Saturday, Patty," I say.

"That's nice. Just the two of you?"

"That's right," I say, looking over at Tim good-naturedly.

"Isn't that nice, Darlene?" Patty asks Darlene, looking at Tim.

Darlene nods. "Father—son. It's nice." She finishes her Pahoehoe greedily and immediately sets upon the fresh one Hiki places in front of her.

"Well, I hope I'm not being too forward if I ask you this," I begin, leaning a little closer to Patty, who reeks of gardenias.

"I'm sure you won't be, Les," Patty says.

Darlene giggles expectantly.

"Jesus," Tim mutters, finally taking a sip of his Mai Tai. I ignore the little bastard.

"What is it?" Darlene asks. "Les?"

"Who are you two ladies here with?" I ask, laughing a little.

"That's it," Tim says, getting off the stool.

"We're here alone," Patty says, looking over at Darlene.

"All alone," Darlene adds.

"Can I have the keys to the room?" Tim asks, holding out his hand.

"Where are you going?" I ask, sobering up slightly.

"To the room," he says. "Where do you think? Christ."

"But you haven't even finished your drink," I say, pointing at the Mai Tai.

"I don't want the drink," he says evenly.

"Why not?" I ask, my voice rising.

"I'll drink it if he doesn't." Darlene laughs.

"Just give me the key," Tim says, exasperated.

"Well, I'll come with you," I tell him, standing there.

"No, no, no, you just stay here and enjoy yourself with Patty and Marlene."

"That's Darlene, honey," Darlene says behind me.

"Whatever," Tim says, his hand still held out.

I reach into my pocket for the key and hand it to him.

"Make sure to let me in," I tell him.

"Thank you," he says, backing off. "Darlene, Patty, it has been a . . . um, uh. I'll see you later." He stalks out of the bar.

"What's wrong with him, Les?" Patty asks, her smile faltering.

"Problems at school," I say drunkenly. I reach for the Mai Tai, bringing it to my mouth, not drinking. "His mother."

I wake Tim early and tell him that we're going to play tennis before breakfast. Tim gets up easily, without protest, and takes a long shower. After he gets out I tell him to meet me down at the courts. When he gets there, fifteen, twenty minutes later, I decide that we should warm up, hit a few balls. I serve, slamming the ball forward. He misses it. I serve again, this time harder. He doesn't even try to hit it, ducking instead. I serve again. He misses it. He doesn't say anything. I serve again. He hits the ball back, grunting with exertion, the bright-yellow ball hurtling at me like some kind of fluorescent weapon. He tumbles forward.

"Not so hard, Dad."

"Hard? You call that hard?"

"Well, uh, yes."

I serve again.

He doesn't say anything.

After I've won all four sets, I try to be sympathetic.

"Aw hell, you win some, you lose some."

Tim says, "Sure."

*   *   *

For some reason it's better on the beach. The ocean calms us, the sand comforts. We are polite to each other. We lie side by side on chaise longues beneath two short, wide palm trees in the sand. Tim reads a Stephen King paperback he picked up in the gift shop in the lobby and listens to his Walkman. I read *Hawaii*, every now and then looking up, concentrating on the sun's warmth, the sand's heat, the smell of rum and suntan lotion and salt. Darlene passes by and waves. I wave back. Tim lowers his sunglasses.

"You were pretty rude to them last night," I tell him.

Tim shrugs catatonically and pushes his sunglasses back up. I'm not sure he heard what I said, due to the Walkman, but he realized I spoke. It is impossible to know what he wants. Looking at Tim, one cannot help feeling great waves of uncertainty, an absence of aim, of purpose, as if he is a person who simply doesn't matter. Trying not to worry about it, I concentrate on the calm sea instead, the air. Two of the fags walk by in thin French briefs and sit by the open bar on the beach. Tim motions for suntan oil. I toss it to him. He rubs the lotion over tan, broad shoulders, then sits back, wiping his hands off on muscular calves. My eyes ache from reading small print. I blink a couple of times and ask Tim to get us a couple of drinks, a Mai Tai maybe or another rum and Coke. He doesn't hear me. I tap his arm. He jerks up suddenly and takes his Walkman off. It falls to the sand.

"Shit," he says, picking it up, inspecting it for sand or damage. Satisfied, he puts it back around his neck.

"What?" he asks.

"Why don't you get your dad and yourself a drink?"

He sighs, gets up. "What do you want?"

"Rum and Coke," I tell him.

"Okay." He pulls on a USC sweatshirt and walks listlessly toward the bar.

I fan myself with the copy of *Hawaii* and watch Tim walk

away. Once at the bar, he stands there, not trying to get the bartender's attention, waiting for the bartender to notice him. One of the fags says something to Tim. I sit up a little. Tim laughs and says something back. And then I notice the girl.

She's young, Tim's age, maybe older, and she's tan, with long blond hair, and she's walking slowly along the shore, oblivious to the waves breaking at her feet, and soon she's moving toward the bar and as she moves closer I can make out her face, barely—brown, placid, eyes wide, unblinking even with the brightness of an afternoon sun that is total and complete. She moves languorously, sensually, to the bar, next to Tim. Tim is still waiting for the drinks, daydreaming. The girl says something to him. Tim looks at her and smiles and the bartender hands him a drink. Tim stands there, they talk briefly. She asks him something as Tim begins to walk toward me. He looks back at her and nods, then jogs away, almost tripping. He stops and looks back, then laughs to himself and walks over and hands me the drink.

"Met a girl from San Diego," he says absently, removing the USC sweatshirt.

I smile and nod and lie there with the drink, which is clear and bubbly and not what I ordered, and when I close my eyes I pretend that when I open them, when I look up, Tim will be standing in front of me, motioning me to join him in the water where we will talk about minor things but he's spoiled and I don't care and ignore him and to ask forgiveness is pretending. I open my eyes. Tim dives into a breaker with the girl from San Diego. A Frisbee lands on the sand next to my feet. I spot a lizard.

Later, after the beach, we are both in the bathroom, getting ready for dinner. Tim has a towel wrapped around his waist and is shaving. I'm at the other sink, washing suntan oil off my face before a shower. Tim takes the towel off, unselfconsciously, and wipes lather off his jaw.

"Is it okay if Rachel comes to dinner with us?" he asks.

I look over at him. "Sure. Why not."

"Great," he says, leaving the bathroom.

"She's from San Diego, you said?" I ask, drying my face.

"Yeah. She goes to UC San Diego."

"Who is she here with?"

"Her parents."

"Well, won't they want to have dinner with her tonight?"

"They're in Hilo for the night," he says, underwear on, searching for a shirt. "Some business her stepfather's involved with."

"You like her?"

"Yeah." Tim studies a plain white shirt as if it is a book of answers. "I guess."

"You guess? You were with her all afternoon."

After a shower, I walk into the bedroom and over to the closet. Tim seems happier and I'm glad he's met this girl, relieved that there will be someone else with us at dinner. I put on a linen suit and pour myself a drink from the minibar and sit on the bed, watching Tim put gel in his hair, greasing it.

"Are you glad you came?" I ask.

"Sure," he says, too evenly.

"I thought maybe you didn't want to come."

"Why would you think that?" he asks. He puts some more of the gel on his fingers, rubbing it through thick, blondish hair, darkening it.

"Your mom mentioned that you didn't feel like coming," I say, quickly, offhand. I sip the drink.

He looks at me in the mirror, his face clouding over.

"No, I never said that. I just had this paper to do and, um, no." He combs his hair, inspecting himself. Satisfied, he turns away from the mirror and looks at me, and as I'm confronted with that blank stare, my decision not to pursue it is made.

We meet Rachel in the main dining room. She stands by the piano, talking to the piano player. She has a purple flower in her hair and the piano player touches it and she laughs. Tim and I walk over to the white baby grand. She turns around, her eyes flat and blue, and she flashes a perfect white smile. She touches her shoulder and moves toward us.

"Rachel," Tim says, a little reluctantly. "This is my dad. Les Price."

"Hello, Mr. Price," Rachel says, holding out her hand.

"Hi, Rachel." I take her hand, noticing that she has no polish on her fingernails even though they are long and smooth. I tentatively let go of her hand. She turns to Tim.

"You both look nice," she says.

"You look great," Tim says, smiling at her.

"Yes," I say. "You do."

Tim looks at me, then at her.

"Thanks, Mr. Price," she says.

The maître d' seats us outside. There's a warm night breeze. Rachel sits across from me and she looks even more beautiful in candlelight. Tim, clean-shaven, wearing an expensive Italian suit I bought him over the summer, his tan darker than Rachel's even, his hair combed back slickly, complements Rachel unnervingly, almost as if they were related. Tim seems comfortable with this girl and I'm almost happy for him. I order a Mai Tai and Rachel has a Perrier and Tim has a beer. After drinking the Mai Tai and ordering another and after listening to the two of them drone on about MTV, college, videos they like, a movie about a deformed girl who learns to accept herself, I feel relaxed enough to tell a joke that ends with the punch line: "May I please have some mouthwash please?" When both of them confess to not understand it and I need to explain it to them, I move on.

"What's that stuff in your hair?" I ask Tim.

"It's Tenax, Dad. It's a gel for your hair." He looks at me with mock exasperation and then at Rachel, who smiles at me.

"Just wanted to know," I say idly.

"So what do you do, Mr. Price?" Rachel asks.

"Call me Les," I tell her.

"Okay. What do you do, Les?"

"I'm into real estate."

"I told you that," Tim tells her.

"You did?" she asks, looking at me blankly.

"Yeah," Tim says sourly. "I did."

She finally looks away. "I forgot."

An image of Rachel, naked, hands on her breasts, lying on my bed, flashes past my line of vision and the idea of taking her, having her, does not seem unappealing to me. Tim pretends to ignore my constant staring but I know he's watching me watching Rachel, very carefully. Rachel flirts boldly with me and I keep debating whether to flirt back. Dinner comes. We eat quickly. More drinks are ordered afterward. By this time I am comfortably drunk enough to lean forward and smile suggestively at Rachel. Tim is so deflated it doesn't even seem like he exists.

"Did you know that Robert Waters is here?" Rachel asks us.

"Who?" Tim asks sullenly.

"Come on, Tim," I say. "Robert Waters. He's on 'Flight Patrol,' that TV show."

"I guess I don't watch enough TV," Tim says.

"Yeah, right," I snort.

"You don't know who Robert Waters is?" Rachel asks him.

"No, I don't," Tim says, an edge in his voice. "Do you?"

"I actually met him at Reagan's inauguration," Rachel says, then, "God, I thought everybody knew who Robert Waters is." She shakes her head, amused.

"I don't," Tim says, plainly irritated. "Why?"

"Well, it's kind of embarrassing." Rachel smiles, looks down.

"Why?" Tim asks again, a fraction of coldness evaporating.

"He's here with three guys," I say.

"So?" Tim asks.

"So?" Rachel laughs.

"One of them tried to pick up on Tim today," I tell Rachel, attempting to gauge her response because at first there isn't one but then she starts laughing and then I'm laughing with her. Tim is not laughing.

"Me?" he asks. "When?"

"At the bar," Rachel says. "Today on the beach."

"Him? That guy?" Tim asks, remembering.

"Yeah, him," I say, rolling my eyes.

Tim blushes. "He was nice. He was a nice guy. So what?"

"Nothing," Rachel says.

"I'm sure he was real nice," I say, laughing.

"Real nice," Rachel repeats, giggling.

Tim looks at her, then sharply at me since I'm to blame, and then back at Rachel and his face changes as if he understands something might be heading toward something else and this realization seems to relax him.

"I guess you two would notice," Tim says, still smiling at her, then, grimly, my way. He lights a cigarette, taunting me. But I only smile back and pretend not to notice.

"I guess we would," I say, patting Rachel's arm.

"Come on, Tim," she says, pulling back a little. "They like you. You're probably the youngest guy here."

Tim smiles, takes a deep drag on the cigarette. "I haven't noticed how many 'young guys' are here. Sorry."

"You shouldn't smoke," Rachel says.

"I told you, Tim," I say.

He looks at her, then at me. "Why not?" he asks her.

"It's bad for you," she tells him earnestly.

"He knows that," I say. "I told him last night."

"No. You told me not to smoke because 'we're in Hawaii,' *not* because it's bad for me," he says, glaring.

"Well, it's bad for you too and I find it offensive," I say with no effort.

"I'm not blowing it in your face," he mutters. He looks over at Rachel to save him. "Am I bothering you? I mean, jeez, we're outside. We're outside."

"You just shouldn't smoke, Tim," she says softly.

He gets up. "Well, I'm going somewhere else to finish this cigarette, okay? Since you two don't like it." Pause, then, to me, "Are the odds pretty good tonight, Dad?"

"Tim," Rachel says. "You don't have to. Sit down."

"No," I say, daring him. "Let him go."

Tim begins to walk away.

Rachel turns in her chair. "Tim. Oh God."

He walks past a couple of small potted palms, the piano player, one of the fags, an old couple dancing, then in, then out of the dining room.

"What's wrong with him?" Rachel asks.

The two of us don't say anything else to each other and listen to the piano player and the muffled conversations that float out of the dining room, the background sound of waves breaking along the shore. Rachel finishes a drink I don't remember her ordering. I sign for the check.

"Good night," she says. "Thanks for dinner."

"Where are you going?" I ask.

"Please tell Tim I'm sorry." She begins to walk away.

"Rachel," I say.

"I'll see him tomorrow."

"Rachel."

She walks out of the dining room.

I open the door to our suite. Tim is sitting on his bed, looking out over the balcony, curtains billowing around him. The room is completely dark except for moonlight and, even with the balcony doors open, permeated with marijuana.

"Tim?" I ask.

"What?" He turns around.

"What's wrong?" I ask.

"Nothing." He stands up slowly and closes the doors leading out to the balcony.

"Do you want to talk?" I have been crying.

"What? Did you ask me if I wanted to talk?" He flips on a light, smiling at me with a tainted smile.

"Yes."

"About what?"

"You tell me."

"There's nothing to talk about," he says. He paces beside the bed, slowly, deliberately, trudging.

"Please, Tim. Come on."

"What?" He throws his arms up, smiling, eyes wide and bloodshot. He takes off his jacket and tosses it on the floor. "There is nothing to talk about."

I can't say anything except "Give me a chance. Don't ruin my chances."

"You don't have any chances to ruin, dude." He laughs, then says again, *"Dude."*

"You don't mean that," I say.

"Nothing. There is nothing," Tim says, less sternly than

before. He stops pacing, then sits on the bed again, his back
to me.

"Just forget about it," he says again, yawning. "There's . . .
nothing."

I just stand there.

"Nothing," he says again. "Nada."

I wander around the grounds of the hotel for a long time
and I finally end up sitting on a small bench situated above
the sea, next to a floodlight shining down into the water.
Two manta rays, drawn by the intense light, are swimming in
circles, their fins flapping slowly in the clear, lit waves. There
is no one else watching the manta rays and I stare at them
swimming tirelessly for what seems to be a long time. The
moon is high and bright and pale. A parrot squawks from
across the hotel. Tiki torches burn with gas flames. I'm about
to go to the front desk and get another room, when I hear a
voice behind me.

"*Manta birostris*, also called manta ray." Rachel steps out of
the darkness, wearing sweats and a revealing T-shirt with the
words LOS ANGELES on it, the flower from earlier still in
her hair. "They're relatives of the shark and the skate. They
inhabit warmer ocean waters. They spend most of their lives
either partially buried in the bottom mud or sand of the
ocean or swimming just above the bottom."

She steps over the bench and leans against the floodlight
and watches the two large gray monsters.

"They move by undulating their large pectoral fins and
they steer with their long tails. They feed primarily on crusta-
ceans, mollusks, marine worms." She pauses, looks at me.
"Some manta rays weighing over three thousand pounds and
measuring twenty feet across have been caught. Because of
their size they are greatly feared." She looks back into the
water and continues speaking, as if reading to the blind. "Ac-

tually they have a retiring disposition. They only cause boats to capsize and kill humans when they're being attacked." She looks back at me. "They leave these large eggs that have a dark-green, almost black, leathery covering on them, with little tendrils at each corner that fasten to seaweed. After they hatch, the empty cases drift to shore." She stops, then sighs heavily.

"Where did you learn all that?"

"I got an A in oceanography at UCSD."

"Oh," I sigh, drunk. "That's . . . interesting."

"I suppose so." She looks back at the manta rays.

"Where have you been?" I ask.

"Around," she says, looking off, as if absorbed by something invisible. "Talk to Tim?"

"Yeah." I shrug. "He's okay."

"Don't you two get along?" she asks.

"As well as most fathers and sons," I say, guessing.

"That's too bad, then," she says, looking at me. She moves away from the floodlight and sits next to me on the bench. "Maybe he doesn't like you." She pulls the flower from her hair and smells it. "But I guess that's okay because maybe you don't like him either."

"Do you think my son is handsome?" I ask.

"Yes. Very," she says. "Why?"

"I just wanted to know." I shrug.

One of the manta rays rises to the surface and splashes at the water with its fin.

"What did you talk about with him this afternoon?" I ask.

"Not a lot. Why?"

"I want to know."

"Just . . . things."

"What things?" I press. "Rachel."

"Just things."

We watch the manta rays. One of them swims away. The other one drifts uncertainly in the floodlight's glare.

"Does he talk about me?" I ask.

"Why?"

"I want to know."

"Why?" She smiles coyly.

"I want to know what he says about me."

"He doesn't say anything."

"Really?" I ask, mildly surprised.

"He doesn't talk about you."

The manta ray floats there, paddling.

"I don't believe you," I say.

"You have no choice," she says.

The next day, Tim and I are on the beach, under a calm, seamless sky, playing backgammon. I am winning. He is listening to his Walkman, not really interested in the outcome of the game. I roll double sixes. He gazes listlessly at the beach, his face drained of emotion. He rolls the dice. A small red bird lands on our green umbrella. Rachel walks up to the two of us, wearing a pink lei and a small blue bikini, sipping Perrier.

"Hi, Les. Hi, Tim," she says happily. "Nice day."

"Hi, Rachel," I say, looking up from the backgammon board, smiling.

Tim nods without looking up, without taking off his sunglasses or removing the Walkman. Rachel just stands there, looking first at me, then at Tim.

"Well, see you two later," she stammers.

"Yeah," I say. "Maybe at the luau?"

Tim doesn't say anything. I move two men. Rachel walks away, back up to the hotel. I win the game. Tim sighs and leans back against the chaise longue and takes off his sunglasses and rubs his eyes. Maybe the odds have not been good from the start. I lean back, watching Tim. Tim looks out at the sea, warm, stretching out like a flat blue sheet to the horizon, and maybe Tim is looking out past the horizon, his eyes disappointed at finding even more of the same flatness, and the day begins to seem colder even if there's no wind and later in the afternoon the ocean darkens, the sky turns orange and we leave the beach.

5

SITTING STILL

I do not pull back the curtains of my window until somewhere in New Mexico. I do not open them when the train
leaves New Hampshire and moves down through New York
and I do not open them when the train pulls into Chicago or
after that, when I board another Amtrak train, the train that
will eventually take me to Los Angeles. When I finally do
open the curtains in the small compartment, I am sitting on
my bed and staring at passing images beyond the window as
if they are a movie and the clear square window a screen. I
watch cows grazing beneath overcast New Mexico skies, endless rows of backyards, pale laundry hanging on lines, rusted
toys, bent slides, crooked swing sets, clouds growing darker
as the train passes through Santa Fe. There are windmills in
fields, which begin to turn faster, and yellow daisies that lie
in clumps on the side of wet highways, which tremble as the
train hurtles past, and I'm moved to start humming "This
Land Is Your Land" to myself, which leads to taking the dress
I'm going to wear to my father's wedding out of the suitcase
and laying it out on the small bed and staring at it until the
train stops in Albuquerque and I'm immediately reminded
of the Partridge Family and a song they sing.

My father tells me about the marriage when he visits Camden in November. He takes me into town and buys me a

couple of books, then a tape at the Record Rack. I don't really want the books or the tape but he seems unusually persistent about buying me something so I oblige and try to seem excited over the Culture Club tape and the three books of poetry. I even introduce him to two girls I run into at the Camden bookshop who live in my house and whom I don't like much. My father keeps tightening the scarf around my neck and complains about the early snow, the cold, how nice L.A. is, how warm the days are, how comfortable the nights seem, how I still might get into UCLA or USC and if not UCLA or USC maybe Pepperdine. I'm smiling and nodding and not saying too much, suspicious of what his intentions are.

At lunch in a small café on the outskirts of town, my father orders a white-wine spritzer and doesn't seem to mind when I order a gin and tonic. After we order lunch and he has two more white-wine spritzers he begins to loosen up.

"Hey, how's my little punk rocker doing?" he asks.

"I'm not a punk rocker," I say.

"Oh come on, you look a little, um, punk." He smiles and then, after I don't say anything, asks, "Don't you?" his smile slipping.

Suddenly feeling sorry for him, I say, "A little, I guess."

I finish the drink, chewing on ice, deciding not to let him carry the conversation, so I ask about the studio, about Graham, about California. We eat quickly and I order another gin and tonic and he lights a cigarette.

"You haven't asked about Cheryl," he finally says.

"I haven't?" I ask.

"No." He takes a drag, exhales.

"Yes. I have."

"When?"

"On the way into town. Didn't I?"

"I don't think so."

"I'm pretty sure I did."

"I don't remember that, honey."

"Well, I think I did."

"Don't you like her?"

"How's Cheryl?"

He smiles, looks down, then at me. "I think we're getting married."

"Really?"

"Yes."

"That's, um, so, congratulations," I say. "Great."

He looks at me quizzically, then asks, "Do you really think that's great?"

I lift the glass to my mouth and tap the side to get the ice at the bottom.

"Well, it's, um, slowly dawning on me that you might be serious."

"Cheryl's great. You two get along." He falters again, refrains from lighting another cigarette. "I mean, when you met her."

"I'm not marrying Cheryl. You are."

"When you give me that type of response, baby, I know how you really feel," he says.

I start to touch his hand across the table, then something in me stops myself.

"Don't worry about it," I say.

"I've been so . . . lonely," he says. "I've been alone for what seems like forever."

"Uh-huh."

"You get to a point where you need someone."

"Do not explain this to me," I say quickly, then with less harshness, "because you don't have to."

"I want your approval," he says simply. "That's all."

"You don't need it."

He sits back in his chair, puts down another cigarette he was about to light. "The wedding is in December." He pauses. "When you get home."

I'm looking out the window at hard, cold snow and gray clouds the color of asphalt.

"Have you told Mom?" I ask.

"No."

At lunch on the train, the waiter sits me at a table with an old Jewish man who is reading a small, frayed black book and keeps muttering to himself in what must be Hebrew. The Jewish man doesn't look anything like my father though the way he's holding himself right now is reminiscent of the behavior of many of my father's friends who work at his studio. This man is older and has a beard, but it is the first time since that lunch with my father that I have been this close to a man during a meal. I don't eat too much of the sandwich I order, which is paper thin and stale, or the lukewarm vegetable soup. Instead I finish a small cup of ice cream and drink a Tab and am about to light a cigarette when I realize there's no smoking in the dining lounge. I nibble at the sandwich, stare out over the crowded dining car, noticing that all the waiters are black and that the train's passengers are mainly old people and foreigners. Outside, a sepia landscape passes by, small adobe houses, young mothers wearing cutoff jeans and halter tops hold small red babies up to the train, waving listlessly as it passes by. Empty drive-ins, huge, seemingly deserted junk lots, more houses built of adobe. Back in my room, staring at the dress, my Walkman on, I'm listening to Boy George sing "Church of the Poisoned Mind," a song on the tape he bought me in town last November.

* * *

Nights are bad. I can't sleep even after I take Valium, which only makes me drowsy enough to pace the short length of the compartment, trying to keep my balance as the train speeds through deserts, stopping suddenly, without warning, jerking me forward in the dimly lit cabin. Opening the curtains, I can't see anything except the tip of my cigarette illuminated in the window's reflection. Announcements are usually made about sand being blown onto the tracks and there is one, at about three a.m., that involves a coyote. Falling asleep for a while, I wake up as the train passes through some kind of electrical storm on the border of Arizona. It is completely dark, then suddenly in a flourish of purple, violet lightning streaks across the sky, illuminating small towns for seconds at a time. As the train passes through these towns, you can hear warning bells, the glow of red flashing, the headlights of a lone pickup truck, waiting, as the train passes, lumbering on into the night, and these awful towns pass by, getting smaller, farther apart from each other, and I came by train not because I don't like to fly and not because I wanted to see the country but because I do not want to spend an extra three days in Los Angeles with either my father and Cheryl or Graham or my mother. A closed mall, a neon gas station sign, the train stops, then moves on, the uselessness of postponing the inevitable, the closing of curtains.

The next morning, at breakfast, I meet a rich boy from Venezuela, wearing an Yves Saint Laurent sport jacket, who is also going to L.A. He has recently been to El Salvador and he keeps talking about how beautiful the country is and how people put it down far too often, about the Lionel Richie concert he attended there. While we wait for breakfast, the boy flips through a new copy of *Penthouse* and I stare out the window, at endless patches of fields and rows of refinery towers and trailer parks and radio relay towers jutting up from red clay ground. I open a notebook I brought with me and try to organize some papers I still have to rewrite from last term but I lose interest as soon as I start. The train stops for a long time in front of a Pizza Hut in some nameless city in Arizona. A family of five comes out of the Pizza Hut and one of the kids waves at the train and I'm wondering who takes their kids to Pizza Hut for breakfast and then the Venezuelan boy waves back to the kid in front of the Pizza Hut, then smiles at me.

I eat my breakfast slowly, pretending to concentrate on stale hash browns and hard, black-on-the-bottom pancakes so that the boy from Venezuela will not ask me anything. Sometimes I look up and out the window at pastures and at the cattle grazing in them. I pull a Valium from my pocket and squeeze it between my fingers. Except for the rich boy from Venezuela who has been to El Salvador, the only other person remotely my age is a homely, sad-faced black girl who is staring at me from across the dining car, which causes me to squeeze the Valium harder. I wait for the girl to turn away and when she finally does I swallow the pill.

"Headache?" the Venezuelan boy inquires.

"Yes. A headache." I smile shyly, nodding.

The black girl glances once more at me and then gets up and is replaced by this totally fat couple who are wearing lots of turquoise. The Venezuelan boy actually looks at a centerfold and then at me and grins and my father was probably right when he told me on the phone two weeks ago, "You should just take MGM, baby," but I'm amazed at how every now and then the ground seems to drop out below the train as it passes over rivers the color of chocolate or a ravine.

I call Graham, my brother, from an Amtrak station in Phoenix. He is in a hot tub in Venice.

"He's going through with it," I say, after a while.

"What a scandal," Graham says.

"He's going through with it," I say again.

"Who cares?"

"You sound stoned."

"I'm not."

"You sound sad when you get stoned. You sound stoned."

"I'm not stoned yet."

"I'm looking at a huge slot machine, the size of a double bed," I tell Graham. "You should talk to him." I light a cigarette. It tastes bad.

"What?" Graham asks. "Why are you calling me?" and then, "*Talk* to . . . him?"

"Aren't you going to talk to him?" I ask. "Aren't you going to do something about this?"

"Oh man." I can hear Graham inhale, then blow something out, slowly. His voice drops three octaves. "Like what?"

"Just . . . talk to him."

"I don't even like him," Graham says.

"You just shouldn't sit back and watch him do this."

"Who said I'm watching the fool do anything?"

"You said, Graham, you said . . ." I'm on the verge of tears. I swallow, try to control myself. "You said she has seen *Flashdance* nine times." I start sobbing quietly, biting my fist. "You said it was her"—pause—"favorite movie."

"She's seen it probably . . ." He stops. "Yeah, nine times is probably right."

"Graham, please, just for once . . ."

"She's not that bad," Graham finally says. "In fact she's sort of hot."

Valium, peering past the curtains, Spanish-style train stations, signs that announce NEEDLES or BARSTOW, cars driving through the desert at night toward Las Vegas, raining

again and harder, lightning illuminating billboards on a road
heading to Reno, huge drops of rain hitting the window,
splattering apart. My reaction to being startled: a blink.
Someone calls out over the intercom: "Anyone who speaks
French please come to the lounge area" and the request
seems tempting, seems so beside the point that it moves me
to brush my hair, pick up a magazine and head for the lounge
area even though I don't speak French. When I get to the
lounge area I don't see anyone French or anyone who looks
in need of assistance from anyone French. I sit down, stare
out a window, flip through the magazine, but there's a drunk
woman across from me who seems to be talking to herself
but in fact is talking to the fat couple in turquoise, who are
trying not to pay attention to her. The woman keeps talking
about the movies on HBO she has seen while staying at her
son's house in Carson City.

"Did you ever see *Mr. Mom?*" the drunk asks, her head
lolling forward.

"No," the fat woman says, her arms folded around a turquoise purse that sits on, in, her lap.

"Darling little movie—just darling," the drunk says, pausing, hoping for some sort of response.

A poor-looking couple with three small children walk into
the lounge and the mother starts to play a game involving
rubber bands with one of the children. I'm watching the
smallest kid eat a packet of butter I was hoping he wouldn't.

"You didn't see *Mr. Mom?*" the drunk asks again.

The woman in turquoise says "No." Her husband fingers
his string tie that has a small piece of turquoise at the end of
it and recrosses bulky legs.

The noise from the children, the meanderings of the
drunk woman, two giggling college girls talking about Las
Vegas irritate me but I stay in the lounge area because I
dread going back to the small compartment, which reminds
me of my destination. Another cigarette, lights above flicker,

then dim. The train passes through a tunnel and when it emerges outside again there is no tangible difference. One of the little kids screams playfully, "God is gonna get you, God is gonna get you," and then, louder, "father, father, father," and the little boy who has eaten the pack of butter is pointing at his father, eyes wide, tiny mouth parted, looking up at him for guidance. The father belches, pulls out another Parliament, lights the cigarette, then looks at me and he's not bad-looking.

Back at my compartment, an hour later, a black porter is straightening up the room. He has finished making the bed and cleaning the small stall called a bathroom.

"Where are you going?" he asks me.

"Los Angeles," I tell him, standing in the corridor, waiting for him to leave.

"What's in Los Angeles?"

"Nothing," I finally say.

"I've heard that before." He chuckles grimly, then, "Going for a visit?"

"My father is getting married."

"Is she nice?" The porter lifts a bag from the wastebasket and ties it.

"What?"

"Do you like her?"

The train begins to pull, then slows down, the sound of brakes, the sound of the train sighing.

"No."

"We'll be getting there soon."

I meet Cheryl over the summer when I'm back in L.A., doing nothing. I have heard about her somewhat from my father when he calls my dorm on Sunday nights, but he is always ambivalent and whenever he hints that he is close to her he pulls back shyly and doesn't follow through. What little I have learned comes from Graham: tan, streaked blond hair, thin, twentyish, a vague aspiration to be a newscaster. When I press Graham for more than this, Graham, stoned, offers: Cheryl constantly, desperately reads Sydney Omarr's *Guide to Pisces 1984*; Cheryl loves the movie *Flashdance*, has seen it five times since last year, when it came out, and has ten ripped sweatshirts with the word MANIAC on them; Cheryl works out to Jane Fonda tapes on the Betamax; William fed pizza to Cheryl at Spago. These descriptions are always followed by a barely audible "Get it?" from Graham. When I would start to unravel, ask him *how,* Graham would say, "It's not like you've never dated a ski instructor. It's not like you've ever cared."

I am not even sure if my parents' divorce is finalized, but two days in August, after having stayed at my mother's without being able to find her, I drive down to my father's new condo in Newport Beach and Cheryl suggests that the two of us go shopping. Bullock's, Saks, a Neiman Marcus that just opened, where Cheryl buys a horrible-looking olive leather jacket with Oriental print splattered all over the back of it, something my father will probably wear. Cheryl speaks highly of a book I have never heard of called *Megatrends*. Cheryl and I have fruit juice and tea at an outdoor café across from the mall, called Sunshine, where Cheryl seems to know the young guys working behind the counter. Juice-sweetened tofu, herbal teas, frozen yogurt. Cheryl is wearing a neon-pink sweatshirt, ripped at the shoulder, the word MANIAC in sky blue, and the shirt jolts me out of something and into something else. Cheryl is talking about the soap opera she watches, about a man who is trying to tell his family that he is still alive.

"Are you okay?" Cheryl asks.

"Yeah. I'm fine," I say sullenly.

"But you don't look too good," Cheryl says. "I mean, you're tan but you don't look happy."

"But I'm okay."

"Have you ever taken zinc oxide tablets?"

"Oh yeah," I say. "I take them."

"But are you still smoking?"

"Not as much."

"Your father promised me he's going to quit," Cheryl says, spooning yogurt into her mouth.

"Uh-huh."

"Does Graham smoke?"

"Yeah. A pipe too."

"Not a pipe," Cheryl says, horrified.

"Sometimes. It depends."

"On what?"

"On whether he would rather use rolling papers," I say and then, when this comment is returned with an uncomprehending look, I offer, "Or if he's lost his bong."

"Do you want to join up for that aerobics class I'm taking over at the plaza?"

"Aerobics class?"

"You say that word like you've never heard it before."

"I'm just tired," I say. "I think I want to go."

"This is kiwi tofu," she says. "I know it sounds totally crazy but it's good. Don't make fun, okay?"

"I'm really sorry."

Later, in the new Jaguar my father bought her, Cheryl asks, "Do you like me?"

"I think so." I pause. "I don't know."

"That's not good enough, honey."

"But that's all I can tell you."

The train arrives in L.A. at dusk. The city seems deserted. In the distance are Pasadena hills and canyons and the small

blue rectangles of lit pools. The train passes dried-up reser-
voirs and vast, empty parking lots, running parallel to the
freeway then past a seemingly endless row of vacant ware-
houses, gangs of young boys standing against palm trees or
huddling in groups in alleyways or around cars with headlights on, drinking beer, the Motels playing. The train moves
slowly as it eases toward Union Station, as if it's hesitating,
passing Mexican churches and bars and strip joints, a drive-in
where a horror movie is playing with subtitles. Palm trees are
highlighted against a shifting orange-purple mass, a sky the
color of Popsicles, a woman passes my door, mumbling loudly
to someone, maybe herself, "This ain't no Silver Streak," and
out the window a young Mexican boy in a red Chevrolet
truck sings along with the radio and I'm close enough to
reach out and touch his blank, grave face, staring straight
ahead.

I'm in a phone booth in Union Station. It's hot, even for
December and night. Three black boys break-dance next to
the phone booth. Sitting down, I pull out my phone book
and dial my mother's number carefully, using my father's
credit card number. I hang the phone up quickly and watch
the break-dancers. I light a cigarette, finish it, then redial the
number. It rings thirteen times.
   "Hello?" my mother finally answers.
   "Hi . . . It's me."
   "Oh." My mother sounds flustered in slow motion, her
voice disembodied, a monotone.
   After a while I have to repeat what I just said.
   "Where are you?" she asks tentatively.
   "Were you asleep?"
   "What time is . . . it?"
   "Seven," and then, "at night."
   "Not really," she says, dazed.

"I'm in L.A. right now."

"Um . . ." My mother pauses, confused. "Why?"

"Because. I took a train."

"How was . . . the train?" my mother asks after a long time.

"I . . . liked it."

"Why on earth didn't you take MGM?" my mother asks tiredly.

The boy from Venezuela walks by, sees me and smiles, but when he sees that I'm crying he gets scared and moves quickly away. Outside, a limousine waits, idling at the curb. A driver holds up a sign with my name on it.

"Well, it's nice you're back . . . hmm," my mother says. "Um, yes." Pause. "This is for Christmas, right?"

"Have you spoken to Dad?" I finally ask.

"Why . . . would I speak to . . . him?" she asks.

"So you don't know?"

"No. I don't know."

I sit down in the lounge area as the train begins to pull out of L.A. I have a drink, look through *Vanity Fair,* take a Valium. A couple of surfers come into the lounge and drink beer with the two college girls who were talking about Las Vegas. An elderly woman sits next to me, tired, tan.

"You heading up north?" she asks.

"Yes," I say.

"San Francisco?"

"Near there."

"What a pretty place." She sighs, and then, "I guess."

"Where are you going?"

"To Portland."

"Is that where this train is going?" I ask.

"I hope so," she says.

"Are you from L.A.?" I ask, buzzed from Valium, Tanqueray.

"Reseda."

"That's nice," I murmur, leafing through the magazine, tranquil, having no real idea where exactly Reseda is, only a partial understanding. My eyes skim pages of advertisements that show me the best way to live. "That's so nice." I slowly hand the magazine to the woman, who takes it from me in the same spirit in which it is offered even though it looks as if she doesn't want to.

6

WATER FROM THE SUN

Danny is on my bed and depressed because Ricky was picked up by a break-dancer at the Odyssey on the night of the Duran Duran look-alike contest and murdered. It seems that Biff, Ricky's current lover, called Danny after getting my number from someone at the station and told him the news. I walk in and all Danny says is "Ricky's dead. Throat slit. All of his blood drained from his body. Biff called." Danny doesn't move or explain the tone in which Biff relayed this news and he doesn't take off the Wayfarer sunglasses he's wearing even though he's inside and it's almost eight. He just lies there watching some religious show on cable and I don't know what to say. I'm just relieved that he's still here, that he hasn't left.

Now, in the bathroom, unbuttoning my blouse, unzipping my skirt, I call out, "Did you tape the newscast?"

"No," Danny says.

"Why not?" I ask, pausing before putting on a robe.

"Wanted to tape 'The Jetsons,' " he says dully.

I don't say anything coming out of the bathroom. I walk over to the bed. Danny is wearing a pair of khaki shorts and a FOOTLOOSE T-shirt he got the night of the premiere party at the studio his father is executive in charge of production at. I look down at him, see my reflection, distorted, warped, in the lenses of the sunglasses, and then, carrying my blouse and skirt, walk into the closet and toss them into a hamper. I close the closet door, stand over the bed.

"Move over," I tell him.

He doesn't move over, just lies there. "Ricky's dead. All of his blood drained out of him. He looked black. Biff called," he says again, coldly.

"And I thought I told you to keep the phone off the hook or unplug it or something," I say, sitting down anyway. "I thought I told you that I'll take all my calls at the station."

"Ricky's dead," Danny mutters.

"Someone snapped off my windshield wipers today, for some reason," I say after a while, taking the control box from him and changing the channel. "They left a note. It said 'Mi hermana.' "

"Biff," he sighs, and then, "What did you do? Rip off a Taco Bell?"

"Biff snapped off my windshield wipers?"

Nothing.

"Why didn't you tape the newscast tonight?" I ask softly, trying not to press too hard.

"Because Ricky's dead."

"But you taped 'The Jeffersons,' " I say accusingly, trying not to lose patience. I turn the channel to MTV, a lame attempt to please him. Unfortunately, a Duran Duran video is on.

" 'The Jetsons,' " he says. "Not 'The Jeffersons.' I taped 'The Jetsons.' Turn that *off*."

"But you always tape the newscasts," I'm whining, trying not to. "You know I like to watch them." Pause. "I thought you've seen all 'The Jetsons.' "

Danny doesn't say anything, just recrosses long, sculpted legs.

"And what was the phone doing on the hook?" I ask, trying to sound amused.

He gets up from the bed so suddenly that it startles me. He walks over to the glass doors that open onto the balcony and looks out over the canyons. It's light outside and warm and beyond Danny it's still possible to see heat rising up off the hills and then I'm saying "Just don't leave" and he says "I don't even know what I'm doing here" and I ask, almost dutifully, "Why are you here?" and he says "Because my father kicked me out of the house" and I ask "Why?" and Danny says "Because my father asked me 'Why don't you get a job?' and I said 'Why don't you suck my dick?' " He pauses and, having read about Edward, I wonder if he actually did, but then Danny says, "I'm sick of having this conversation. We've had it too many times."

"We haven't even had it once," I say softly.

Danny turns away from the glass doors, leans against them and swallows hard, staring at a new video on MTV.

I look away from him, following his gaze to the TV screen. A young girl in a black bikini is being terrorized by three muscular, near-naked masked men, all playing guitars. The girl runs into a room and starts to claw at venetian blinds as fog or smoke starts to pour into the room. The video ends, resolved in some way, and I turn back to look at Danny. He's still staring at the TV. A commercial for the Lost Weekend with Van Halen contest. David Lee Roth, looking stoned and with two sparsely dressed girls sitting on either side of him, leers into the camera and asks, "How about a little joyride in my limo?" I look back over at Danny.

"Just don't leave," I sigh, not caring if I sound pathetic.

"I signed up for that," he says, sunglasses still on.

I reach over, disconnecting the phone, and think about the window wipers being snapped off.

"So you signed up for the Lost Weekend contest?" I ask. "Is that what we were talking about?"

* * *

I'm having lunch with Sheldon in a restaurant on Melrose. It's noon and the restaurant is already crowded and quiet. Soft rock plays over a stereo system. Cool air drifts from three large slowly spinning silver fans hooked to the ceiling. Sheldon sips Perrier and I wait for his response. He sets down the large iced glass and looks out the window and actually stares at a palm tree, which I find momentarily distressing.

"Sheldon?" I say.

"Two weeks?" he asks.

"I'll take one if that's all you can get me." I'm looking at my plate: a huge, uneaten Caesar salad.

"What is this week for? Where are you going?" Sheldon seems actually concerned.

"I want to go somewhere." I shrug. "Just take some time off."

"Where?"

"Somewhere."

"Where is somewhere? Jesus, Cheryl."

"I don't know where somewhere is, Sheldon."

"Are you falling apart on me, baby?" Sheldon asks.

"What is this, Sheldon? What the fuck's going on? Can you get me the week off or not?" I pick up a spoon, stab at the salad, lift lettuce to my mouth. It falls off, back onto the plate. I put the spoon down. Sheldon looks at me, so bewildered that I have to turn away.

"You know, um, I'll try," Sheldon says soothingly, still stunned. "You know I'd do anything for you."

"You'll *try*?" I ask, incredulous.

"You lack faith. That's your problem," Sheldon says. "You lack faith. And you haven't joined a gym."

"My agent is telling me that *I* lack faith?" I ask. "My life must really be a disaster."

"You should work out." Sheldon sighs.

"I don't lack faith, Sheldon. I just need to go to Las Cruces for a week." I start to pick at the salad again, making sure Sheldon notices I've picked up a fork. "I used to work out," I mutter. "I used to work out all the time."

"I'll see what I can do. I'll talk to Jerry. And Jerry will talk to Evan. But you know what they say." Sheldon sighs, looking out at the palm tree. "Can't get water from the sun."

"What the hell are you talking about?" I say, then, "Are you on dope or something, Sheldon?"

The check comes and Sheldon pulls out his wallet and then a credit card.

"You still living with that pretty boy?" he asks with what sounds like definite disdain.

"I like him, Sheldon," I say and then, with less confidence, "He likes me."

"I'm sure. I'm sure he does, Cheryl," Sheldon says. "You didn't want dessert, did you?"

I shake my head, tempted, finally, to eat the rest of the unfinished salad, but the waiter comes and takes the plate away. Everyone in the restaurant, it feels, recognizes me.

"Turn that frown upside down," Sheldon says. He's putting his wallet back in his pocket.

"What would that get me—an upside-down frown, what?"

From the way Sheldon is looking at me, I try to smile and put my napkin on the table, mimicking a normal person.

"Your phone has been, um, busy lately," Sheldon mentions softly.

"You can get hold of me at the station," I say. "It doesn't mean anything."

"Talk to William lately?"

"I don't think I want to talk to William."

"I think he wants to talk to you."

"How do you know?"

"I've seen him a couple of times." Sheldon shrugs. "Around."

"Jesus," I'm saying. "I don't want to see that creep."

A young Mexican boy clears away our water glasses.

"Cheryl, most people I know will speak to their ex-husband if their ex-husband wants to speak to them. It's no biggie. What is this? You can't even talk to him on the phone?"

"He can get hold of me at the station," I say. "I don't want to talk to William. He's pathetic." I'm looking out the window again, at two teenage girls with short blond hair, wearing miniskirts, who are walking by with a tall blond boy and the boy reminds me of Danny. It isn't that the boy looks exactly like Danny—he does—it's more the apathetic shuffle, the way he checks himself out in the window of this restaurant, the same pair of Wayfarers. And for a moment he takes off his sunglasses and stares right at me even though he doesn't see me and his hand runs through short blondish hair and the two girls lean up against the palm tree Sheldon was staring at and light cigarettes and the boy puts his sunglasses back on and makes sure they are not crooked and turns away and walks down Melrose and the two girls leave the palm tree and follow the boy.

"Know him?" Sheldon asks.

William calls me at the station around three. I'm at my desk working on a story about the twentieth anniversary of the Kitty Genovese slaying when he calls. He tells me that my phone has been busy lately and that we should have dinner one night this week. I tell him that I've been busy, tired, that there's too much work to complete. William keeps mentioning the name of a new Italian restaurant on Sunset.

"What about Linda?" I realize I should not have said this, that it will give William the idea that I might be considering his offer.

"She's in Palm Springs for a couple of days."

"What about Linda?"

"What about her?"

"What about Linda?"

"I think I've missed you."

I hang up the phone and stare at pictures of Kitty Genovese's body and William doesn't call back. In makeup, Simon talks about a screenplay he's working on about break-dancing in West Hollywood. Once the news begins I stare straight into the camera and hope that Danny is watching since it's really the only time he ever looks at me. I smile warmly before each commercial break even if it's grossly inappropriate and at the end of the broadcast I'm tempted to mouth "Good night, Danny." But at the Gelson's in Brentwood I see a badly burned little boy in a basket and I remember the way William said "I think I've missed you" right before I hung up on him and when I come out of the market the sky is light and too purple and still.

There is a white VW Rabbit parked next to Danny's red Porsche in the driveway, which is parked next to a giant tumbleweed. I drive past the cars and park my Jaguar in the carport and sit there for a long time before I get out and carry the bag of groceries inside. I set them on the kitchen table, then open the refrigerator and drink half a Tab. There is a note on the table from the maid, written in broken English, about William calling. I walk over to the phone, unplug it and crumple the note up. A boy, maybe nineteen, twenty, with short blond hair and tan, wearing only blue shorts and sandals, walks into the kitchen, stopping suddenly. We stare at each other for a moment.

"Uh, hello?" I say.

"Hi," the boy says, starting to smile.

"Who are you?"

"Um, I'm Biff. Hi."

"Biff?" I ask. "You're Biff?"

"Yeah." He begins to back out of the kitchen. "See you around."

I stand there with the note about William still crumpled in my hand. I throw it away and walk up the stairs. The front door slams shut and I can hear the sound of the VW Rabbit starting, backing out of the driveway, moving down the street.

Danny is lying under a thin white sheet on my bed, staring at the television. Wadded-up pieces of Kleenex are scattered on the floor by the side of the bed, next to a deck of tarot cards and an avocado. It's hot in the room and I open the balcony doors, then walk into the bathroom, change into my robe and move silently over to the Betamax and rewind the tape. I look over my shoulder at Danny, still staring at the TV screen I'm blocking. I press Play and a Beach Boys concert comes on. I fast-forward the tape and press Play. There isn't anything on it except for the Beach Boys.

"You didn't tape the newscast tonight?"

"Yeah. I did."

"But there's nothing there." I'm pointing at the Betamax.

"Really?" He sighs.

"There's nothing there."

Danny thinks about it a moment, then groans, "Oh man, I'm sorry. I had to tape the Beach Boys concert."

Pause, then, "You *had* to tape a Beach Boys concert?"

"It was the last concert before Brian Williams died," Danny says.

I sigh, drum my fingers on the Betamax. "It wasn't Brian Williams, you moron. It was Dennis Wilson."

"No, it wasn't," he says, sitting up a little. "It was Brian."

"You've missed taping the show two nights in a row now." I walk into the bathroom and turn on the faucets in the bathtub. "And it was Dennis," I call out.

"I don't know where the hell you heard that," I hear him say. "It was Brian."

"It was Dennis Wilson," I say loudly, bending down, feeling the water.

"No way. You're totally wrong. It was Brian," he says. He gets up from the bed with the sheet wrapped around him, grabs the remote control and lies back down.

"It was Dennis." I walk out of the bathroom.

"Brian," he says, turning the channel to MTV. "You are wrong to the max."

"It was Dennis, you little asshole," I scream at him as I leave the room and walk downstairs, flip on the air-conditioning and then, in the kitchen, open a bottle of white wine. I take a glass out of a cupboard and walk back upstairs.

"William called this afternoon," Danny says.

"What did you tell him?" I pour myself a glass of wine and sip it, trying to calm down.

"That we were dry humping and you couldn't make it to the phone," Danny says, grinning.

"Dry humping? So you weren't exactly lying."

"Right." He snorts.

"Why didn't you just leave the goddamned phone unplugged?" I scream at him.

"You're crazy." He sits up suddenly. "What is this shit about the phone? You're crazy, you're . . . you're . . ." He trails off, unable to find the right word.

"And what was that little surfer doing in my house?" I finish one glass of wine, a little nauseated, then pour another.

"That was Biff," Danny says defensively. "He doesn't surf."

"Well, he looked real upset," I say loudly, sarcastic, taking off my robe.

In the bathroom I ease myself into warm water, turn the faucets off, lie back, sipping the wine. Danny, with the sheet wrapped around him, walks in and throws Kleenex into the wastebasket and then wipes his hand on the sheet. He puts the toilet seat down and sits and lights a joint he's holding. I close my eyes, take a large swallow of wine. The only sounds: music coming from MTV, one of the faucets dripping, Danny sucking on a thinly rolled joint. I'm just noticing that sometime today Danny bleached his hair white.

"Want some weed?" he asks, coughing.

"What?" I ask.

"Some weed?" He holds the joint out to me.

"No," I'm saying. "No weed."

Danny sits back and I'm feeling self-conscious, so I roll over onto my stomach, but it's uncomfortable and I roll over onto my side and then onto my back but he's not looking at me anyway. His eyes are closed. He speaks.

In monotone: "Biff was down on Sunset today and he came to a stoplight and he told me he saw this old deformed woman with a totally big head and long puffy fat hands and she was, like, screaming and drooling, holding up traffic." He takes another hit off the joint, holds it in. "And she was naked." He exhales, then says, benignly, "She was at a bus stop way down on the Strip, maybe near Hillhurst." He takes another hit off the joint, holds it in.

I picture the image clearly and, after thinking about it, ask, "Why in the hell did you tell me that?"

He shrugs, doesn't say anything. He just opens his eyes and stares at the red tip of the joint and blows on it. I reach over the side of the tub and pour another glass of wine.

"You tell *me* something," he finally says.

"Like, trade information?"

"Whatever."

"I . . . want a child?" I say, guessing.

After a long pause, Danny shrugs, says, "Bitchin'."

"Bitchin'?" I close my eyes and very evenly ask, "Did you just say bitchin'?"

"Don't mock me, man," he says, getting up, going over to the mirror. He scratches at an imaginary mark on his chin, turns away.

"It's no use," I say suddenly.

"I'm too young," he says. "Duh."

"I can't even remember when I met you," I say, quietly, then I look up at him.

"What?" he asks, surprised. "You expect *me* to remember?" He drops the sheet and, nude, walks back to the toilet and sits down and takes a swig from the bottle of white wine. I notice a scar on the inside of his thigh and I reach out and touch his leg. He pulls back, takes a drag on the joint. My hand stays there, in space, and I bring it back, embarrassed.

"Would a smart person make fun of me for asking you what you're thinking?"

"I have—" He stops, then slowly continues. "I have been thinking about how awful it was, losing my virginity." He pauses. "I have been thinking about that all day."

"It usually is when you lose it to a truck driver." A long, hateful pause. I turn away. "That was stupid." I want to touch him again but sip Chardonnay instead.

"What makes you so fucking perfect?" His eyes narrow, the jaw sets. He gets up, bends over, picks up the sheet, walks back into the bedroom. I get up out of the tub and dry off and, a little drunk, walk into the room, naked, holding the bottle of wine and my glass, and I get under the sheet with him. He turns channels. I do not know why he is here or where we met and he's lying next to me, naked, gazing at videos.

"Does your husband know about this?" he asks, a tone of false amusement. "He says the divorce isn't finalized. He says he's not your ex."

I don't move, don't answer, for a moment I don't see Danny or anything else in the room.

"Well?"

I need another glass of wine but I force myself to wait a few minutes before I pour it. Another video. Danny hums along with it. I remember sitting in a car in the parking lot of the Galleria and William holding my hand.

"Does it matter?" I say once the video ends. I close my eyes, easily pretend that I'm not here. When I open them it's darker in the room and I look over at Danny and he's still staring at the TV. A photograph of L.A. at night is on the screen. A red streak flies over the neon landscape. The name of a local radio station appears.

"Do you like him?" Danny asks.

"No. I really don't." I sip the wine, easing toward tired. "Do you like . . . him?"

"Who? Your husband?"

"No," I say. "Biff, Boff, Buff, whatever."

"What?"

"Do you like him?" I ask again. "More than me?"

Danny doesn't say anything.

"You don't have to answer immediately." I could say this stronger but don't. "As if you're capable."

"Don't ask me this," he says, his eyes a dull gray-blue, blank, half closed. "Just don't ask me this. Don't do this."

"It's just all so typical." I'm giggling.

"What did Tarzan say when he saw the elephants coming over the hill?" he asks, yawning.

"What?" I'm still giggling, my eyes closed.

"Here come the elephants over the hill."

"I think I've heard this one before." I'm picturing Danny's long tan fingers and then, less appealing, where his tan line stops, starts again, the thick unsmiling lips.

"What did Tarzan say when he saw the elephants come over the hill with raincoats on?" he asks.

I finish the wine and set the glass on the nightstand, next to an empty bottle. "What?"

"Here come the elephants over the hill wearing raincoats." He waits for my response.

"He . . . did?" I ask, finally.

"What did Tarzan say when he saw the elephants come over the hill with sunglasses on?"

"I don't think I really want to know this, Danny," I say, my tongue thick, closing my eyes again, things clogged.

"Nothing," Danny says lifelessly. "He didn't recognize them."

"Why are you telling me this?"

"I don't know." Pause. "To keep me amused maybe."

"What?" I say, drifting. "What did you say?"

"To keep me amused?"

I fall asleep next to him for a minute, then wake up but don't open my eyes. My breathing steady, I feel the touch of two dry fingers trailing up my leg. I lie perfectly still, eyes closed, and he touches me, no heat in the touch, and then he climbs gently on top of me and I lie perfectly still but soon I have to open my eyes because I'm breathing too hard. The instant I do, he softens, rolls off. When I wake up in the middle of the night, he's gone. His lighter, which looks like a small gold handgun, is on the nightstand next to the empty bottle of wine and the large glass and I remember that when he first showed it to me I thought he was actually going to fire it and when he didn't I felt my life become an anticlimax and looking into his eyes, his gaze rendering everything inconsequential, pools incapable of remembering anything, I moved deeper into them until I was comfortable.

Music from downstairs wakes me at eleven. I hurriedly throw on a robe, walk downstairs, but it's only the maid washing the windows in the den, listening to Culture Club. I say gracias and look outside the window the maid is cleaning and notice that the maid's two young children are swimming in the shallow end of the small pool. I get dressed and wait around the house for Danny to come back. I walk outside, stare at the space where his car was parked, and then I look around for signs of the gardener, who has, for some reason, not shown up in three weeks.

I meet Liz for lunch in Beverly Hills and after we order water I spot William, wearing a beige linen sport jacket, white pleated pants and expensive brown sunglasses, standing at the bar. He makes his way over to our table. I excuse myself and walk to the rest rooms. William follows me and I stand outside the door and ask him what he's doing here and he says that he always comes to this place for lunch and I tell him it's too much of a coincidence and he says, admits, that maybe he talked to Liz, that maybe she had mentioned something to him about lunch with me today at the Bistro Gardens. I tell William that I don't want to see him, that this separation was, inadvertently or not, his idea, that he met Linda. William answers my accusations by telling me that he simply wants to talk and he takes my hand and squeezes it and I pull away and walk back to the table and sit down. William follows and squats by my chair and after he asks me three times to come by his house to talk and I don't say anything he leaves and Liz mumbles apologies and I suddenly, inexplicably, become so hungry that I order two appetizers, a large salad and a bitter-orange tart and eat them quickly, ravenous.

After lunch I walk aimlessly along Rodeo Drive and into Gucci, where I almost buy Danny a wallet, and then I'm walking out of Gucci and leaning against one of the gold columns outside the store in white heat and a helicopter swoops down

low out of the sky and back up again and a Mercedes blares
its horn at another Mercedes and I remember that I have to
do the eleven o'clock edition on Thursdays and I'm shielding
my eyes from the sun and I walk into the wrong parking lot
and after walking another block find the right one.

I leave the station after the newscast at five ends, telling
Jerry that I'll be back for the eleven o'clock edition by ten-
thirty and Cliff can do the promos and I get into my car and
drive out of the parking lot of the station and find myself
driving to the airport, to LAX. I park and walk over to the
American Airlines terminal and go to a coffee shop, making
sure I get a seat by the window, and I order coffee and watch
planes take off, occasionally glancing at a copy of the *L.A.
Weekly* I brought with me from the car, and then I do some
of the cocaine Simon gave me this afternoon and get diarrhea
and then I roam the airport and hope someone will follow
me and I walk from one end of the terminal to the other,
looking over my shoulder expectantly, and I leave the American Airlines terminal and walk out to the parking lot and
approach my car, the windows tinted black, two stubs leaning
against the windshield where the wipers used to be, and I get
the feeling that there's someone waiting, crouched in the
backseat, and I move toward the car, peer in, and though it's
hard to tell, I'm pretty sure there's no one in there and I get
in and drive out of the airport and as I move past motels that
line Century Boulevard leading to LAX I'm tempted, briefly,
to check into one of them, just to get the effect, to give off
the illusion of being someplace else, and the Go-Go's are
singing "Head Over Heels" on the radio and from LAX I
drive to West Hollywood and find myself at a revival theater
on Beverly Boulevard that's playing an old Robert Altman
movie and I park the Jaguar in a towaway zone, pay for a
ticket and walk into a small, empty theater, the entire room

bathed in red light, and I sit alone up front, flip through the
L.A. Weekly and it's quiet in the theater except for an Eagles
album that's playing somewhere and someone lights a joint
and the sweet, strong smell of marijuana distracts me from
the *L.A. Weekly*, which drops to the floor anyway after I see
an advertisement for Danny's Okie Dog, a hot dog stand on
Santa Monica Boulevard, and the lights dim and someone in
back yawns and the Eagles fade, a tattered black curtain rises
and after the movie ends I walk back outside and get in the
car and when the car stalls in front of a gay bar on Santa
Monica I decide not to go to the station for the eleven o'clock
newscast and I keep turning the key and when the engine
starts up again I drive away from the bar and past two young
guys yelling at each other in a doorway.

Canter's. I walk into the large, fluorescent-lit delicatessen
to get something to eat and buy a pack of cigarettes so that I
will have something to do with my hands since I left the *L.A.
Weekly* on the floor of the revival theater. I get a booth near
the window and study the Benson & Hedges box, then stare
out the window and watch streetlights change colors from
red to green to yellow to red and nothing passes through
the intersection and the lights keep changing and I order a
sandwich and a diet Coke and nothing passes, no cars, no
people, nothing passes through the intersection for twenty
minutes. The sandwich arrives and I stare at it disinterest-
edly.

A group of punk rockers sit in a booth across from mine
and they keep looking over at me, whispering. One of the
girls, wearing an old black dress and with short, spiked red
hair, nudges the boy sitting next to her and the boy, probably
eighteen, lanky and tall, wearing black with a blond Mohawk,
starts up and walks to my table. The punks suddenly become
silent and watch the boy expectantly.

"Um, aren't you on the news or something?" he asks in a high voice that surprises me.

"Yes."

"You're Cheryl Laine, right?" he asks.

"Yes." I look up, trying to smile. "I want to light a cigarette but I don't have matches."

The boy looks at me, made briefly helpless by this last statement, but he recovers and asks, "No matches either but hey, listen, can I have your autograph?" Staring at me hatefully, he says, "I'm, like, your biggest fan." He holds out a napkin and scratches his Mohawk. "You're, like, my favorite anchorperson."

The punks are laughing hysterically. The girl with the red spiked hair covers her pale face with tiny hands and stamps her feet.

"Sure," I say, humiliated. "Do you have a pen?"

He turns around and calls out, "Hey, David, you gotta pen?"

David shakes his head, eyes closed, face contorted with laughter.

"I think I have one," I say, opening my purse. I take a pen out and he hands me a napkin. "What would you like it to say?"

The boy looks at me blankly and then over at the other table and he starts laughing and shrugs. "I don't know."

"Well, what's your name?" I ask, squeezing the pen so tight I'm afraid it will snap. "Let's start there."

"Spaz." He scratches at the Mohawk again.

"Spaz?"

"Yeah. With an *s*."

I write: "To Spaz, best wishes, Cheryl Laine."

"Hey, thanks a lot, Cheryl," Spaz says.

He walks back to the table where the punks are laughing, even harder now. One of the girls takes the autograph from

Spaz and looks it over and groans, covering her head with her hands and stamping her feet again.

I very carefully place a twenty-dollar bill on the table and take a sip of the diet Coke and then try, inconspicuously, to get up from the table and I head for the rest room, the punks calling out "Bye, Cheryl" and laughing even louder and once in the ladies' room I lock myself in a stall and lean against a door that's covered with Mexican graffiti and catch my breath. I find Danny's lighter at the bottom of my purse and light a cigarette but it tastes sour and I drop it in the toilet and then walk back through Canter's, which is basically empty, walking all the way around its perimeter, keeping to the rim of the room, avoiding the punks' table and then I'm in my car looking at my reflection in the rearview mirror: eyes red, black smudge on chin, which I try to wipe off. Starting the car, I head for a phone booth on Sunset. I park the car, leaving the engine running, the radio loud, and call my number and I stand in the booth waiting for someone to answer and the phone keeps ringing and I hang up and walk back to the car and drive around, looking for a coffee shop or a gas station so I can use a rest room but everything seems closed and I drive down Hollywood Boulevard looking up at movie marquees and finally I end up getting back on Sunset and driving to Brentwood.

I knock on William's door. It takes him a while to answer it. He asks, "Who's there?" I don't say anything, just knock again.

"Who's there?" he asks, his voice sounding worried.

"It's me," I say, then, "Cheryl."

He unlocks the door and opens it. He's wearing a Polo bathing suit and a T-shirt that has CALIFORNIA written across it in bright-blue letters, a T-shirt I bought him last year, and he has glasses on and doesn't seem surprised to find me standing outside his door.

"I was just going to go in the Jacuzzi," William says.

"I have to use your bathroom," I say quietly. I walk past him and across the living room and into the bathroom. When I come out, William is standing at the bar.

"You couldn't . . . find a bathroom?" he asks.

I sit in a reclining chair in front of a huge television set, ignoring him, then, deciding not to, say, "No."

"Would you like a drink?"

"What time is it?"

"Eleven," he says. "What do you want?"

"Anything."

"I've got pineapple juice, cranberry, orange, papaya."

I had thought he meant alcohol but say, again, "Anything."

He walks over to the TV set and it turns on like a sudden flash, booming, and the news is just beginning and he turns the volume up in time to hear the announcer say: ". . . the channel nine news team with Christine Lee filling in for Cheryl Laine . . ." and William walks back to the bar and pours the two of us drinks and he, mercifully, doesn't ask why I'm not there. I turn the television off at the first commercial break.

"Where's Linda?" I ask.

"Palm Springs," he says. "At a colonic seminar." A long, dull silence and then, "Supposedly they're fun."

"That's nice," I murmur. "You two still getting along?"

William smiles and brings me a drink that smells strongly of guava. I sip it cautiously, then put the glass down.

"She just finished redecorating the condo." He motions with his arms and sits down on a beige couch across from the reclining chair. "Even though the condo is temporary." Pause. "She's still at Universal. She's fine." He sips his juice.

William doesn't say anything else. He sips his juice again

and then crosses his tan, hairy legs and looks out the window at palm trees lit by streetlamps.

I get up from the chair and walk nervously around the room. I move over to the bookshelf and pretend to look at the titles of the books on the large glass shelf and then at the titles of films on tape in the shelves below.

"You don't look too good," he says. "You have ink on your chin."

"I'm fine."

It takes five minutes for William to say, "Maybe we should have stayed together." He removes his glasses, rubs his eyes.

"Oh God," I say irritably. "No, we shouldn't have stayed together." I turn around. "I knew I shouldn't have come here."

"I was wrong. What can I say?" He looks down at his glasses, then at his knees.

I walk away from the bookshelf and over to the bar and lean against it and there's another long pause and then he asks, "Do you still want me?"

I don't say anything.

"You don't have to answer me, I guess," he says, sounding confused, hopeful.

"This is no use. No, William, I don't." I touch my chin, look at my fingers.

William looks at his drink and before he sips it says, "But you lie all the time."

"Don't call me anymore," I say. "That's why I came over. To tell you this."

"But I think I still"—pause—"want you."

"But I"—I pause awkwardly—"want someone else."

"Does he want you?" he asks with a quiet emphasis, and the fact refuses to escape me untouched and I slump down on a high gray barstool.

"Don't crack up," William says. "Don't go to pieces."

"Everything's wrecked."

William gets up from the couch, puts his glass of papaya juice down and carefully walks over to me. He puts a hand on my shoulder, kisses my neck, touches a breast, almost knocking my glass over. I move away to the other side of the room, wiping my face.

"It's surprising to see you like this," I manage to say.

"Why?" William asks from across the room.

"Because you've never felt anything for anybody."

"That isn't true," he says. "What about you?"

"You were never there. You were never there." I stop. "You were never . . . alive."

"I was . . . alive," he says feebly. "Alive?"

"No, you weren't," I say. "You know what I mean."

"What was I, then?" he asks.

"You were just"—I pause, look out over the expanse of white carpet into a massive white kitchen, white chairs on a gleaming tiled floor—"not dead."

"And, uh, this person you're with is?" he asks, an edge in his voice.

"I don't know. He's"—I stammer—"nice. Nice. Good for me."

"He's 'good' for you? What is he? A vitamin? What does that mean? He's good in bed or what?" William raises his arms.

"He can be," I mutter.

"Well, if you met *me* when I was fifteen—"

"Nineteen," I say, cutting him off.

"Jesus Christ, nineteen," he spits out.

I head for the door, leaving a not unfamiliar scene, and I turn back, once, to look at William and feel a pang of reluctance, which I don't want to feel. I'm imagining Danny, waiting in a bedroom for me, dialing a phone, calling someone, a phantom. Back at my house, the television is on and so is the Betamax. The bed is unmade. A note on top of it reads,

"Sorry—I'll see you around. Sheldon called and said he had good news. Set the timer for 11 so the show should be taped. I'm sorry. So long. P.S. Biff thinks you're hot," and below that Biff's phone numbers. The bag of clothes he kept by the bed is gone. Rewinding the tape, I lie down and watch the eleven o'clock edition.

7

DISCOVERING JAPAN

Heading straight into darkness, staring out the window of a plane at a starless black canvas beyond the window, placing a hand to a window that's so cold it numbs my fingertips and staring at my hand, I withdraw my hand slowly from the window and Roger makes his way down the darkened aisle.

"Set your watch ahead, man," Roger says.

"What, man?" I ask.

"Set your watch ahead. There's a time difference. We're landing in Tokyo." Roger stares at me, his smile slipping. "Tokyo in, um, Japan, okay?" No response, and Roger runs his hand through short blond hair until he's fingering a ponytail in back, sighing.

"But I . . . can't . . . see . . . anything, man," I tell him, slowly pointing to the darkened window.

"That's because you're wearing sunglasses, man," Roger says.

"No, that's not . . . it. It's . . . real"—I think of the right word—"um . . . dark," and then, ". . . man."

Roger looks at me for a minute.

"Well, that's because the windows are, um, tinted," Roger says carefully. "The windows on this plane are tinted, okay?"

I don't say anything.

"Do you want some Valium, a 'lude, some gum, what?" Roger offers.

I shake my head, answer, "No . . . I might OD."

Roger slowly turns around, makes his way up the aisle toward the front of the jet. Pressing my fingertips, still cold from the window, to my forehead causes my eyes to shut tightly.

Naked, waking up bathed in sweat, on a large bed in a suite in the penthouse of the Tokyo Hilton, sheets rumpled on the floor, a young girl nude and sleeping by my side, her head cradled by my arm, which is numb, and it surprises me how much effort it takes to lift it, finally, my elbow brushing carelessly over the girl's face. Clumps of Kleenex that I made her eat, stuck to the sides of her cheeks, her chin, dry, fall off. Turning over, away from the girl, is a boy, sixteen, seventeen, maybe younger, Oriental, nude, on the other side of the bed, arms dangling off the edge, the smooth beige lower back covered with fresh red welts. I reach for a phone by the nightstand but there is no nightstand and the phone is on the floor, disconnected, on top of damp white sheets. Panting, I reach across the boy, connect the phone, which takes about fifteen minutes, finally ask someone on the other end for Roger but Roger, I am told, is at a fruit-eating contest and is not available for comment.

"Get these two kids out of here, okay?" I mumble into the receiver.

I get out of bed, knocking an empty vodka bottle over onto a bourbon bottle which spills onto potato chip bags and an issue of *Hustler Orient* that this girl on the bed is in this month and I kneel down, open it up, feeling weird while studying how different her pussy looks in the layout compared to how it looked three hours ago and when I turn around and look at the bed, the Oriental boy's eyes are open, staring at me. I just stand there, unembarrassed, nude, hungover, and stare back into the boy's black eyes.

"You feel sorry for yourself?" I ask, relieved when two

bearded guys open the door and move toward the bed, and I walk into a bathroom and lock the door.

Turning on the bathwater full blast, willing the sound of rushing water hitting the mammoth porcelain tub to drown out the noise of two roadies dragging the girl and boy out of the bed, out of the room, taking their turn, I lean toward the tub, making sure only cold water pours out of the faucet. I move toward the door, press my ear against it to hear if anybody's still in the room, and pretty sure no one is, I open it, peer out, and nobody's in the room. From a small refrigerator I take out a plastic ice bucket and then move toward the ice machine that was placed at my request in the middle of the suite and get some ice. Then, on my way back to the bathroom, I kneel by the bed and open a drawer and take out a bag of Librium and then I'm back in the bathroom and locking the door and pouring the bucket of ice into the tub, making sure there's enough water at the bottom of the bucket so that I can wash the Librium down my throat, and I step into the tub, lie down, only my head above water, unsettled by the fact that maybe the freezing water and the Librium aren't really such a great combo.

In the dream I'm sitting in the restaurant on top of the hotel near a wall of windows and staring out over the blanket of neon lights that pass for a city. I'm drinking a Kamikaze and sitting across from me is the young Oriental girl from *Hustler* but her smooth brown face is covered with geisha makeup and the geisha makeup and the tight, fluorescent-pink dress and the expression creasing her flat, soft features and the gaze in the blank dark eyes are predatory, making me uneasy, and suddenly the entire blanket of lights flickers, fades, sirens are wailing and people I never noticed are running out of the restaurant, screams, shouts from the black city below, and huge arcs of flame, orange and yellow highlighted against a black sky, shoot up from points on the ground and I'm still staring at the geisha girl, the arcs of flame reflected in her black eyes, and she's mumbling something to me and there's no fear in those large and slanted wet eyes because she's smiling warmly now, saying the same word again and again and again but the sirens and screams and various explosions drown the word out and when I'm shouting, panicked, asking her what she's saying, she just smiles, blinking, and takes out a paper fan and her mouth keeps moving, forming the same word, and I'm leaning toward her to hear the word but a huge claw bursts through the window, showering us with glass, and it grabs me and the claw is warm, pulsing with anger and covered with a slime that drenches the suit I'm wearing and the claw pulls me out the window and I twist toward the girl, who says the word again, this time clearly.

"Godzilla . . . Godzilla, you idiot . . . I said Godzilla . . ."

Screaming silently, I'm lifted toward its mouth, eighty, ninety stories up, looking through what's left of the smashed wall of glass, a cold black wind whipping furiously around me, and the Oriental girl with the pink dress on is now standing on the table, smiling and waving her fan at me, crying out "Sayonara" but it doesn't mean goodbye.

Sometime later, after I climb nude and sobbing from the bathtub, after Roger calls on one of the extensions and tells me that my father has called seven times in the last two hours (something about an emergency), after I tell Roger to tell my father that I'm asleep or out or anything or in another country, after I smash three champagne bottles against one of the walls in the suite, I'm finally able to sit in a chair I've moved over to a window and look out over Tokyo. I'm holding a guitar, trying to write a song, because for the past week a number of chord progressions have been repeating themselves in my head but I'm having a hard time sorting them out and then I'm playing old songs I wrote when I was playing with the band and then I stare at broken glass on the floor that surrounds the bed, thinking: that's a cool album cover. Then I'm picking up a half-empty package of M&M's and washing them down with some vodka and then since it makes me sick I have to head for the bathroom but I trip over the telephone cord and my hand slams into a thick piece of champagne-bottle glass and for a long time I'm staring at my palm, at a thin rivulet of blood racing down my wrist. Unable to shake the glass out, I pull it out and the hole in my hand looks soft and safe and I take the jagged stained piece of glass that still has part of a Dom Perignon label on it and seal the wound by placing it back into it where it looks complete, but the glass falls out and streaming blood covers the guitar I'm beginning to strum and the bloodied guitar will make a pretty good record cover too and I'm able to light a cigarette, blood soaking it only a little. More Librium and I'm asleep but the bed shakes and the earth moving is part of my dream, another monster approaching.

The phone starts ringing at what I can only guess is noon.

"Yeah?" I ask, eyes closed.

"It's me," Roger says.

"I'm sleeping, Lucifer."

"Come on, get up. You're having lunch with someone today."

"Who?"

"Someone," Roger says, irritated. "Come on, let's play."

"I need, like, something," I mumble, opening my eyes, the sheets, the guitar next to the sheets, covered with brown dried blood, some of it in patches so thick it moves me to open my mouth, then swallow. "I need something, man."

"What?" Roger's saying. "Your Mr. Potato Head broke? What?"

"No, a doctor, man."

"Why?" Roger sighs.

"Cut my hand."

"Really?" Roger sounds bored.

"It was bleeding, um, pretty bad."

"Oh, I'm sure it was. How did you do this?" Roger asks. "In other words: did you have help?"

"I did it shaving—who the fuck cares? Just . . . get a doctor."

After a while, Roger asks, "If it's not bleeding anymore, does it matter?"

"But there was a lot of . . . blood, man."

"But does it even hurt?" Roger asks. "Can you even feel it?"

A long pause, then, "No, um, not really." I wait a minute before saying, "Sort of."

"I'll get you a doctor. Jesus."

"And a maid. A vacuum. I need a . . . vacuum, man."

"You *are* a vacuum, Bryan," Roger says. I can hear giggling in the background, which Roger silences by hissing, then he tells me, "Your father keeps calling." I can hear Roger lighting a cigarette. "For what it's worth."

"My fingers, um, Roger, won't move."

"Did you hear me or, like, what's the bloody story?"

"What did he want? Is that what you want me to ask?" I sigh. "How did he know where I am?"

"I don't know. Some emergency. Your mom's in the hospital? I'm not sure. Who knows?"

I try to sit up, then with my left hand light a cigarette. When it becomes apparent to Roger that I'm not going to say anything else, Roger says, "I'll give you three hours to get cleaned up. Do you need longer? I hope to holy Christ *not*, okay?"

"Yeah."

"And wear something with long sleeves," Roger warns.

"What?" I ask, confused.

"Long sleeves, man. Wear long sleeves. Something poofy."

I look down at my arms. "Why?"

"Multiple choice: *(a)* you look nice in long sleeves; *(b)* you have holes in your arms; *(c)* you have holes in your arms; *(d)* you have holes in your arms."

A long pause that I finally break up by saying, "*C*?"

"Good," Roger says, then hangs up.

A producer from Warner Brothers who is in Tokyo to meet with Japanese representatives from Sony is thirty and balding and has a face like a death mask and is wearing a kimono with tennis shoes, pacing languidly around his suite, smoking a joint, and it's all really fab and to die over and Roger is flipping through *Billboard,* sitting on a giant unmade bed, and the producer has been on the phone forever and whenever he is put on hold he points at Roger and says, basically, "That minipony is really nifty," and Roger, pleased that the producer has noticed the small tuft of hair, nods, turns around, shows the thing off.

"Like Adam Ant?" the producer asks.

"You bet." Roger, who should be mortified, turns back to *Billboard.*

"Help yourself to sake."

Roger leads me by the hand out to the balcony, where two Oriental girls, maybe fifteen, fourteen, sit at a table piled with plates of sushi and what looks like waffles.

"Wow," I say. "Waffles."

"Please don't feel like you're saying too much," Roger says.

"Why don't you just ignore me?" I plead.

"On second thought," Roger says, making a terrible face, "why don't you just sit this one out?"

One of the Oriental girls is wearing pink satin underwear and no top and she's the one I was with last night and the other girl, wearing a POLICE T-shirt, has a Walkman on and glazed eyes. The producer moves over to the balcony doors and is now talking to Manuel about having some deli but no pickles and it's really fab. He clicks off, snaps his fingers as he sits down with a pained expression, motioning for the girl with pink satin underwear to cover herself. The girl, who has a heart of ice, stands up, walks slowly back into the room, turns the television on and falls to the floor with a thump.

The producer sits next to the Oriental girl with the Walk-man, sighs, takes a hit off the joint. He offers it to Roger, who shakes his head, then to me. Roger shakes his head for me too.

"Sake?" the producer asks. "It's chilled."

"Great," Roger says.

"Bryan?" the producer asks.

Roger shakes his head again.

"Anybody feel the earthquake?" the producer asks, pouring the sake straight from the bottle into champagne glasses.

"Yeah, I did," Roger says, lighting a cigarette. "Really terrifying," and then, after glancing over at me, "Well, not so scary."

"Don't trust these fucking Japs," the producer says. "I hope it got some of them."

"Who does, man?" Roger sighs, nodding tiredly in agreement.

"They're building an artificial ocean," the producer says. "Several, in fact."

I adjust my sunglasses, look at my hands. Roger readjusts my sunglasses. This moves the producer to get down to business.

He begins gravely. "An idea for a movie. It's actually an idea that has been halfway realized. It is, as we speak, sitting in a vault being guarded by some of the most dangerous men at Warners." Pause. "You're sensing it's a really hot property." Pause. "The reason we came to you, Bryan, is because there are people who remember how intense that movie turned out about the life of the band." His voice gets high and trails off and he studies my face for a reaction, a tough job.

"I mean, holy Jesus, the four of you guys—Sam, Matt and . . ." The producer stops, snaps his fingers, looks at Roger for help.

"Ed," Roger says. "His name was Ed." Pause. "Actually, at the time the band formed it was Tabasco." Pause. "We changed it."

"Ed, gosh," the producer says, pausing awkwardly with such a false reverence that it almost moves me to tears. "What is known as a 'real tragedy.' A real shame. Real upsetting too, I bet, no?"

Roger sighs, nods. "They were already broken up by then."

The producer takes a huge toke off the joint and while inhaling manages to say the following: "You guys were probably one of the pioneering forces in rock during the last decade and it's a shame you broke up—can I interest you in some waffles?"

Roger delicately sips sake, says, "It is a shame," and then looks at me. "Right?"

I sigh. "Sí, señor."

"Since the flick turned out to be so cool and profitable without exploiting anyone, we thought that, um, with your" —the producer glances at Roger for help, falters—"presence, you'd be interested and thrilled to actually star in a movie."

"We receive so many scripts," Roger sighs, adding, "Bryan turned down *Amadeus,* so he's got rather high standards."

"The movie," the producer continues, "is basically the rock-star-in-outer-space thing. An alien creature, this E.T., sabotages the—"

I clutch Roger's arm.

"E.T. An extraterrestrial," Roger says softly.

I let go. The producer continues.

"The E.T. sabotages the dude's limo after a gig at the Forum and after a rather large and fiery chase takes him to this planet where the rock star is held captive. I mean, yadda whatever and there's a princess, who is basically a love interest." The producer pauses, looks at Roger hopefully. "We're thinking Pat Benatar. We're thinking a Go-Go."

Roger laughs. "Oh, that's bloody great."

"The only way the guy can get released is to record songs and perform a concert for the planet's emperor, who is basically a, um, tomato." The producer grimaces, shuddering, then looks worriedly at Roger.

Roger is squeezing the bridge of his nose and saying, "So it's madcap, right?"

"It's *not* tacky and you have a copy," the producer tells Roger. "And everyone is getting excited by the thing in the vault."

Roger smiles, nods, looks over at the Oriental girl and sticks his tongue out, winking. He tells the producer, "I'm not bored."

I actually remember the movie that was made about the band and the movie had gotten it pretty much right except the filmmakers forgot to add the endless paternity suits, the time I broke Kenny's arm, clear liquid in a syringe, Matt crying for hours, the eyes of fans and "vitamins," the look on Nina's face when she demanded a new Porsche, Sam's reaction when I told him Roger wanted me to do a solo record—information the filmmakers seemed to not want to deal with. The filmmakers seemed to have edited out the time I came home and found Nina sitting in the bedroom in the house on the beach, a pair of scissors in her hand, and they cut out the shot of a punctured, leaking water bed. The editor seemed to have misplaced the scene where Nina tried to drown herself one night at a party in Malibu and they cut the sequence that followed where her stomach was pumped and also the next shot, where she leaned into the frame next to my face and said, "I hate you," and she turned her face, pale and swollen, her hair still wet and plastered to her cheeks, away from me. The movie had been made before Ed jumped from the roof of the Clift Hotel in San Francisco so the filmmakers had an excuse for that scene not being in the movie but there seemed to be no excuse for the rest to have been omitted and for the movie's being made up of bones, an X ray, a set of dull facts, that became wildly popular.

A green lantern hanging from a rafter that shields the balcony pulls me back into the conversation: percentage points, script approval, gross against net profits, terms that, even now, I still find strangely unfamiliar, and I'm staring into Roger's flute of sake and the Oriental girl, inside, is writhing, kicking at the floor, moving in circles, sobbing, and the producer stands up, still talking to Roger, closes the door and smiles when I say, "I'm grateful."

I call Matt. It takes the operator a swift seven minutes to connect me to the number. Matt's fourth wife, Ursula, answers, sighing when I tell her who it is. I wait five minutes for her to come back and I'm imagining Matt standing next to Ursula in the kitchen of a house in Woodland Hills, head bowed down. Instead Ursula says, "He's here," and Matt's voice comes over the line.

"Bryan?"

"Yeah, man, it's me."

Matt whistles. "Whoa." Long pause. "Where are you?"

"Japan. Tokyo, I think."

"Has it been . . . two, three years?"

"No, man, it hasn't been . . . that long," I say. "I don't know."

"Well, man, I heard you were, um, touring."

"World Tour '84, man."

"I heard something about that. . . ." His voice trails off.

Tense, awkward silence broken only by "yeah"s and "um"s.

"I saw the video," he says.

"The one with Rebecca De Mornay?"

"Er, no, the one with the monkey."

"Oh . . . yeah."

"I heard the album," Matt finally says.

"Did . . . you like it, man?" I ask.

"Are you kidding, man?" he says.

"Is that . . . good, man?" I ask.

"Great backup. Really tight."

Another long silence.

"It's, um, valid, man, valid," Matt says. Pause. "The one about the car, man?" Pause. "I saw John Travolta buy a copy at Tower." Long pause.

"I'm, um, really gratified by your response, man," I say. "Okay?"

Long pause.

"Are you, um, doing anything, like, now?" I ask.

"I've fooled around with some stuff," Matt says. "Might be ready to go into the studio in a couple of months."

"Ter-rif-ic," I say.

"Uh-huh."

"Have you . . . talked to Sam?" I ask.

"Just about . . . well, maybe it was a month ago? One of the lawyers? Ran into him somewhere. By accident."

"Sam is . . . okay?"

Not sounding too sure, Matt says, "He's great."

"And . . . his lawyers?"

He answers by asking, "How's Roger?"

"Roger is . . . Roger."

"Out of rehab?"

"A long time ago."

"Yeah, I know what you mean." Matt sighs. "I know what you mean, man."

"Well, man." I breathe in, tense up. "I wonder if maybe you'd like to, oh I don't know, if maybe you would like to get together and write some songs when I get finished with this tour, maybe record some stuff . . . man?"

Matt coughs, then after not too long says, "Oh man I don't know y'know the old days are over man and I really don't think so."

"Well, fuck, it's not like—" I stop in midsentence.

"You gotta move on."

"I . . . I am, you know, but." I start to kick my foot against a wall and my fingernails have somehow dug themselves so hard into the bandaged wound that it becomes spotted with red.

"It's over, y'know, man?" Matt is saying.

"Am I, like, lying, man?"

I'm not saying anything, just blowing on my palm.

"I was watching some of those old movies that Nina and Dawn took in Monterey," Matt is saying.

I'm trying not to listen, thinking *Dawn?*

"And the weirdest thing but also the grooviest thing is that Ed looked really good. He looked great, in fact. Tan and in good shape and I don't know what happened." Pause. "I don't know what the fuck happened, man."

"Who cares, man?"

"Yeah." Matt sighs. "You've got a point."

"Because I don't care, man."

"I guess I don't care either, man."

I hang up, pass out.

* * *

On the way to the arena, sitting in the back of the limo, watching television, sumo wrestling, what could be an old Bruce Lee movie, the same commercial about a blue lemonade seven times, throwing ice cubes I've sucked on at the small square screen, I roll the glass partition down and tell the chauffeur I need a lot of cigarettes and the chauffeur reaches into the glove compartment, tosses back a pack of Marlboros, and cocaine I'd taken earlier isn't doing much of anything, which I expected, and dismayingly it just seems to intensify the pain in my hand and I keep swallowing but residue keeps tickling the back of my throat in an insistent, annoying kind of way and I keep drinking Scotch which almost takes away the taste.

The stage reeks of sweat and it's a hundred degrees on-stage and we have been playing for about fifty minutes and all I want to do is sing the last song, which the band, when I mention this in between breaks, thinks is a pretty bad idea. All the songs are from the last three solo albums but from the front row I can hear Orientals crying out in thick, r-less accents the names of big hits I played with the band and this band launches into the biggest hit off the second solo LP and I can't really tell if the audience is enthused even when they applaud loudly and behind me a four-hundred-foot tapestry —BRYAN METRO WORLD TOUR 1984—billows in back of us and I'm moving slowly across the large expanse of stage, trying to peer out into the audience but bright blinding spotlights turn the arena into this moving mass of gray darkness and as I begin to sing the second verse of the song I forget the lyrics. I sing "Another night passes by and still you wonder what happened" and then I freeze. A guitarist suddenly jerks his head up and a bassist moves closer toward me, the drummer still keeping beat. I'm not even playing my guitar anymore. I start the second verse again: "Another night passes by and still you wonder what happened . . . ," then nothing. The bassist yells out something. I turn my head toward him, my hands killing me, and the bassist urges "You give the world one more try" and I'm saying "What?" and the bassist calls out "You give the world one more try" and I'm saying "What?" and the bassist yells "You give the world one more try—Jesus" and I'm thinking to myself why in the hell would I sing this and then who the fuck wrote this piece of shit and I motion for the band to go into the chorus and we finish the song okay and there's no encore.

Roger rides with me in the limo back to the hotel.

"Terrific show, Bryan." Roger sighs. "Your concentration and showmanship really cannot be improved upon. I would be lying if I said they could. I'm all out of superlatives."

"My hands are . . . fucked up."

"Just the hands?" he says, not even really sarcastically, no edge in his voice, a muffled complaint maybe, an observation not worth making. "We'll just tell the promoters you had an uneven synth mix," Roger says. "We'll just tell people that your mother died."

We pass a crowded street diagonal to the hotel and everyone is trying to peer into the tinted windows as the limo rolls toward the Hilton.

"Jesus," I'm mumbling to myself. "All these fucking gooks. Just look at them, Roger. Just look at all these fucking gooks, Roger."

"All those fucking gooks bought your last album," Roger says, then adds, under his breath, "You brain-dead asshole."

I'm sighing, putting my sunglasses on. "I'd like to get out of this limo and tell these gooks what I think of them."

"That's not gonna happen, baby."

"Why . . . not?"

"Because you aren't presentable for direct contact with the public."

"Think of all the words that rhyme with my name, Roger," I say.

"Are there a lot?" Roger asks.

Roger and I are standing in an elevator.

"Get me a maid or something, okay?" I ask him. "My room is like a total wreck, man."

"Clean it yourself."

"No. Unh-uh."

"I'll move you, okay?"

"Okay."

"You've got the whole floor, you cadaver. Take your pick."

"Why can't you just get me a maid?"

"Because housekeeping at the Tokyo Hilton seems to think that you raped two of their maids. Is this true, Bryan?"

"Define, um, rape, Roger."

"I'll have room service send up a dictionary." Roger makes a terrible face.

"I'm going to move."

Roger sighs, looks at me and says, "You're getting the feeling that you're not going to move, right? You're realizing that you were going to consider it but now you're coming to the conclusion that it would not be worth the effort, that you don't have the strength or something, right?" Roger turns away, the elevator gradually slowing, reaching his floor. Roger turns a key so that the elevator is locked into going to my floor and not anywhere else, like I even want it to.

* * *

The elevator stops at the floor that Roger has put a lock on and I step into an empty, dim-lit corridor and start walking toward my door, breaking the hush by screaming loudly, twice, three, four times, and I fumble for the key that will open the door and I turn the handle and it's open anyway and inside is a young girl sitting on my bed, dried blood everywhere, leafing through *Hustler*. She looks up from the magazine. I close the door, lock it, stare at her.

"Was that you screaming?" the girl asks in a small, tired voice.

"Guess," I say and then, "Have you made friends with the ice machine yet?"

The girl is pretty, blond, dark tan, large wide blue eyes, Californian, a T-shirt with my name on it, faded tight cutoff jeans. Her lips are red, shiny, and she puts the magazine down as I slowly move toward her, almost tripping over a used dildo that Roger calls The Enabler. She stares back, nervously, but the way she gets up off the bed, walking slowly backward, seems too calculated and when she finally hits the wall and stands there breathing hard and I reach her, I have to put my hands around her neck, softly at first, then tightening the grip, and she shuts her eyes and I bring her toward me then slam her head against the wall which doesn't seem to faze her and this worries me, until she opens her eyes and grins and in one swift movement lifts her hand, the fingernails long and sharp and pink, and rips a two-hundred-dollar T-shirt down the front, scratching my chest. I bunch my fist and hit her hard. She claws at my face. I push her down on the floor and she's spitting at me, plugging my mouth with her fingers, squealing.

I'm in the bathtub taking a bubble bath. The girl has lost a tooth and is nude and sitting on the toilet seat, holding an ice pack from room service (who left several) up to the side of her face. She stands unsteadily and limps over to the mirror and says, "I think the swelling's gone down." I pick up a piece of ice that floats in the water and put it in my mouth and chew it, concentrating on how slowly I am chewing. She sits back down on the toilet and sighs.

"Don't you want to know where I'm from?" she asks.

"No," I say. "Not really."

"Nebraska. Lincoln, Nebraska." A long pause.

"You had a job at the mall, right?" I ask, eyes closed. "But the mall closed down, right? It's all empty now, huh?"

I can hear her light a cigarette, smell its smoke, then ask, "Have you been there?"

"I've been to a mall in Nebraska," I say.

"Yeah?"

"Yeah."

"It's all flat."

"Flat," I agree.

"Totally."

"Totally flat."

I stare down at torn skin on my chest, at the pink swollen lines that crisscross the skin below, over my nipples and I'm thinking, There goes another photo shoot without a shirt on. I touch the nipples lightly, brush the girl's hand away when she tries to touch them. Once she's properly lubricated I slide into her again.

A gram and I'm ready to call Nina at the house up in Malibu. The phone rings eighteen times. She finally answers.

"Hello?"

"Nina?"

"Yeah?"

"It's me."

"Oh." Pause. "Wait a minute." Another pause.

"Are you there?"

"You sound like you care," she says.

"Maybe I do, babe."

"Maybe you don't, asshole."

"Jesus."

"I'm fine," she says quickly. "Where are you now?"

I close my eyes, lean up against the headboard. "Tokyo. A Hilton."

"Sounds classy."

"It is far and away the nicest place I have ever lived."

"That's great."

"You don't sound too enthusiastic, babe."

"Yeah?"

"Oh shit. Just let me talk to Kenny."

"He's on the beach with Martin."

"Martin?" I ask, confused. "Who the hell is Martin?"

"Marty, Marty, Marty, Marty—"

"Okay, okay, yeah, Marty. How's Marty?"

"Marty's great."

"Yeah? That's great, even though I have no idea who he is, but, um, can I talk to Kenny, babe?" I ask. "I mean, can you go out to the beach and get him and not like freak out?"

"Some other time, okay?"

"I would like to talk to my kid."

"But he doesn't want to talk to you."

"Let me talk to my kid, Nina." I sigh.

"This is pointless," she says.

"Nina—just go get Kenny."

"I'm going to hang up on you now, okay, Bryan?"

"Nina, I'll get my lawyer."

"Fuck your lawyer, Bryan, just fuck him. I've gotta go."

"Oh Jesus—"

"And it's not a good idea if you call here too often."

A long silence because I don't say anything.

"It is never a good idea if you talk to Kenny, because you scare him," she says.

"And you don't?" I ask, appalled. "Medusa?"

"Never call back." She hangs up.

Sitting in the empty coffee shop (which Roger had "cor-doned off" because he was afraid "people would see you") in the bottom of the Tokyo Hilton, Roger tells me that we are going to be watching the English Prices eat lunch. Roger is wearing huge black sunglasses and an expensive pair of pajamas, chewing bubble gum.

"Who?" I ask. *"Who?"*

"The English Prices," Roger enunciates clearly, again. "New group. MTV discovered them and has made them big." Pause. "Real big," he adds grimly. "They're from Anaheim."

"Why?" I ask.

"Because-they-were-born-there." Roger sighs.

"Uh-huh," I say.

"They want to meet you."

"But . . . why?"

"Good question," Roger says. "But does it really matter to you?"

"Why are they here?"

"Because they are on tour," Roger says. "Are you doing coke?"

"Grams and grams and grams of it," I say. "If you knew how much you would choke."

"I suppose it's better than the angel dust routine from '82." Roger sighs warily.

"Who are these people, Roger?" I ask.

"Who are you?"

"Um . . . ," I say, confused by this question. "Who . . . do you think?"

"Someone who tried to set his ex-wife on fire with a tiki torch?" he suggests.

"I was married to her then."

"I suppose it was a good thing that Nina threw herself in the ocean." Roger pauses. "Of course it was three months later, but considering how smart she was when you first met, I was glad her reflexes had improved." Roger lights a cigarette, thinks everything over. "Christ, I can't believe she got custody. But then I hate to think what would've happened to that kid if you had gotten custody. Mothra would have made a better parent."

"Roger, who are these people?"

"Have you seen the cover of the new *Rolling Stone*?" Roger asks, snapping his fingers at a young, nervous Oriental waitress. "Oh, I forgot. You don't read that publication anymore."

"Not after that shit they pulled with Ed's death."

"Touchy, touchy." Roger sighs. "The English Prices are hot. A hot album, *Toadstool,* and a video game made about them that you should play, er, sometime." Roger points to his coffee cup and the waitress, head bowed dutifully, pours. "It sounds tacky but it's not. Really."

"Jesus, I'm a wreck."

"The English Prices are big," Roger reminds me. "Stratosphere isn't an inappropriate word."

"You said that already and I still don't believe you."

"Just be cool."

"Why the fuck do I have to be cool?" I look straight at Roger for the first time since we entered the coffee shop.

Roger looks down at his cup and then at me and enunciates each word very carefully: "Because I am going to be managing them."

I don't say anything.

"They'll bring in a lot more people," Roger says. "A *lot* more people."

"For what? For who?" I ask, instantly realizing the question is useless, better left unanswered.

"For you, babes," Roger says. "We've been drawing sizable crowds, but still."

"There isn't gonna be another tour, man," I say. "This is it."

"That's what you think, baby," Roger says casually.

"Oh man" is all I say.

Roger looks up. "Oh shit—here the little bastards come. Just be cool."

"Jesus fucking Christ." I sigh. "I *am* cool."

"Just keep telling yourself that and roll your sleeves down."

"I am becoming aware of just how lost inside my life you really are," I say, rolling my sleeves down.

Four members of the English Prices walk into the coffee shop and each of them has a young Oriental girl by his side. The Oriental girls are very young and pretty and wearing striped miniskirts and T-shirts and pink leather boots. The lead singer of the English Prices is very young also, younger than the Oriental girls in fact, and he has a short platinum-blond burr of hair on his head and smooth tan skin and he's wearing mascara and red eyeliner and is dressed in black leather and has a spiked bracelet wrapped around the wrist he holds out. We shake hands.

"Hey, man, I've been a fan of yours like forever," I hear him say. "Forever, man."

The other members nod their heads sullenly in agreement. It's impossible for me to smile or nod. We're all sitting at a large glass table and the Oriental girls keep staring at me, giggling.

"Where's Gus?" Roger asks.

"Gus has mono." The lead singer turns to Roger, eyes still on me.

"I'll have to send him some flowers," Roger says.

The singer turns back to me, explains, "Gus is our drummer."

"Oh," I say. "That's . . . nice."

"Sushi?" Roger asks them.

"No, I'm a vegetarian," the singer says. "Plus we already had a big breakfast of SpaghettiOs."

"With who?"

"A big important record executive."

"Hip," Roger says.

"Anyway, man," the lead singer says, turning his full attention back to me. "Like, I was listening to your records—well, the band's records—since I can remember. In, like, well, a long time ago, and I'm not guessing when I tell you that you"—he stops and has trouble pronouncing the next word—". . . influenced us."

The rest of the English Prices nod, mumbling in unison.

I try to look the singer in the eyes. I try to say "Great." No one says anything.

"Hey," the lead singer says to Roger. "He's pretty, uh, subdued."

"Yes," Roger says. "We call him, in fact, Sub Dude."

"That's . . . cool," the lead singer says apprehensively.

"Who were *you* listening to, man?" one of them asks me.

"When?" I ask, confused.

"In, like, when you were a little kid, in, like, high school and stuff. Influences, man."

"Oh . . . lots of things. Um, I don't really remember. . . ." I look at Roger for help. "I'd prefer not to say."

"Do you want me to, like, repeat the question, man?" the lead singer asks.

I just stare at him, frozen, unable to move.

"That's life," the lead singer finally says, sighing.

"Captain Beefheart, the Ronettes, antiestablishment rage, you know," Roger says blithely, then, "Who are your friends?" He laughs slyly and the lead singer laughs, barking, and that's the cue for the rest of the band to follow.

"These girls are great."

"Yes sir," one of them says in a deep monotone with a lisp. "Can't understand one bit of American but they fuck like rabbits."

"Can't you?" the lead singer asks the girl sitting next to him. "You a good fuck, bitch?" he asks, a sincere expression on his face, nodding. The girl looks at the expression, takes in the nod, the smile, and she smiles back a worried, innocent smile and nods and everyone laughs.

The lead singer, nodding and smiling, asks another girl, "You give real good head, right? You like it when I slap your face with my fat leathery cock, you gook bitch?"

The girl nods, smiling, looks at the other girls, and the band laughs, Roger laughs, the Oriental girls laugh. I laugh, finally taking off my sunglasses, loosening up a little. Silence takes over and everyone at the table is left, momentarily, to his own uneasy devices. Roger tells the band to order some drinks. The Oriental girls giggle, adjust tiny pink boots, the lead singer keeps glancing at my bandaged hand and I see myself in the same naive curled grin, in the blur of a photo session, in a hotel room in San Francisco, in a zillion dollars, in another ten months.

In a dressing room at the arena before we are supposed to go on, I just sit in a chair in front of a huge oval mirror staring at my reflection through Wayfarers, at myself nibbling radishes. I start to kick my foot against the wall, my fists clenched. Roger walks in, sits down, lights a cigarette. After a while I say something.

"What?" Roger asks. "You're mumbling."

"I don't want to go out there."

"Because why?" Roger asks as if speaking to a child.

"I don't feel too good." I stare at my reflection, uselessly.

"Don't say that. You have a distinctly upbeat air about you."

"Yeah, and you're gonna win Mr. Congeniality any fucking year now," I growl, then, calmed down, "Get Reggie."

"Get ready for what?" he asks and then, seeing that I am about to pounce on him, relents. "Just a joke."

Roger makes a phone call, ten minutes later someone is wrapping something around my arm, a vein is slapped, pinpricks, vitamins, saying yeah, weird warmness rushing through me, flushing out the coldness, fast at first, then, more slowly, yeah, sure.

Roger sits back down on the couch and says, "Don't beat up any more groupies, all right? Can you hear me? *Lay* off."

"Oh man," I say. "They . . . like . . . it. They like to pet me. I let them pet . . . me."

"Just *cool* it. Do you hear me?"

"Oh man fuck you man I'll do it again."

"What did you say to me?"

"Man, I'm Bryan—"

"I know who you are," Roger cuts me off. "You're the same awful asshole who beat up *three* girls on the last tour, threatened one with a *carving* knife. These are girls we are still paying off. Do you remember that bitch from Missouri?"

"Missouri?" I giggle.

"The one you almost killed?" Roger says. "Does that refresh your memory?"

"No."

"We are *still* paying her and some scumbag lawyer off—"

"You're getting heavy, man, and when you're getting heavy . . . you must, um, leave me alone."

"Do you remember how you fucked that one up?"

"Don't dwell on the past, dude."

"Do you know how much we still have to pay that bitch off every fucking *month*?"

"Leave me alone," I whisper.

"She was in a wheelchair for a year."

"I have something to tell you."

"So don't give me that oh-man-I-know-it shit. You *don't* know," Roger says. "You don't know shit."

"I have something to tell you."

"What? You're announcing your retirement?" Roger hisses. "Let me guess—you're going to sell out big-time?"

"I hate Japan," I say.

"You hate everywhere," Roger groans. "You loathsome fuck."

"Japan's so . . . different," I say, finally.

"That's a joke. You say every place is different." Roger sighs. "Focus, focus, focus, for Christ sakes, focus."

I stare back into the mirror, hear screaming coming from the arena.

"Adjust my dreams for me, Roger," I whisper. "Adjust my dreams for me."

On the plane leaving Tokyo I'm sitting alone in back twisting the knobs on an Etch-A-Sketch and Roger is next to me singing "Over the Rainbow" straight into my ear, things changing, falling apart, fading, another year, a few more moves, a hard person who doesn't give a fuck, a boredom so monumental it humbles, arrangements so fleeting made by people you don't even know that it requires you to lose any sense of reality you might have once acquired, expectations so unreasonable you become superstitious about ever matching them. Roger offers me a joint and I take a drag and stare out the window and I relax for a moment when the lights of Tokyo, which I never realized is an island, vanish from view but this feeling only lasts a moment because Roger is telling me that other lights in other cities, in other countries, on other planets, are coming into view soon.

8

LETTERS FROM L.A.

Sept 4 1983

Dear Sean,

Guess you didn't expect to hear from me. Talk about getting away from it all! Here I am—all away across the country in California, sitting on my bed, drinking diet Coke and listening to Bowie. Pretty weird, isn't it? I've been in L.A. a week and I still can't quite believe it. All this summer I knew that I'd be coming out here but somehow the idea wasn't quite real. It's just as well that I didn't spend too much time thinking about it because *nothing* would have prepared me. L.A. is something else.

I got into LAX last Tuesday afternoon, half-crazy from lack of sleep and wondering what the hell I was doing here. It was like walking into another world. 100 degrees out and all these beautiful blond tan people (specimens!) staring into outer space, walking around me and toward their cars. I felt so pale—kind of like what it would feel being the only blond girl in Egypt or something. And I got this awful feeling that all of them were looking at me: no tan, not blond, not beautiful, let's ignore her! All I did those first few days was chainsmoke Export A's and look at the pavement and wish I was back at Camden. I'm not sure how one fits in here. Get a tan? Dye my hair blond? I know it sounds paranoid but I really feel this hostility toward me. I'm getting used to it but still.

My grandparents were overjoyed when they saw me. They

aren't very emotional people but I've always been their favorite granddaughter and they were positively bubbling over with excitement. On the way back to their house my grandfather, who looked so tan and healthy it was positively eerie, patted my hand and said, "From now on we're going to take care of you—you won't lack for *any*thing," and he didn't seem to be joking.

This last week I spent doing mostly touristy stuff and going to parties and trying to catch up on my sleep. We spent a day at Disneyland, which was a real trip. I've seen pictures of the place but let me tell you, Sean, seeing this place in reality was altogether something else. My grandfather's assistant took something like twenty roles of pictures: me standing with Mickey Mouse (feeling utterly foolish), me in front of the Matterhorn, me staring pensively at Space Mountain, some pervert dressed up as Pluto coming on to me (disgusting), me with the Haunted Mansion in the background, etc. etc. etc. I got lost at Disneyland, which was most embarrassing. The place is a little smaller than I anticipated but it's wonderful-looking. We also went to four wax museums and then went driving up and down Sunset Boulevard (L.A. by night is so pretty). Actually the nightlife is pretty hot. On Friday night I went out with this couple, Mr. and Mrs. Fang (she's an executive at Universal and he's a record producer) to some exclusive club and danced and got drunk and had great fun. And I had thought I wouldn't have much of a social life! This couple and I became great friends and he promised to introduce me to his sister who is about my age and at Pepperdine next time I'm down in Malibu with them and all their friends. They're even going to give me the key to their (well, actually his) penthouse in Century City so that whenever I want to get away from my grandparents I can go and stay there. They also want me to go with them next time they go to the Springs (which is what everyone calls Palm Springs).

The city is so quiet though. Especially compared to New

York. And everything seems so clean and to move so much more slowly in a very relaxed way. But yet I don't feel too safe here yet. I feel vulnerable—like I'm in this big open environment. But my grandparents assure me that it's pretty safe and they live in supposedly the best part of Bel Air so I don't need to worry. Just the same I'm so used to my padded little Manhattan-Camden existence that being here seems like a real shock. I look at all these people roaming around: the beautiful, healthy, tan men and the elegant women and everyone drives a Mercedes and it's just so hard to describe it.

All in all I feel happier and more free than I have in a long, long time. And I am so glad that I came. I think it's an incredibly healthy move. I think it's a good thing that I took a term off and came out here.

"I'm just a million miles away," the Plimsouls are singing on KROQ and I have to think that songs sometimes are uncannily appropriate. I really am so far away from everything. But it's a good feeling. I'm going to be out here until February, which means I'll be back at school in March. I'm going to be helping my grandfather at the studio a lot and reading scripts and stuff like that (I'm pretty excited) and I guess I'll be going down to Malibu and hanging around Palm Springs (I'm glad that there are a couple of places I can get away to if I ever tire of L.A. which I can't possibly imagine). Well, I'll hope you write me back. I really would love to hear from you. I'd appreciate it a lot.

Love,
Anne

Sept 9 1983
Dear Sean,
Hello! I thought of you at Camden today. Hanging out at the Café, chain-smoking, getting your classes together. Is it going all right for you there or is "grace under pressure" still

an apt phrase? I worry about you which is pretty silly of me but then again I worry about a lot of things so it's not necessarily out of context. So—how are you? How is it back at school? Who are you hanging out with? What classes are you taking? Have you been forced to wear your Wayfarers a lot? (God knows, I have!) Has anything changed? Are you okay? As you can tell, I'm full of questions, Sean. I really, really hope you write me. I'm dreadfully sorry if my little infatuation bothered you. I get so caught up in things that I simply lose all perspective. But even before I got all infatuated with you I was still fond of you, and I would hate to lose your friendship because of . . . whatever. I know we really don't know each other that well and because of how busy we were at Camden we couldn't talk a whole lot. I still hope you and I can become better acquainted (sp?). What I guess I mean is that there are things I want to know about you. I don't know. I wish you'd write.

I'm still having a great time. At least I think I am. I feel so relaxed that it's hard to say for sure. I'm sitting out by the pool now. I have the beginnings of a tan—and believe it or not I've cut down on my smoking! I'm getting healthy. Can you totally, like, believe it? (That's L.A. lingo for you.)

Love,
Anne

P.S. Did you get my last letter? Please do write.

Sept 24 1983
Dear Sean,
Hi(?). I feel sort of awkward writing to you because I guess you're pissed at me or something. Or are you? It must have been something I said in that last letter. Maybe you think I got carried away? I can understand that, I suppose. I tend to get a little extreme in my enthusiasm. You know you could have just written to me and told me to cut it out and that

would have been cool. Please, Sean, understand that this is kind of rough for me. Can you forgive me for whatever it was I did? Oh God, I just had this vision of me coming back to Camden in March and seeing you and feeling embarrassed and not knowing what to do. And maybe you won't even talk to me or something horrible like that. Could you write me and explain it all to me? Please? Please?

Anyway I'm sitting out by the pool in this great house in Palm Springs. It's late morning and I have done nothing for the last few hours but sit in the sun and stare at the palm trees. It's so tempting to go swimming and lay out by the pool and get drunk or do any of the innumerable decadent things one does in Palm Springs. But I'm just too lazy and the thought of mingling with all these obnoxious suntanned people fills me with dread. Really, the most mindless people are at the house right now: middle-aged studio execs with joints hanging from their lips and gold lighters they have for just these occassions. Dumb blond bunnies reeking of suntan oil and sex. Old rich women with gorgeous young boys (who for some reason are all gay). I checked out the bookshelves in this house and was embarrassed to find all these pornography books with titles like *Stud Ranch* and *Gestapo Pussy Ranch*. Sickening, isn't it?

About a week ago I was sitting in L.A.'s chicest nightclub with a few friends and the DJ was playing Yaz and Bowie and the videos were on and I was on my third gin and tonic and I realized that no matter where I am it's always the same. Camden, New York, L.A., Palm Springs—it really doesn't seem to matter. Maybe this should be disturbing but it's really not. I find it kind of comforting. There's a pattern out here that I've become accustomed to and I like it. Is this healthy? Is this the way it will be for the rest of my life? The rest of the time I'm in L.A.? I don't know. All I can think is that nothing is going to change overnight and the best I can do is keep trying. This might sound like I'm unhappy or depressed, which isn't true. I'm more content and relaxed than I've been in years. I've been away from New York for a month (I still kind of miss it) but it has done wonders for my psyche. I can't say that I've reverted back to the wholesome, idealistic little girl I was five years ago, but I'm a lot less depressed and I feel a lot less desperate and confused. Things are coming easier. I think you were right when you told me that night that I should "get the hell out of here and go to L.A." (do you remember that? you were very drunk). Your advice was good. Well, if I don't come back happier, I'll definitely come back healthier. I'm really into the whole health food scene out here. I'm popping vitamins like there's no tomorrow.

What can I say about life with my grandparents? They're a pretty normal couple and they're really nice to me. They buy me everything and anything I want (I must admit that I don't mind being spoiled out here). They seem to love buying me things and taking me to restaurants. The nicest thing is that they don't expect too much of me so they can't possibly be let down.

I seem to be getting more philosophical these days, especially here in the desert outside L.A. Or maybe it's just survival tactics. One thing I'm learning is not to expect too much from people. If I do I always feel let down. And there really isn't any need to feel that way. Of course, I still make a lot of mistakes but I'm learning. "Aha!" you're probably thinking, "I bet she's alluding to me." Well, you might be right. Letters are curious the way they can give a person away. Since I'm really not sure what you're thinking, all I can do is write and hope that you aren't ripping up the letters. Are you? Maybe you should stick a piece of paper in your typewriter and type out "Stop It" and send it to me (you do have my address in L.A., don't you? . . . do you even have a typewriter?). And that would do it. I'm not insensitive to out-and-out denials even though I'd be sorry to lose your friendship (we are friends, aren't we?). I seem to have this knack for making things complicated for myself. Do I make you feel like things are messy and uncomfortable between us? How awful. Can't we just simply be friends and just forget about whatever is messy and uncomfortable? Maybe I'm being foolish or simplistic to believe that things can be as easy as that, but why not?

So anyway, how are you? Are things okay up there in New Hampshire? Who do you hang out with? And how do you spend your days? What do you think about? Are you still painting? I am curious about your impressions of the place now. What do you see? What is your mood like after three terms there? Please write and tell me.

I just went to the kitchen for a Perrier and I overheard this fat old producer croon to this young man who bears a startling resemblance to Matt Dillon that he wants him and needs him. Why am I not surprised? I've been in L.A. for a long time, Sean. Nothing surprises me(!). Will you write me?

Love,
Anne

Sept 29 1983
Dear Sean,
Did you get my last letter?

My grandfather got very drunk last night and told me that everything is decaying and that we are coming to the end of something. My grandparents (who are *not* the most intelligent people) feel that they lived in the Golden Age and they told me that they are glad that they are going to die when they do. Last night my grandfather told me, over a huge bottle of Chardonnay, that he fears for his children and he fears for me. That was the first time I ever sensed any sincerity from him. But he truly meant it. And looking around and seeing

on TV about those poor boys in Beirut or Lebanon or wherever the hell they are and hearing about these drug dealers
who were all stabbed to death in the hills last night, I have to
agree with him to a certain extent. I keep feeling that people
are becoming less human and more animalistic. They seem
to think less and feel less so that everyone is operating on a
very primitive level. I wonder what you and I will see in our
lifetimes. It seems so hopeless yet we must keep on trying,
Sean. (I told you I was becoming more philosophical lately.)
I guess we can't escape being a product of the times, can we?
Write back, please? Still having fun in the sun!

Love,
Anne

Oct 11 1983
Dear Sean,
Did you get my other letters? I'm not even sure if you are
getting them. I just keep writing you letters and sending
them off and I feel like I might as well be stuffing them into
bottles and tossing them into the Pacific off of Malibu.
   I can't believe I've been here six weeks! My grandparents
told me a few days ago that they very much desire for me to
stay here for a year. I didn't have the heart to tell them that
I'd rather be locked in the Galleria for a year! Yes, I do like
being out here. I've had more adventures and know more
about the world than I'd have thought possible. L.A. is an
exciting place to be and my depression has left. But there is
a difference between visiting here and staying, living here. I
don't think I could stand being here forever. L.A. is like
another planet. I mean, all these thousands of blond-haired,
blue-eyed tan surfers with perfect bodies wandering the
streets, driving to the beach to catch the waves in their new
Porcshe's (and they are all *stoned*) and the beautiful older
women listening to KROQ in long black Rolls-Royces, trying

to find a parking space on Rodeo Drive—I don't know, it all strikes me as a bit odd. I am kind of tired of hanging out at the same clubs night after night and laying by the pool doing all this incredible coke. (Yes, I've tried some of the white powder—everybody, simply everybody, does it out here and I must agree with them: it definitely does make the days go by faster.) I use to enjoy it and it's not *that* bad but I don't know how much longer I can take it! Each day seems exactly like the day before. Each day seems the same. It's weird. It's like watching yourself in the same film but with a different sound track each time you watched it. If you saw me here in L.A. at Voila's or After Hours, you'd probably tell me what you told Kenneth when he asked you (I told him to ask you! Surprise!) what you thought of me and you said "That is a very sad, affected girl." (Oh, don't be embarrassed—I don't hold it against you. I forgive you, so don't worry.) Well, that's only part of my life in L.A.

My time at the studio is much more interesting and exciting. I've met *so many* famous actors and actresses the past month or so. My grandfather seems to know them all. I must have been to about a million screenings. And I've looked at twice as many scripts. Also, I'm picking up a fair amount of "studio lingo" and a lot of the business aspect. It's all very exciting.

I know I should write about this place but I can't come out with a coherent story. I don't have a firm enough grasp or base to write from. There's really not a whole lot to assimilate or see. It's just that I don't have enough time, with all the parties and screenings and my job at the studio and all. . . . By the way, how is your painting going? Are you still painting? I know you're busy and you don't have to do this if you don't want to but I would love it if you would send me a poem or a sketch or anything you've produced lately but even more than that I hope you are as happy and as healthy and as fulfilled as I am. And if your life is not too turbulent I would be very happy to get a letter from you. Just one.

Love,
Anne

Oct 22 1983
Dear Sean,
I'm sitting in the penthouse apartment of some friends in Century City. It's kind of late in the afternoon and I'm very relaxed. Someone gave me a Dalmane (I think I've spelled it right) because I had a headache and they told me it would help it. I feel very comfortable and relaxed right now. This is the first time I can remember since I was a kid that I am glad and content to be where I am. I don't know if you have ever felt like this, but I've always felt very uncomfortable and impatient with wherever I happen to be after a certain point. I get bored and irritated and everything I think is in the future tense (maybe like the way you got up suddenly that night when we were all sitting in the Café and you looked at me and abruptly left). I've always felt jumpy, like I couldn't stay in one place for any length of time. But something's changing. Totally rad (short for "radical"), as we say around here.

This is not going to be much of a letter because we're about to go out to dinner soon because someone made reservations at Spago and we're leaving in an hour to an hour and a half, someone says. What I want to tell you mostly is that I'm thinking about you and I hope you are all right. Are you? Will you write me? I want to hear from *you*. Please?

Love,
Anne

* * *

Oct 29 1983

Dear Sean,

There's something luxorious and wonderful about living in L.A. I feel like this is how I want to live forever. Every day there is some new adventure, some new person to talk to, different things to look at every night. This is the first time I've felt like I've found myself or something. Even during the worst moments I feel relaxed. Sometimes I get lonely but those moments are far and few between the other ones.

My relationships here with people aren't tense or trying because no one requires a whole lot of serious emotional investment at all. They're very safe—but don't get the idea that they're superficial. They're not. I mean, sure I feel kind of anxious and depressed because of them sometimes, but otherwise the sun is always out and the pool is always clean and heated so it's never cold and I'm happy with people out here.

Part of this has to do with the people I spend time with. They are all alive and interesting and *fun*. A lot of them are in the record industry or work at the studios and they are all people who are old enough to realize they don't want to waste their lives in a vacuum. They seem supportive and give me advice from their own experience.

Well, have you gotten all my letters? I can't remember how many I've sent—maybe four or five? Not a single letter from you, Sean. I'm shocked. No—just kidding. I'm not shocked, not really, I guess. I understand that your mood might be such that you wouldn't feel much like writing. But see, I'd like to know just what your mood *is*.

Love,
Anne

* * *

Nov 10 1983

Dear Sean,

How are you? Your long silence has not unnerved me (should it?). I figure that your life is what it is and I can fully understand you not having the energy or inclination to write. But I hope you don't mind the onslaught of letters from my direction.

It's interesting to me what I want to write about to you. I could be telling you all the details of my sexual adventures and bragging about my latest conquests. But that stuff seems pretty silly. I mean, it sounds cool but in reality it's awfully unoriginal. After a while it's like, so what? Drugs and alcohol and the sex that stems from them are pretty damn common (well, a bit more out here, but *still*) wherever you happen to be. It's all lost a lot of glamour for me. It's fun but that's all it is. I don't know at what stage you are emotionally or how your life is going or how much karma you have and where it's at but I feel pretty good about where I am. I mean, out here it's kind of fun coasting around, meeting all these totally gorgeous guys (they're stupid but oh so cute. Jealous? You shouldn't be) and hanging out with all these rich, spoiled Beverly Hills kids in clubs and going to the beach and going to sleep every day on Valium, dressing up, staying out all night dancing and drinking and whatever at someone's house on top of Mulholland. It's all fun but it's kind of getting boring. But I met this guy . . .

He's head of production at some studio out here and we were introduced at one of my grandfather's infamous bashes and we became friends. He has a Ferrari 308-GTB and we drive out to the desert, to Palm Springs, and go to his house and talk. Sean, the man is fascinating. His name is Randy and he's thirty years old and going out with this model who's off in New York this week for a shoot and he's been all over the world—as we say: a total intellectual, very distanced and existential in the best sense of the word. I told him all about myself and about New York and Camden, about my life, and I let him read some of my stories. He liked them but was honest enough about them to tell me he didn't think they were very commercial. Anyway he told me he'd love to read some more of my stuff. He also told me that he knows three vampires who live in Woodland Hills but out here you learn to take the good with the bad.

Randy is just one of the many interesting people out here whom I've met.

Just read this fabulous screenplay. A remake of Camus's *The Stranger* with Meursault as a bi break-dancing punk rocker. Randy showed it to me. I loved it. Randy thinks "basically unfilmable" and that filming an orange rolling around a parking lot for three hours would draw a bigger audience.

Well, I hope you do manage to write me, but if you don't . . . well, what can I say?

Love,
Anne

Nov 20 1983
Dear Sean,

I have to tell you more about Randy (remember? the studio exec?). He and I went up to his house on Mulholland, where we sat on his patio and watched the sunset. The moon was full and already visible as the sun was going down. Everything was so still and all there was was Randy and myself and his Ferrari, the wind, the Jacuzzi, the deepening colors of the sky. We shared a joint (yes, I smoked a little of it) and I thought of how lovely and relaxing it was to be away from everything and everyone. It helps me think more clearly, feel more clearly. Especially out in Palm Springs, where I am completely surrounded by desert—it's so comforting. You figure it out. I'm sure there is a psychological explanation for it. But I feel so mellow, so peaceful, so relaxed. And I think I help Randy too. When he tells me that he feels hollow and lost, I tell him not to be and he seems to understand. I've written some more stuff and when he isn't tired he reads it and even though all he really says is that it's a little more commercial than my earlier stuff and would probably do okay in foreign markets—it's still constructive criticism, right? I think he's right most of the time.

Randy's helped me so much in the last couple of months. He's made me less defensive. He has traveled so much, experienced so much and read so much more than I have. I trust his opinions. He is really my best friend here. The person to whom I confide everything. It's a little amazing—here I am in Los Angeles and my closest friend is a thirty-year-old studio executive. Life is odd, isn't it?

Listen, do take care of yourself and if you do find some spare time, I'd love to hear from you. By the way, if you want to call me you can get me either at my grandparents' house (213-275-9008) or at the studio (just ask for Anne) or at Randy's place (986-2030; it's unlisted). So if you're in the mood.

Love,
Anne

Nov 27 1983
Dear Sean,
Hi! So I'm sitting in a bungalow at the Beverly Hills Hotel visiting some friends of Randy's. I just got my best night's sleep since I've been in L.A. (I was taking tranquilizers for a while which really, like, screwed up my sleeping habits.) So far today I've done nothing but watch MTV and lie out by the pool. I told Randy (you remember Randy, don't you?) and some other people that I might go out with them tonight but I might not. Oh dear, what a life. Did I tell you that I've

been lying about my age? Everyone out here seems so young, *is* so young, that I've begun to feel old so I tell everyone that I'm seventeen or eighteen (I'm twenty). Randy thinks I'm sixteen. Can U believe it? A lot of the time I have to remind myself, yes, Anne, you are a college sophomore. It's curious and a little confusing but I guess it's not so very important. Well, I've got to go now. Drop me a letter? A note? Please?

> Love,
> Anne

Nov 30 1983
Dear Sean,
So here I am again writing to you. A lot of people are going out to Palm Springs this weekend. It's kind of hard to say no. I had a dream with you in it a few nights ago. (Me and my weird dreams—remember the one I told you about last term? I was so interested in that one that I wrote a paper for a psychology class two terms ago. Don't worry, though— no names were mentioned! Why didn't I tell you this at the time? Probably because I thought you'd be embarrassed.) This dream was pretty strange. You were living in L.A. and we were both a lot older and you invited me to your birthday party and I had to fly from somewhere and had a horrible time of it. Then the rest of the dream was about the party. Everyone who was there was old and it was depressing be- cause no one had really changed and even though it was wonderful to see you and you were as endearing as ever, I felt strange and out of place and I hated everyone. Not really hated but just couldn't cope.

Sean, I'm really thinking seriously about staying here a little longer. I've sort of forgotten what New York and Cam- den look like and I've forgotten a lot of faces from there and I don't know if I can face going back. I probably won't stay here but I've been thinking about it. I'm dreading seeing those people who I called my friends. I'd rather stay out here and *not*, as you so often put it, "deal with it," y'know? Everyone out here lives such exciting and interesting lives, going back seems so anticlimactic. (God, this letter is awfully meandering—I wonder if it makes any sense to you. If you find it unintelligible, then promise me you'll be nice enough to skim over it, okay?)

Well, everything out here is interesting and stimulating. L.A. (as usual) is a lot of fun. I've been really getting into the social life. (Met Duran Duran out here! It was so exciting I could have died—*right*.) I've been seeing a lot of really nice English boys. (There are a lot of English boys out here— don't ask why.) They're all really young and tan and work at stores on Melrose. Randy's friends with a lot of them. One of them in particular that Randy hangs out with is Scotty, whom I met over at Randy's place one day. He's 17 and psychic and works at Flip and is energetic and possibly the best-looking person I have ever seen. We're already planning to go down to the beach and go to the Springs and to some parties.

I'm also friends with Scotty's girlfriend, Christie (who Randy doesn't like; Christie doesn't like Randy either), who is a model (she's been in five Levi jeans commercials and a ZZ Top video—she's gorgeous—you'd recognize her if you saw her). Christie spends a lot of time in L.A. and in New York (she's basically bicoastal). She's half German and very, very sweet. And then there's Carlos, who is Randy's "confidante." He's about 18 and fascinating and models swimwear for *International Male*. He's always drunk and trying to tell jokes. He's basically a riot. Carlos is becoming one of the people I am closest to out here. Plus he thinks I make an incredible blond and has a lot of Valium and he practices a new kind of voodoo he picked up in Bakersfield.

Anyway I'm very busy. I go to this aerobics class with Christie in the morning and I've also been going to the beach a lot, working on my tan. I really haven't been to the studio too much. I've also been dancing and trying to do stuff.

Yesterday, Randy was really bummed out for some reason and so we took his Ferrari down to the Springs and he was really talking about offing himself, you know? He said to me, "I just want to die—I want it to end," and stuff like that. Well, I showed him some new leotards I bought and cheered him up and everything's okay now, but it kind of freaked me out. Well, we came back to L.A. and went to the beach and watched the sunset and everything was okay. Randy's stopped talking about how he feels that he's disintegrating. (Yeah, disintegrating—weird, huh?) Please, please, I'm begging you—write me? Okay, Sean?

Love,
Anne

Dec 5 1983
Dear Sean,

I bet you can't guess who is writing to you once more. Yes, it's me again. D'ya mind? I just had a very full day and I need to unwind a little. I don't feel like reading or being creative. I just want to sorta pour out my thoughts.

Typical Saturday. I got up late and shared a joint with Randy and Scotty who both slept outside together—while I slept upstairs in Randy's bed. Then we watched MTV for a long time and then we went to the beach and after that we went and watched the filming of this new Adam Ant video in Malibu—the English Prices were there. It was wild. Then I had an aerobics class and then Randy and I had a couple of drinks and watched some more MTV. And then we tried to go to sleep. Some nights we play all the new records Randy gets in the mail. He gets all these promotional copies to every damn record pressed. It's wild. And we listen to those sometimes. Anything to get Randy off his suicide kick. He's back on it, Sean. It scares me. Well, time to go to aerobics again in half an hour. Write me *please*.

Love,
Anne

Dec 7 1983
Dear Sean,
It rained for the first time since I've been here. The temperature dropped to about sixty-five and it rained. Randy and I laid around the house and I read some scripts and watched some MTV. Met Michael Jackson at a party in Encino. It wasn't that great. I'm still worried about Randy. Randy thinks that I'm going to leave him. He keeps talking about how everyone out here is just passing through, that no one has specific reasons for being here. Randy beat up Scotty and will only let Carlos (who is now his astrologer) and me into his house. I seem to be staying here all the time now. My grandparents don't seem to notice or mind. This sounds like I'm not too thrilled. But I am. It's still fun out here. Write me. I haven't gotten one letter from you, Sean. Please write.

Love,
Anne

Dec 10 1983
Dear Sean,
So once again I've been tempted to write a letter to someone back East. At the moment I am laying in Randy's bed because it's too fucking hot to do anything else. Smoking some really good grass and watching videos. So what else is new, right? But I like days like this. I hope it stays this way forever. December is the best month for parties (or so I've

heard) in L.A. The end of the year is coming nearer, with all the promise and hope of a whole other year to come. Think of how much things can change after only a year. Jesus Christ. When I think about what I was doing last December and compare it to *now*, it's hard to imagine that that person was me. Thank God time passes.

Randy is still going through rough times. He still feels "in limbo." He's laying right next to me now. Well, actually he's on the floor and I'm in the bed. Carlos is outside trying to get what sun is left. I deal with Randy as best I can. He's getting so thin. Randy's laughing right now. Wait . . . okay, he's all right now. Oh, Sean, I don't know if I'm going back to Camden. The thought of going back to all those stupid pseudo-intellectuals sounds terrible. I don't think I can handle it. There's really no reason for me to go back to school. I mean, I'd absolutely love to see you. But going back to New Hampshire seems like a bummer.

Is there anything you'd like me to send you? How about a big supply of Valium (which everyone seems to have). No—I won't contribute to your drug habit (ha ha). Randy seems to have everything here. Stuff I don't even know the names of. (Los Angeleans aren't very shy about their pills.)

We (Randy, Carlos, someone named Wallace the Roachclip and I) might be going to Palm Springs for Christmas. It depends on how Randy is feeling. My grandparents want me to stay with them but I don't know if I'm going to. I might. I might not.

It seems so easy to stay here in L.A. and get into the record industry or work at my grandfather's studio (I don't know yet—even if I haven't been there a whole lot in the last month). But my grandparents don't really notice my absence. They're both tranquilizer addicts. I recently found out they're both heavily into Librium. Carlos just came in— Carlos says "hi" and is asking if you are cute. What do you think I told him? You'll never know.

I'll be 21 when you get this or 18—depending on who you ask. Where will we be in ten years? I wonder what's going to be happening then? I wonder what's happening now.

A friend of Carlos was found dead in a garbage can in Studio City. He had been shot in the head and skinned. How awful, huh? Carlos doesn't seem very sad but Carlos is a very strong person so that doesn't surprise me. Carlos just put in a new videotape. We've been watching *Night of the Living Dead* and *Dawn of the Dead*. Have you ever seen them? Randy plays them all the time. I've seen them a lot since I've been here. They're both really fun. Carlos is trying to wake Randy up to watch the movie. Carlos says L.A. is swarming with vampires. I'm taking a Valium.

Listen, Sean. I've decided that I'm not going to write to you anymore unless I get a letter from you in return. I'm not going to plead anymore. If you don't write me, I simply won't write back. So write me and take care.

Love,
Anne

Dec 26 1983
Dear Sean,

I just reread a first draft of this letter and realized that it says nothing about what's happening specifically. Sorry, I seem to be incapable of writing a newsy letter. Descriptions bore me, I guess, and the best I can do are these scribbles, which may not make much sense to you. How's everything with you? How was your Christmas? I hope you're enjoying yours. I'm at Christie's right now, sitting by the pool. I went shopping earlier and bought earrings, two pairs of slippers, a bag of oranges and then had lunch with someone from the studio, who juggled for me, then peed on a potted palm.

Randy OD'd a week ago (I think it was a week ago). Well, at least that's what they say he died of. They all told me that

Randy OD'd, but Sean, I saw the room where they found him and there was so much blood. It was everywhere. There was blood on the ceiling, Sean. How can blood get on the ceiling if you OD? How can it get there anyway? (Scotty says only if you explode.) Well, I went to the beach with Lance (this really gorgeous punker who works at Poseur on Melrose) and Lance gave me some Seconal, which helped a lot. I feel much better now. I really do.

I've been talking to my stepmother about staying here. I won't be living with my grandparents but at Randy's place (it's all cleaned up, so don't worry) with Carlos. And I also get Randy's Ferrari, so it's not like I'm left empty-headed. But nothing is definite yet. Haven't been thinking too much about it. Are you going to write?

Love,
Anne

Jan 29 1984
Dear Sean,
Doesn't it seem like a long time since I've written you? I guess I'm not much into it anymore. Well, I'm still around and alive, so don't worry. Can you believe I'm actually staying here? That I've already been here five months? Oh God. Well, I guess I won't be going back to Camden in the fall. I've gotten so used to things out here. I've been driving around a lot and I go to the studio sometimes. Sometimes I go out to Palm Springs. It's quiet at night.

I'm collaborating on a screenplay with this guy I met at the studio named Tad. I can't really talk too much about it but it's about these camp counselors and a big snake and it's really scary. (Maybe I'll send you a copy.) Tad's really an artist (he paints these fantastic murals in Venice) but he wants to write screenplays. No one has seen Carlos for weeks. Last I heard, he was in Vegas, though someone else told me that they found both of his arms in a bag off La Brea. He was going to write the screenplay with me. I've shown part of it to my grandmother. She liked it. She said it was commercial.

Love,
Anne

9

ANOTHER GRAY AREA

I'm kind of looking at Christie dancing next to the wide-screen television set. Fun Boy 3's on MTV, singing "Our Lips Are Sealed," and Christie's dancing rhythmically, spaced out, hands running over her bikini, her eyes closed. I'm bored but won't admit it and Randy is lying on the floor, immobile, looking up at Christie, and Christie almost steps on him, both wasted. I'm sitting in the beige chair next to the beige couch that Martin is lying on. Martin is wearing a pair of Dolphin shorts, Wayfarers, browsing through the new issue of *GQ*. The video ends and Christie falls to the floor giggling, mumbling that she is very high. Randy lights another joint and inhales deeply and coughs and hands it to Christie. I look back at Martin. Martin keeps staring at a particular picture in the magazine. Now the Police are on MTV in black and white and Sting's huge blond head stares straight out at the four of us and starts singing. I look away from the screen and over at Christie. Randy hands me the joint and I take a toke and close my eyes but I'm so stoned right now that the hit doesn't do anything, just moves me to the pseudorealization that I am located somewhere beyond communication. "God, Sting is gorgeous," Christie moans or maybe it's Randy. Christie takes another hit off the joint, rolls over onto her stomach and looks up at Martin. But Martin only nods, adjusts his sunglasses. Christie keeps looking up at him. Martin has not said a word during the past twelve videos. I have kept count. Christie is my girlfriend, a model who I think is from England.

I stand up, sit down, stand up again, pull on my shorts and walk out to the balcony and stand there with my hands on a railing, staring at Century City. The sun is setting and the sky is orange and purple and it seems to be getting hotter. Take a deep breath, trying to remember when Christie and Randy came over, when Martin let them in, when they turned on MTV, when they ate the first pineapple, when they lit the second joint, the third, the fourth. But now, inside, the video has changed and a boy gets sucked into a giant cloud shaped like a television, the colors of a rainbow. Christie is on top of Martin on the couch. Martin still has his sunglasses on. The issue of *GQ* he was holding is now on the beige floor. I walk past them, step over Randy and walk into the kitchen and pull a bottle of apricot-and-blueberry juice out of the refrigerator and walk back to the patio. I finish the juice and watch the sky get dark some more and when I turn back, I see that Martin and Christie are probably in Martin's room, probably nude on beige sheets with the stereo on, Jackson Browne singing, softly. I walk over to Randy and look down on him.

"Want to go and get something to eat?" I ask.

Randy doesn't say anything.

"Want to go and get something to eat?"

Randy starts to laugh, eyes still closed.

"Want to go and get something to eat?" I ask again.

He grabs the *GQ* and, still laughing, puts it over his face.

"Want to go and get something to eat?" I ask.

On the cover is John Travolta and it almost looks like John Travolta is lying on the floor, giggling, wasted, wearing only a pair of cutoff jeans. I turn away and look at the TV screen: a toy airplane with a rock star inside it trying to control the panels in mock desperation and he's singing to a girl not looking at him, doing her nails. I walk out of the apartment and drive onto Wilshire and then to some café in Beverly

Hills called Café Beverly Hills where I order a salad and an iced tea.

I wake up out of some kind of stupor at eleven-twenty and when I walk into the kitchen looking for an orange or some matches for my bong I find a note written on Beverly Hills Hotel stationery that tells me to meet someone for lunch at a house up in the hills above Sunset where someone is directing a video for a band called the English Prices. Someone has left an address and directions and after about an hour of lying on the balcony, dreaming beneath the sun in my Jockey shorts, listening to the sound of videos flashing by in a soothing, endless hum, I decide to meet someone for lunch. Before I leave, Spin calls and tells me that ever since Lance left for Venezuela he's had a hard time finding good coke and that there are lots of frightened people in town and that he might drop out of USC if he can't find the right Mercedes in the fall and that the service at Spago is getting worse.

"But what do you want?" I ask, turning the TV off.

"Need some coke. Anything. Four, five ounces."

"I can get you that by, uh . . ." I stop. "Um, Saturday."

"Dude," Spin says. "Like I need it before Saturday."

"Not Saturday? Like when?"

"Like tonight."

"Like Friday?"

"Like tomorrow."

"Like Friday," I sigh. "I could get it for you tonight but I don't really want to."

"Dude," he sighs. "Bogus but okay."

"Okay? Just come over sometime Friday," I say.

"Friday, right? I appreciate this. There are a lot of frightened people in this town, dude."

"Yeah, I know," I tell him. "I sort of understand what you're talking about."

"Friday, right?" he asks.
"Uh-huh."

I park the car outside the house and walk up the steps leading to a front door. Two girls, young and tan and blond, wearing ripped sweatshirts and headbands, are sitting on the steps staring off into space, not saying anything to each other, ignoring me as I walk past them into the house. I can hear music coming from above and then it stops. I walk slowly upstairs, into a large room that seems to take up the entire second floor of the house. I stand in the doorway and watch as Martin talks to a cameraman and points at Leon, who is the lead singer of the English Prices, and he's smoking a cigarette and holding a gun, a toy, in one hand and in the other a small hand mirror that he keeps checking his hair in. Behind Leon is a long table with nothing on it and behind that the rest of the band and someone has painted the backdrop behind the band a pale pink with green stripes and Martin is walking over to Leon who puts the hand mirror away after Martin slaps his wrist and Leon hands Martin the toy gun. I move into the room and lean against a wall, being careful not to step on any wires or cables. There's a girl sitting on a pile of pillows next to where I'm standing and she's young and tan and blond and wearing a ripped sweatshirt and a pink headband holding up a lot of hair and when I ask her what she's doing here she tells me that she kind of knows Leon and she doesn't look at me when she says this and I turn away from her and look at Martin who is now on the table and he rolls off it and onto the floor and looks up into the camera, pointing the toy gun at the lens, and then Leon rolls off the table and onto the floor and looks up into the camera, pointing the toy gun at the lens, and then Martin rolls off the table and onto the floor and looks up into the camera, pointing the toy gun at the lens, and then Leon rolls off the table and onto the floor and looks up into the camera, pointing the toy gun at the lens. Leon is now standing, his hands on his hips, shaking his head, and Martin lies on the floor looking up into the camera and he can see me and he gets up and walks over, leaving the gun on the floor, and Leon picks it up and smells it and there is basically nobody here.

"What's going on?" Martin asks.

"You left me a note," I say. "Something about having lunch."

"I did?"

"Yeah," I say. "You left me a note."

"I don't think I did."

"I saw a note," I say, unsure.

"Well, maybe someone did." Martin doesn't look too sure either. "If you say so, dude. But if you think it was me you're freaking me out, dude."

"I'm pretty sure there was a note," I say. "I could have been hallucinating, but not today."

Martin looks over at Leon tiredly. "Well, um, okay, uh, yeah, I'll be able to get out of here in around twenty minutes and, uh." He calls out to the cameraman, "Smoke machine still busted?"

The cameraman is now on the floor and he calls back, flatly, "Smoke machine busted."

"Okay, well." Martin looks at his Swatch and says, "We just have to get this shot right and"—Martin's voice rises but only a little—"Leon's being a real jerk about it. Isn't that right, Leon?" Martin is rubbing his hand across his face slowly.

Across the room Leon looks up from the gun and makes his way very slowly toward Martin.

"Martin, I'm not gonna jump off that fucking table onto the fucking floor and look into the fucking camera and wink. No fucking way. That's fucking lame."

"You said fucking five times, you piece of trash," Martin says.

"Oh boy," Leon says.

"You're gonna do it, man," Martin says, sort of sounding like he means it.

"No, Martin, I'm not. It sucks and I'm not going to do it."

"But you were in a video with singing frogs," Martin protests. "You were in a video where you turned into a bewildered tree, a plate full of water and a large, talkative banana, respectively."

One of the band members says, "He's got a point."

"So what?" Leon shrugs. "You've got viral herpes, Rocko."

"Has anybody forgotten that I'm directing this?" Martin asks air.

"Hey, I wrote the fucking song, stooge." Leon looks over at the girl who kind of knows him, sitting on the pile of pillows. The girl smiles at Leon. Leon looks at her, confused, then away, then back again at the girl and then away again, then back again, then away.

"Leon," Martin's saying. "Listen, the video doesn't make sense without this shot."

"But you're missing the point, which is I don't *want* it to make sense. It doesn't need to make sense," Leon's saying. "What are you talking about? Sense? Jesus." Leon looks at me. "Do you know what sense is?"

"No," I say.

"See?" Leon says accusingly to Martin.

"You want all those retards in whatchamacallit, Nebraska, staring at your video on MTV openmouthed, not realizing that it's all a joke, thinking that after you shot your girlfriend in the head and the guy she was partying with that you *meant* it? Huh? You didn't mean it, Leon. You liked the girl you shot in the head. The girl you shot in the head was a flower to you, Leon. Your image, Leon. I'm just helping you shape your image, okay? Which is of a nice friendly guy from Anaheim who is so fucking lost the mind reels, okay? Let's just do it that way. It took someone four months to write this script—that works out to a month a minute, which is pretty impressive if you think about it—and it's your image," Martin persists. "Image, image, image, image."

I put my hands to my head and look at Leon, who doesn't seem that different than when I saw him with Tim at Madame Wong's last Tuesday but maybe a little different, in a way I'm not sure about.

Leon is looking at the floor and sighing and then at the girl and then at me and then back at Martin and I have the feeling I'm not going to be able to have lunch with Martin, which is a loss of some kind.

"Leon," Martin says, "this is Graham, Graham this is Leon."

"Hi," I say softly.

"Yeah?" Leon mutters.

There's a longer pause, this one more distinct. The cameraman stands up, then sits back down on the floor and lights a cigarette. The band just stand there, no evidence of motion, staring at Leon. The cameraman says "Smoke machine busted" again and one of the girls from outside walks in and asks if anyone has seen her KAJAGOOGOO T-shirt lying around anywhere and then if Martin needs to use her anymore.

"No, baby, I've used you all up," Martin says. "That's not to say you weren't great but someday I'll give you a buzz."

She nods, smiles, leaves.

"She's pretty hot," Leon says, watching her walk away. "Did you do her, Rocko?"

"Don't know" is Rocko's answer.

"Yeah, she's pretty hot, she stays in shape, she's fucked everyone I know, she's an angel, she has a hard time remembering her phone number, her mother's name, to breathe," Martin sighs.

"But the point is I could fuck her quite easily," Leon says.

The girl sitting on the pillows who kind of knows Leon looks down.

"You would be fucking an abyss," Martin says, yawning, stretching. "A clean, vaguely talented abyss. But an abyss nonetheless."

I put my hands to my head again, then in my jeans.

"Well," Martin starts. "This was all refreshing. What are we doing here, Leon? Huh? What are we doing here?"

"I don't know." Leon shrugs. "What are we doing here?"

"I'm asking you—what are we doing here?"

"I don't know," Leon says, still shrugging. "I don't know. Ask him."

Martin looks at me.

"I don't know what we're doing here either," I say, startled.

"You don't know what we're doing here?" Martin looks back at Leon.

"Shit," Leon says. "We'll talk about it later. Let's take a break. I'm vaguely hungry. Does anyone know anyone who has beer? Hal, do you have any beer?" he asks the cameraman.

"The smoke machine is busted," the cameraman says.

Martin sighs. "Listen, Leon."

Leon is now staring into the hand mirror, checking his hair, a huge, stiff, white-blond pompadour.

"Leon, are you listening to me?" Martin whispers.

"Yes," Leon whispers back.

"Are you listening to me?" Martin whispers.

I start to walk away, move out the door, past the girl on the pile of pillows, who is pouring a bottle of water over her head, in a sad way or not I can't tell. I walk down the stairs, past the girls, one who says "Nice Porsche," the other, "Nice ass," and then I'm in my car, driving away.

* * *

After finishing part of a salad made up of ten different kinds of lettuce, the only thing she ordered, Christie mentions that Tommy from Liverpool was found somewhere in Mexico last weekend and that maybe there was a hint of foul play since his body was completely drained of blood and his neck was hacked open and his vital organs were missing even though the Mexican authorities are telling people that Tommy "drowned," and if he didn't drown exactly then maybe it was just a "suicide," but Christie is sure that he definitely did not drown and we're in some restaurant on Melrose and I don't have any cigarettes left and she doesn't take off her sunglasses when she tells me that Martin's a nice guy so I can't see where her eyes are focused which would probably tell me nothing anyway. She says something about immense guilt and the check comes.

"Forget it," I say. "I'm not really sorry you brought it up in the first place."

"He is a nice guy," she says.

"Yeah," I say. "He's a nice guy."

"I don't know," she says.

"You slept with him?"

She breathes in, then looks at me. "He's supposedly 'staying' at Nina's."

"But he told me Nina is, um, insane," I tell her. "Martin told me that Nina is insane and that she makes her child work out at a gym and that the child is four." Pause. "Martin told me that he had to spot him."

"Just because he's a child doesn't mean he should be in lousy shape," Christie says.

"I see."

"Graham," Christie starts. "Martin is *noth*ing. You were just on edge last week. I couldn't deal with you just sitting in a chair saying nothing and holding that giant avocado."

"But aren't we, like, seeing each other or something?" I ask.

"I guess." She sighs. "We're together now. I'm eating a salad with you now." She stops, lowers Martin's Wayfarers, but I'm not looking at her anyway. "Forget Martin. Besides, who cares if we see other people? Don't tell me one of us."

"See or fuck?" I ask.

"Fuck." She sighs. "I think." Pause. "I guess."

"Okay," I say. "Who knows, right?"

Later she asks, grinning, rubbing suntan oil over my abs, "Did you care that I slept with him?" and then, "Nice definition."

"No," I finally say.

The sound of gunshots wakes me up. I look over at Martin, who is lying on his stomach, nude, breathing deeply, Christie between us along with two fluffy calico cats and a guinea pig I have never seen before wearing a small diamond necklace, and another couple of shots are fired and they both flinch in their sleep. I get out of bed and put on a pair of Bermuda shorts and a FLIP T-shirt and take the elevator down to the lobby, put on my sunglasses since my eyes are puffy. As the elevator doors open, two more shots are fired. I walk slowly through the dark lobby. The night doorman, young guy, tan, blond, maybe twenty, a Walkman around his neck, stands by the door, looking outside. On Wilshire there are seven or eight police cars parked outside the building across the street. Another shot is fired from the apartment building. The doorman stares, dazed, mouth open, Dire Straits coming from the Walkman. A big blue Slurpee glows from where it's sitting on the front desk.

"What's going on?" I ask.

"I don't know. I think some guy has his wife up there and is, like, threatening to shoot her or something. Something like that," the doorman says. "Maybe he's already shot her. Maybe he's already killed a whole bunch of people."

I walk over next to him mainly because I like the song on the Walkman. It's so cold in the lobby our breath steams.

"I think there's a SWAT team up in the building trying to talk him down," the doorman says. "I don't think you should open the door."

"I won't," I say.

Another shot. Another police car arrives. Then an ambulance. My stepmother for about ten months, who I ended up sleeping with twice, gets out of a van and is lit, positioned in front of a camera. I yawn, shivering.

"Did the shots wake you up?" the doorman asks.

"Yeah." I nod.

"You're the guy who lives on the eleventh floor, right? The guy who directs videos, Jason or something, visits you a lot?"

"Martin?" I say.

"Yeah, hi. I'm Jack," the doorman says.

"I'm Graham." We shake hands.

"I've talked to Martin a couple of times," Jack says.

"About . . . what?"

"Just that he knows someone in a band I was almost in." Jack takes out a pack of clove cigarettes, offers me one. Three more shots, then a helicopter starts circling. "What do you do?" he asks.

"Go to school."

Jack lights my cigarette. "Yeah? Where do you go to school?"

"I go to school at . . ." I stop. "Um, I go to school at U . . . at, um, USC."

"Yeah? What are you? Freshman?"

"I'll be a sophomore in the fall," I tell him. "I think."

"Yeah? Cool." Jack thinks about this for a minute. "Do you know Tim Price? Blond guy? Really good-looking but, like, the worst person in the world? I think he's in a fraternity?"

"I don't think so," I tell him. There's a horrible scream from across Wilshire, then smoke.

"How about Dirk Erickson?" he asks.

Pretending to think about it for a minute, I answer, "No, I don't think so." Pause. "But I know a guy named Wave." Pause. "He's very fit and his family basically owns Lake Tahoe."

Another police car arrives.

"Do you go to school?" I ask, after a while.

"No, I'm an actor, really."

"Yeah?" I ask. "What have you been in?"

"A commercial for gum. Boyfriend in a Clearasil spot." Jack shrugs. "Unless you're willing to do some pretty awful things it's hard getting a job in this town—and I'm willing."

"Yeah, I guess."

"I really want to get into video," Jack says.

"Yeah," I say. "Video, dude."

"Yeah, that's why Mark's a really good contact." There's a huge crashing sound, then more smoke, then another ambulance.

"You mean Martin," I say. "It would probably help out a lot, dude, if you get the names straight."

"Yeah, Martin," he says. "He's a good contact."

"Yeah, he's a good contact," I say slowly. I finish the cigarette and stand by the door, waiting for the sound of more gunfire. When it looks like nothing much is going to happen, Jack offers me a joint and I shake my head and say that I've got to drink some juice then get some more sleep. "There are two calico cats and a guinea pig I have never seen before upstairs in my bed." Pause. "Plus I need to drink some more juice."

"Yeah, sure, dude, I understand," the doorman says, sparking up. "Juice, man. It's good."

The pot smells sweet and I kind of want to stay. Another shot, more screams. I head toward the elevator.

"Hey. I think maybe something's gonna happen," the doorman says as I step into the elevator.

"What?" I ask, holding the doors open.

"Maybe something will happen," the doorman says.

"Yeah?" I say, unsure of what to do. I stare at the doorman, standing in the lobby, smoking a joint, then at the Slurpee, and we both wait.

I get a conference call from my mother, my father's lawyer and someone from the studio he works at, at eleven the next morning. I listen, then tell them I'll fly to Las Vegas today, and I hang up to make flight reservations. Martin wakes up, looks over at me, yawning. I wonder where Christie is.

"Oh man," Martin groans, stretching. "What time is it? What's going on?"

"It's eleven. My father died."

A long pause.

"You . . . had a dad?" Martin asks.

"Yeah."

"What happened?" Martin sits up, then lies back down, confused. "How, man?"

"Plane crash," I say.

I take the pipe off the nightstand, look for a lighter.

"Are you serious?" he asks.

"Yeah."

"Are you okay about it?" he asks. "Can you deal?"

"Yeah, I guess," I say, inhaling.

"Wow," he says. "I guess I'm sorry." There's a pause. "Should I be?"

"Don't," I say, dialing information for LAX.

I walk up to the crash site with a Cessna 172 engine special-ist who has to take photos of the condition of the engine for his company's files and a ranger who acts as our guide up the mountain and was the first person to appear at the wreckage on Friday. I meet the two guys at my suite at the MGM Grand and we take a jeep up to about the midway point on the mountain. From there we walk a narrow path that is steep and covered with dead leaves. On the way up to the crash site I talk to the ranger, actually a young guy, maybe nineteen, about my age, good-looking. I ask the ranger what the body looked like when he found it.

"You really want to know?" the ranger asks, a smile appearing on his calm, square face.

"Yeah." I nod.

"Well, this'll sound awful funny but when I first saw it, I don't know, it kind of looked to me like a . . . like a miniature hundred-and-ten-pound Darth Vader," he tells me, scratching his head.

"A what?" I ask.

"Yeah, like a Darth Vader. Like a little Darth Vader. You know. Darth Vader from *Star Wars*, right?" the ranger is saying with a faint accent I can't place.

The ranger, who I guess I'm starting to flirt with, sort of, continues. The torso and head were completely skinless and they were sitting upright. What was left of the arm bones was resting on where the steering column should have been. None of the cabin was left. "The torso was just sitting there, right on the ground. It was like completely charred black, down to the bone in a lot of places." The ranger stops walking and looks up at the mountain. "Yeah, it looked pretty bad but I've seen a lot worse."

"Like what?"

"I once saw a large group of black ants carry part of someone's intestine to their queen."

"That's . . . impressive."

"I'd say so."

"What else?" I ask. "Darth Vader? Wow, man."

The ranger looks at me and then at the engine specialist ahead of us and continues up the path. "You really interested?"

"I guess," I say.

"That was about it," the ranger says. "There were a lot of flies. Some smell. But that's about it."

After walking for another forty minutes we reach the site of the crash. I look around at what's left of the plane. The cabin was almost totally destroyed and so there's nothing much left except the tips of the wings and the tail, which is intact. But there's no nose and the engine is completely smashed. No one has found the propeller even though there has been an extensive search for it. There is no dashboard either, not even melted parts. It seems that the plane's aluminum frame crunched on impact and then melted.

Since small Cessnas are such lightweight planes, I'm able to lift the entire tail and flip it over. The specialist tells me that the fire that melted the plane was probably caused by impact rips in the fuel tanks. On a Cessna the fuel tanks are in the wings on both sides of the cabin. I also find bits of bone in the ashes and pieces of my father's camera. I stand against a rock next to the ranger as the Cessna specialist hesitantly takes some photographs of us that I want.

I also talk to the pathologist later that day, after a nap, and he tells me that the body was shaken up on its trip down the mountain in the plastic bag, since what he received in the pathology lab is quite different from what the primary sighting reports indicate. The pathologist tells me that he found most of the organs unrecognizable "as organs" due to the devastating impact and severe burning damage suffered by my father. Since the body is unrecognizable as my father, identification is done on his fake teeth. My father's original teeth were lost in an automobile accident on PCH when he was twenty, I find out.

* * *

On the flight back to L.A. I sit next to an old man who keeps drinking Bloody Marys and mumbling to himself. As the plane makes its descent he asks me if this is my first time in L.A. and I say "Yeah" and the man nods and I put the headset back on and listen to Joan Jett and the Blackhearts sing "Do You Wanna Touch Me?" and tense up as the plane breaks through smog to land. As I get up, taking out my overnight bag from the overhead compartment, I drop my lighter in the old man's lap and he hands it to me, smiling, and, sticking his tongue out a little, offers me a role in a porn film starring some good-looking black guys. The only things in my overnight bag are a couple of T-shirts, a pair of jeans, one suit, a copy of *GQ*, an unopened letter from my father that was never sent, my bong, and a handful of ashes in a small black film container, the rest having been gambled away at a blackjack table in the casino of Caesars Palace. I close the overhead compartment. The old man, wrinkled and drunk, winks at me and says "Welcome to L.A." and I say "Thanks, dude."

I open the door of the apartment and walk in and turn on the television and put the overnight bag down in the sink. Martin's not here. I pull a bottle of apricot-apple juice out of the refrigerator and sit on the balcony waiting for Martin or Christie. I get up, open the overnight bag and find the *GQ* and read it out on the balcony and then I finish the juice. The sky gets dark. I wonder if Spin called. I don't hear Martin open the door. The ice machine in the refrigerator clanks out cubes of ice.

"Man, it was hot today," Martin says, holding a beach towel and a volleyball.

"Was it?" I ask him. "I heard it snowed."

"Do any gambling?"

"I lost about twenty thousand dollars. It was okay."

After a while Martin says, "Spin called."

I don't say anything.

"He's a little pissed, Graham," Martin says. "You should have called him."

"Oops big-time," I say. "I'll give him a call."

"We have reservations at Chinois at nine."

I look up. "Great."

The music from the television carries out to the balcony. Martin turns away and walks back into the apartment. "I'm gonna peel a pomegranate, then take a shower, okay?"

"Yeah. Okay." I move off the balcony too and try to find Spin's number but then I'm following Martin into the bathroom and later I find Christie's Guess jeans by the side of Martin's bed and underneath that is a bayonet.

Next day we're sitting at Carny's and Martin's eating a cheeseburger and he can't believe that an ex-girlfriend of mine is on the cover of this week's *People*. I tell him I can't believe it either. I finish my french fries, take a swallow of Coke and tell Martin I want to get stoned. Martin also slept with the girl on the cover of this week's *People*. I watch as a red Mercedes passes by slowly in the heat, a shirtless guy at the wheel, who Martin also slept with, and in an instant my and Martin's reflection flashes by in the side of the car. Martin starts complaining that he hasn't finished the English Prices video yet, that Leon's causing hassles, that the smoke machine still doesn't work, will probably never work, that Christie is a drag, that yellow is his favorite color, that he recently made friends with a tumbleweed named Roy.

"Why do you shoot those things?" I ask.

"Videos? Why?"

"Yeah."

"I don't know." He looks at me and then at the cars passing by on Sunset. "Not everyone has a rich mommy and daddy. I mean, mommy. And"—he takes a swallow of my Coke—"not everyone deals drugs."

"But your parents are loaded," I protest.

"Loaded can be interpreted in a lot of ways, dude," Martin says.

I sigh, pick at a napkin. "You're a real . . . enigma."

"Listen, Graham. I feel bad enough crashing out at your place. You footing the bill for Nautilus, Maxfield's. All that."

Another red Mercedes passes by.

"Listen," Martin's saying. "After these next two videos I'll be hot."

"Hot?" I ask.

"Yeah, hot," he says.

"Like, how hot? Medium hot? How hot?" I ask.

"Maybe really hot. Maybe spicy," he says. "The English Prices are big. Heavy rotation on MTV. Opening for Bryan Metro. Big."

"Yeah?" I ask. "Hot and big?"

"Sure. Easy. Leon is a star."

"Did you sleep with Christie while I was gone?" I ask.

He looks at me, groaning. "Oh man, of course I did."

Christie and I are standing in line for a movie in Westwood. It's almost midnight and hot and Westwood is packed. The sidewalks are so crowded in fact that the movie line merges with the people walking along the street and the people on the other side of the movie line coming out of shoe stores and places that sell frozen yogurt and posters. Christie is eating Italian ice cream and telling me that Tommy is actually hanging out in Delaware and that it was Monty and not Tommy who was found hacked to death in San Diego, not

Mexico, his blood drained, not Tommy's, like she heard, because she got a postcard with Richard Gere on it from Tommy but Corey *was* found sealed in a metal drum buried in the desert. She asks me if Delaware is a state and I tell her that I'm not too sure but that I'm really certain I saw Jim Morrison at a car wash on Pico this morning. He was drinking soda and minding his own business. Christie finishes the ice cream and wipes her lips with a napkin, complains about her implants.

Two people in front of us are talking about a drug bust in Encino last night, how the new year is approaching steadily. I watch as a young Hispanic girl crosses the street, moving toward the theater. As she crosses the street in long, purposeful strides, a black convertible Rolls-Royce almost hits her, braking suddenly, swerving. The people on the sidewalk watch silently. One girl, maybe, says "oh no." The driver of the Corniche, a tan guy, shirtless and wearing a sailor's cap, smoking a cigar, yells "Watch out, you dumb spic" and the girl, not shaken at all, walks calmly to the other side of the street. I wipe sweat off my forehead and watch as the girl, unfazed, walks over to a palm tree and leans against it, her white T-shirt with the word CALIFORNIA on it soaked with sweat, her breasts outlined beneath the cotton, a gold cross hanging from her neck, small, a glimmer, and even when she notices me looking at her I keep staring at the smooth brown face and the vacant black eyes and the calm, bored expression, and now she's moving away from the palm tree and making her way toward where I stand, still staring, transfixed, and she walks up to me slowly, the warm winds blowing, the crowd parting slightly, the sweat on her face drying as she gets closer to me and she says, eyes widening, in a low, hushed whisper, "Mi hermano."

I don't say anything, just stare back.

"Mi hermano," she whispers again.

"What?" Christie's saying. "What do you want? Do you know her, Graham?"

"Mi hermano," she says once more, urgent this last time, and then she moves on. I lose sight of her in the crowd.

"Who was she?" Christie asks as the line begins to move toward the theater.

"I don't know," I tell her, looking back at where the girl, who looks worth following, went.

"Really—they're overrunning the city," Christie says. "She was probably stoned out of her mind." She pulls out her ticket, handing me mine. The people who were talking about the drug bust and 1985 turn around, look at Christie like they recognize her.

"What did she say?" I ask.

"Me hermano? I think it's a kind of chicken enchilada with a lot of salsa," Christie says. "Maybe it's a taco, who knows?" She shrugs uncomfortably. "These implants are killing me and it's so hot."

We walk into the theater and sit down and the movie starts and after the movie, driving down Wilshire, back to the apartment, we come to another red light and at the bus stop are five Mexican punk rockers standing around, wearing T-shirts with black crosses and skulls the color of sulfur painted on them and they glare at the two of us in Christie's convertible BMW and I gaze back and back at the apartment we have sex and Martin watches part of the time.

Tonight Martin mentions something about a new club that opened on Melrose, way down Melrose, and so we drive down to Melrose in Martin's convertible, which Nina Metro gave him as a Halloween present, and Martin knows the owner at the club and we get in free with no hassles. Animotion is blasting out, people are dancing, the shower scene from *Psycho* is playing nonstop on the video screens above the bar and we do some coke in a bathroom and I meet a girl named China who tells me I look like a taller Billy Idol and I bump into Spin.

"Hey, where have you been?" he asks, screaming over the music, staring at Janet Leigh getting stabbed over and over again.

"Las Vegas," I tell him. "Brazil. Inside a tornado."

"Yeah? How about a quarter ounce?" he asks.

"Sure. Anything," I tell him.

"Yeah?" he says, leaving. "I must talk to China. I think Madonna's here."

"Madonna?" I ask him. "Where?"

He can't hear me. "Great. Call you Friday. Let's do Spago."

"I'm not in a hurry," I say.

I wave and he walks away and I end up dancing with Martin and two of these blond girls he knows who work at RCA and then we all go back to the apartment on Wilshire and get really stoned and take turns with these three high school kids we meet outside, waiting in a parking lot, across the street from the club on Melrose.

I drive to the Beverly Center and wander around, lingering in clothing stores, flipping through magazines in bookstores, and at around six I sit in an empty restaurant on the top floor of the mall and order a glass of milk and a pastry, which I don't eat, unsure of why I even ordered it. At seven, after most of the shops have closed, I decide to go to one of the movies at one of the fourteen small theaters on the top floor of the mall, not too far from where I'm sitting. I pay my admission and buy some wafers and sit in one of the small rooms and watch a movie in a daze. After the movie ends I decide to sit through the first part again since I don't remember what happened before I started to pay attention. After sitting through the first forty minutes again I move into a similar but smaller theater, not really caring if any of the ushers see me switch, and I sit there in the dark, breathing slowly. By midnight I'm pretty sure I have been in all of the theaters for some length of time, so I leave. I come to the entrance where I came in and find it closed and locked and I turn around and make my way to the other end of the mall and find that exit closed also. I move onto the second floor and find both exits closed and locked. I walk down the escalators, which have been shut off, to the first floor and come to one end of the mall and find it closed. But I find the other end open and walk out that exit and to where I parked my car and I get into the Porsche and drive past the closed ticket-attendant booths, tossing my unvalidated ticket out the window, and turn the radio on.

I'm waiting alone at the stoplight on Beverly and Doheny, turning the radio up even louder. A black boy runs out of the parking lot of the Hughes supermarket on the corner of Beverly and past my car. Two store clerks and a security guard follow him. The boy throws something in the street and runs away into the darkness of West Hollywood, followed by the three men. I sit in the Porsche, very still, while the light turns green, a tumbleweed blows by. I get out of the car, cautiously, and walk into the intersection and look around to see what the black boy dropped. There are no cars coming from any of the four streets that intersect here and no noise either, except for the humming of fluorescent streetlights and the Plimsouls coming from the radio and I pick up what the black boy dropped. It's a package of filet mignon, and staring at it beneath the overhead glare of a neon light, I can see that some of the juice seeping from the Styrofoam is running down the length of my hand to my wrist, staining the cuff of a white Commes des Garçons shirt I'm wearing. I put the piece of meat back down, carefully, wipe my hand on the back of my jeans, then get into my car. I turn the volume on the radio down and the light turns green again and I come to another yellow, now red, light and I turn the radio off and put a tape in and drive back to the apartment on Wilshire.

10

THE SECRETS OF SUMMER

I'm trying to pick up this ok-looking blond Valley bitch at
Powertools and she's sort of into it but not drinking enough,
only pretending to be drunk, but she goes for me, like they
all do, and says she's twenty.

"Uh-huh," I tell her. "Right. You look really young," even
though I know she can't be more than sixteen, maybe even
fifteen if Junior is working the doors tonight and which is
pretty exciting if you consider the prospects. "I like them
young," I tell her. "Not too young. Ten? Eleven? No way.
But fifteen?" I'm saying. "Hey, yeah, that's cool. It may be
jailbait, but so what?"

She just stares at me blankly like she didn't hear a word,
then checks her lips in a compact and stares at me some
more, asks me what a wok is, what the word "invisible"
means.

I'm getting totally psyched to get this bitch back to my place
in Encino and I even get a medium hard-on waiting for her
while she's in the ladies' room telling her friends she's leaving
with the best-looking guy here while I'm at the bar drinking
red-wine spritzers with my medium hard-on.

"What are these little fellas called?" I ask the bartender, a
cool-looking dude my age, wondering, gesturing toward the
drink.

"Red-wine spritzers," he says.

"I don't want to get too drunk, though," I tell him while he pours a group of frat guys another round. "No way. Not tonight."

I turn and look out at everyone dancing on the dance floor and I think I banged the DJ about a million years ago but I'm not too sure and she's playing some god-awful nigger rap song and I'm getting hungry and want to split and then here the girl comes, all ready to go.

"It's the anthracite Porsche," I tell the valet and she's impressed. "This is gonna be great," I'm saying. "I'm totally jazzed," I tell her but trying not to seem too eager.

She plays some Bowie tape while we drive toward the Valley. I tell her an Ethiopian joke.

"What's an Ethiopian with sesame seeds on his head?"

"What's an Ethiopian?" she asks.

"A Quarter Pounder," I say. "That really cracks me up."

We get to Encino. I open the garage door with the garage opener.

"Wow," she says. "You've got a big house," and then, "You'll take me home afterwards, later?"

"Yeah. Sure," I say, opening a bottle of fumé blanc. "Some chicks are stupid but I like that in a fuck."

We go into the bedroom and she's wondering where all the furniture is. "Where's the furniture?" she whines.

"I ate it. Just shut up, pop in a coil and lay down," I mutter, pointing her toward the bathroom, and then, "I'll give you some coke afterwards," even though I don't say what afterwards means, don't even hint.

"What do you mean? A coil?"

"Yeah. You don't want to get pregnant, do you? End up giving birth to something awful. A monster? Some kind of beast? You want that?" I ask. "Jesus, even your abortionist would freak out."

She looks at the bed and then at me and then tries to open the door to the other room.

"No way." I stop her. "Not *that* room." I shove her toward

the bathroom door. She looks at me, still pretending to be drunk, then goes in, closes the door. I actually hear her fart.

I turn the lights off, with a Bic, light candles I bought at the Pottery Barn last night. I take off my clothes, touching myself, already stiff, stretch out on the bed, waiting, starving now.

"Come on come on come on."

The toilet flushes, she uses the bidet and then she comes out, shoes in hand, and seems shocked to find me lying on the bed with this giant hard-on but she plays it cool. She doesn't want to do this and she knows she's way out of her league and she knows it's too late and this turns me on even more and I have to giggle and she takes her clothes off, asking "Where's the coke? Where's the coke?" and I say "After, after" and pull her toward me. She doesn't really want to fuck so she tries to give me head instead and I let her for a little while even though I cannot feel a thing, so then I start fucking her really hard, looking into her face when I'm coming and, like always, she freaks out when she sees my eyes, shiny black, and she sees the horrible teeth, the ruptured mouth (what Dirk thinks looks like "the anus of an octopus"), and I'm screaming on top of her, the mattress below us sopping wet with her blood and she starts screaming too and then I hit her hard, punching her in the face until she passes out and I carry her outside to the pool and by the light coming from underwater and the moon, high in Encino tonight, bleed her.

I meet Miranda at the Ivy on Robertson for a late supper and she's looking, in her own words, "absoloutly fabulous." Miranda is "forty," with jet-black hair pulled back tight, a jagged white streak running through it on the side, a pale-tan complexion and high, gorgeous cheekbones, teeth the color of lightning, and she's wearing an original hand-beaded velvet dress by Lagerfeld from Bergdorf Goodman she bought when she was in New York last week to bid on a water bottle at Sotheby's that eventually went for a million dollars and to check out a private fund-raising party for George Bush, which, according to Miranda, was "just smashing."

"Even though you're older than me by, like, twenty years, you always seem incredibly youthful," I tell her. "You are definitely one of my favorite people to hang out with in L.A."

Tonight we're on the patio and it's hot and we're talking quietly about how Donald is used rather promiscuously in a layout on linen suits in the August issue of *GQ* and how if you look very carefully at the model next to him you can see four tiny purple dots on his tan neck that the airbrusher missed.

"Donald is absoloutly wicked," Miranda says.

I agree and ask, "What's the definition of superfluous? Ethiopian after-dinner mints."

Miranda laughs and tells me that I'm wicked too and I sit back, sipping my limeade and Stoli, very pleased.

"Oh look, there's Walter," Miranda says, sitting up a little. "Walter, Walter," she calls out, waving.

I despise Walter—fiftyish, faggot-clone, agent at ICM whose main claim to fame in some circles is that he bled every person in the Brat Pack except Emilio Estevez, who told me one night at On the Rox that he wasn't into "Dracula and shit like that." Walter saunters over to our table, wearing a completely tacky Versace tuxedo, and he drones on about the screening at Paramount tonight and how this film will do $110 million domestic and that he played fucky with one of the film's stars even though the film is a piece of shit and he flirts shamelessly with me and I'm not impressed. He slinks off—"What a slime, what a homo," I mutter—and then it's only me and Miranda.

"So tell me what you've been reading, darling," she asks, after the N.Y. steaks, blood rare and extra au jus on the side, arrive and we both dig in. "By the way, this is"—she cocks her head, chewing—"delish," and then, "Oh, but what a headache."

"Tolstoy," I lie. "I never read. Boring. You?"

"I absoloutly love that Jackie Collins. Marvelous trash," she says, chewing, a dark line of juice dripping down her pale chin as she pops two Advil, washing them down with the cup of au jus. She wipes her chin and smiles, blinking rapidly.

"How's Marsha?" I ask, sipping a red-wine spritzer.

"She's still in Malibu with . . ." and now Miranda lowers her voice, mentions one of the Beach Boys.

"No way, dude," I exclaim, laughing.

"Would I lie to you, baby?" Miranda says, rolling her eyes up, licking her lips, polishing that steak off.

"Marsha for the longest time was only into animals, right?" I ask. "Cows? Horses, birds, dogs, pets, you name it, right?"

"Who do you think controlled the coyote population last summer," Miranda says.

"Yeah, I heard about that," I murmur.

"Baby, she would go to Calabasas, out to the stables, and bleed a fucking horse in thirty minutes flat," Miranda says. "I mean, holy shit, baby, things were getting ridiculous for a while."

"I personally cannot stand horses' blood," I'm saying. "It's way too thin, too sweet. Other than that, I can deal with just about anything, but only when I'm feeling gloomy."

"The only animal I cannot abide is a cat," Miranda says, chewing. "That's because so many of them have leukemia and lots of other poo-poo diseases."

"Dirty, filthy creatures," I shudder.

We order two more drinks and split another steak before the kitchen closes and then Miranda confides to me that she almost got herself into a gang bang the other night over at Tuesday's place with all these frat boys from USC.

"I'm, like, completely taken aback by this," I say. "Miranda, you can be so lousy." I drink the rest of the spritzer, which is a little too bubbly tonight.

"Darling, believe me, it was some kind of accident. A party. Lots of young gorgeous men." She winks, fingering a tall glass of Moët. "I'm sure you can guess how that turned out."

"You're just, like, wicked," I tell her, chuckling. "How did you extract yourself from the . . . situation?"

"What do you think I did?" she says teasingly, gulping down the rest of the champagne. "I sucked the living shit right out of them." She looks around the mostly empty patio, waves over to Walter as he steps into his limo with a girl who looks about six, and Miranda says, softly, "Semen and blood is a delightful combo, and do you know what?"

"I'm captivated."

"Those ridiculous USC boys loved it." She laughs, throwing her head back. "Lined up again and I of course was only too happy to please them again and they all passed out." She laughs harder and I'm laughing too and then she stops, looking up at a helicopter crossing the sky, a searchlight sending down a cone of white. "The one I liked lapsed into a coma." She looks sadly out onto Robertson at a small tumbleweed the valets are playing soccer with. "His neck fell apart."

"Don't be sad," I say. "It's been a delightful evening."

"Let's catch a midnight flick in Westwood," she suggests, eyes brightening at her own suggestion.

We go to the movies after dinner but we first buy two large raw steaks at a Westward Ho and eat them in the front row and I flirt with a couple of sorority girls, one of whom asks me where I got my vest, meat hanging from my mouth, and Miranda even bought napkins.

"I adore you," I tell her, once the previews start. "Because you've got the right idea."

* * *

I'm at another club, Rampage (but pronounce it French), and I find a pseudo-hot-looking Valley bitch and she seems really slow and stupid like she's completely stoned or drunk or something but she's got great tits and a pretty hot body, not too heavy, maybe a little too skinny, and basically her emptiness thrills me.

"I usually hate skinny chicks," I'm telling her. "But you look great."

"Skinny chicks suck?" she asks.

"Hey—that's pretty funny," I tell her.

"Is it?" she asks, slack, washed out.

"I'm into you anyway."

We take my car and drive over to the Valley, into Encino. I tell her a joke.

"What do you call an Ethiopian wearing a turban?"

"Is this a joke?"

"Q-Tip," I say. "That really cracks me up. Even you must admit it's riotous."

The girl is too stoned to respond to the joke but she manages to ask, "Does Michael Jackson live around here?"

"Yep," I say. "He's a buddy."

"I'm really impressed," she says ungratefully.

"I only went to one party after the Victory tour and it was really shitty," I tell her. "I hate hanging out with niggers anyway."

"That's not exactly the nicest thing you could say."

"Mellow out," I groan.

In my room she's into it and we're fucking wildly and when she starts to come I begin to lick and chew at the skin on her neck, panting, slavering, finding the jugular vein with my tongue, and I start bleeding her and she's laughing and moaning and coming even harder and blood is spurting into my mouth, splashing the roof, and then something weird starts to happen and I get really tired and nauseous and I have to roll off her and that's when I realize that this girl is not drunk or stoned but that she's on some, as she puts it now, "way-out fucking drugs."

"Ecstasy? LSD? Is it smack?" I'm gagging.

She lies there silently.

"Oh Christ no," I say, feeling it. "It's . . . heroin," I croak. "Oh shit. Now I'm majorly tripping."

I roll off the bed onto the floor, naked, my head killing me, this poison cramping my stomach up, and I crawl toward the bathroom, and all the time this fucking drugged-out bitch who has snapped out of her stupor is now crawling along with me, squealing "Let's play let's play let's play you're a cowboy and I'm a squaw, got it?" and I growl at her, trying to scare her, showing her my teeth, the fangs, my horrible transformed mouth, my eyes black, lidless. But she doesn't freak out, just laughs, completely high. I finally make it to the toilet and on my back vomit up her blood in geysers and then pass out with the door closed, on the floor. I wake the next night, groggy, her blood dried all over my face and neck and chest. I wash it off in a long, hot shower with a loofah and then I walk into the bedroom. On the bed, written on a matchbook from California Pizza Kitchen, is her name and phone number and below that, "Had a *wild* time." I go to the other room, swallow some Valium, open up my coffin and take a little nap.

I wake up later, restless, still kind of weak, grateful for the new customized coffin I had this guy out in Burbank build for me: FM radio, tape cassette, digital alarm clock, Perry Ellis sheets, phone, small color TV with built-in VCR and cable (MTV, HBO). Elvira is the hottest-looking woman on TV and she hosts this horror-movie show on Sunday nights which is my favorite show on TV and I would like to meet Elvira one day and maybe one day I will.

I get up, take my vitamins, work out with weights while playing Madonna on CD, take a shower, study my hair, blond and thick, and I'm thinking about calling Attila, my hairdresser, and making an appointment for tomorrow night and then I call and leave a message. The maid has come and cleaned, which she is supposed to do, and I have specified to her that if she ever tries to open the coffin I will take her two little children and turn them into a human tostada with extra lettuce and salsa and eat them, muchas gracias. I get dressed: Levi's, penny loafers, no socks, a white T-shirt from Maxfield's, an Armani vest.

I drive over to the Sun 'n' Fun twenty-four-hour tanning parlor on Woodman and get ten minutes of rays, then head over to Hollywood to maybe visit Dirk, who is mostly into pretty boys, hustlers down on Santa Monica, in bars, at gyms. He likes chain saws, which are okay if you have your place soundproofed like Dirk does. I pass an alley, four parking lots, a 7-Eleven, numerous police cars.

It's a warm night and I pop open the sunroof, play the radio loud. Stop off at Tower Records and buy a couple of tapes, then it's to the twenty-four-hour Hughes on Beverly and Doheny and pick up a lot of steak in case I don't feel like going out next week because raw meat is okay even though the juice is thin and not salty enough. The fat chick at checkout flirts with me while I write a check for seven hundred and forty dollars—the only thing I bought is filet mignon. Stop off at a couple of clubs, places where I have a free pass or know the doormen, check out the scene, then drive around some more. Think about the girl I picked up at Powertools, the way I drove her to a bus stop on Ventura Boulevard, dropped her off, hoping she doesn't remember. I drive by a sporting goods store and think about what happened to Roderick and shudder, get queasy. But I take a Valium and soon I'm feeling pretty good, passing by the billboard on Sunset that says DISAPPEAR HERE and I wink over at two blond girls, both wearing Walkmen, in a convertible 450SL at a stoplight we're at and I smile back at them and they giggle and I start following them down Sunset, think about stopping for maybe some sushi with them, and I'm about to tell them to pull over when I suddenly see that Thrifty drugstore sign coming up, the huge neon-blue lowercase *t* flashing off and on, floating above buildings and billboards, the moon hanging low behind, above it, and I'm getting closer to it, getting weak, and I make this totally illegal U-turn, and still feeling sort of sick but better the farther I get from it, my rearview mirror turned down, I head over to Dirk's place.

Dirk lives in a huge old-style Spanish-looking place that was built a long time ago up in the hills and I let myself in through the back door, and walking through the kitchen, I can hear the TV blaring up above. There are two hacksaws in a sink filled with pink water and suds and I smile to myself, hungry. Whenever I hear about some young guy on the news who was found near the beach, maybe part of his body, an arm or a leg or a torso, sucked clean in a bag near a freeway underpass, I have to whisper to myself, "Dirk." Take two Coronas out of the fridge and run upstairs to his room, open the door and it's dark. Dirk's sitting on the couch, wearing a PHIL COLLINS T-shirt and jeans, a sombrero on his head and Tony Lamas, watching *Bad Boys* on the VCR, rolling a joint, and he looks full, a bloody towel in the corner.

"Hey, Dirk," I say.

"Hey, dude." He turns around.

"What's going on?"

"Nothing. You?"

"Just thought I'd stop by, see how it's hanging." I hand him one of the Coronas. He twists the top off. I sit down next to him, pop mine open, throw my cap over at the bloody towel, below a poster of the Go-Go's and a new stereo. A mound of damp bones stains the felt on a pool table, beneath it a bundle of wet Jockey shorts spotted violet and black and red.

"Thanks, guy." Dirk takes a swallow. "Hey"—he grins—"what's brown and full of cobwebs?"

"Ethiopian's asshole," I say.

"Right on." We slap high five.

On the patio, a bag filled with flesh, heavy with blood, hangs from a wooden beam and moths flutter around it, and when it drips they scatter, then regroup. Beneath that someone has strung white Christmas lights around a large thorny tumbleweed. A blond bat flaps its wings, repositions itself in the rafters above the bag of flesh and the moths.

"Who's that?" I ask.

"That's Andre."

"Hey Andre." I wave.

The bat squeaks a reply.

"Andre's got a hangover," Dirk yawns.

"Bummer."

"It takes a long time to pull someone's skull out of their mouth," Dirk's saying.

"Uh-huh." I nod. "Can I have a seltzer?"

"Can you?"

"Nice toucan," I say, noticing a comatose bird in a cage that hangs near the french doors that lead out to a veranda. "What's its name?"

"Bok Choy," Dirk says. "Hey, if you're gonna get a seltzer, make me a mimosa, will you?"

"Jesus," I whisper. "The things that toucan has seen."

"The toucan doesn't have a clue," Dirk says.

Body bags lie out by the Jacuzzi, lit candles surround the steaming water, a reminder of relatives who will not be as anguished as they should be, a test they will not pass.

I go back downstairs, get a seltzer, make Dirk a mimosa, then we hang out, watch the movie, drink some more beer, look through worn copies of *GQ*, *Vanity Fair*, *True Life Atrocities*, smoke some pot, and that's around the time I can smell the blood, coming from the next room, so fresh it's pulsing.

"I think I have the munchies," I say. "I think I may go berserk."

Dirk rewinds the movie and we start watching it again. But I can't concentrate. Sean Penn keeps getting beat up and I get hungrier but don't say anything and then the movie's over and he turns the channel to HBO, where *Bad Boys* is on, so we start watching it again and we smoke some more pot and finally I have to stand up and walk around the room.

"Marsha's with one of the Beach Boys," Dirk says. "Walter called me."

"Yeah," I say. "I had dinner with Miranda at the Ivy the other night. Can you dig it?"

"Gnarly. I can dig it." He shrugs. "I haven't talked to Marsha since"—he stops, thinks about something, says, hesitantly—"since Roderick." He switches the channel, then back again.

No one mentions Roderick a whole lot anymore. Last year, Marsha and Dirk were supposed to have dinner with Roderick at Chinois and when they stopped by his place in Brentwood, they found, at the bottom of Roderick's empty swimming pool, a wooden stake (which was really a Wilson 5 baseball bat crudely whittled down) driven into the concrete near the drain, which had been all scratched up (Roderick prided himself on long, manicured claws), and gray-black sand and dust and chunks of ash were scattered in piles in one corner. Marsha and Dirk had taken the stake, which was slathered with Lawry's garlic powder, and burned it in Roderick's empty house, and no one has seen Roderick since.

"I'm sorry, man," Dirk says. "It scares the shit out of me."

"Aw, come on, dude, let's not talk about that," I say. "Come on."

"Righty-o, Professor." Dirk does his Felix the Cat impersonation, slaps his Wayfarers on and smiles.

I'm walking around the room now, in the dark, shouts coming from the TV, moving toward the door, the smell rich and very thick, and I take another deep breath and it's sweet too and definitely male. I'm hoping I'll be offered some but I don't want to act like a leech and I lean up against the wall and Dirk is talking about stealing pints from Cedars and I'm moving toward that door, stepping over the towel drenched with blood, trying casually to open it.

"Don't open that door, dude," Dirk says, his voice low, raspy, sunglasses still on. "Don't go in there."

I pull my hand away real quick, put it in my pocket, pretend I was never going to check it out, whistle a Billy Idol song that I can't get out of my head. "I wasn't gonna go in there, dude. Chill out."

He nods slowly, takes off the sombrero, switching to another channel, then back to *Bad Boys*. He sighs and flicks something off one of his cowboy boots. "He's not dead yet."

"No, no, I get it, dude," I tell him. "Just mellow out."

I go downstairs, bring up some more beer, and we smoke some more pot, tell some more jokes, one about a koala bear and one about black people, another about a plane crash, and then we watch the rest of the movie, basically not saying a lot, long pauses between sentences, even words, the credits are rolling and Dirk takes off his sunglasses, then puts them back on, and I'm stoned. He looks at me and says, "Ally Sheedy looks good beaten up," and then outside, like ritual, a storm arrives.

I'm hanging out at Phases over in Studio City and it's getting late and I'm with some young girl with long blond hair who could be maybe twenty who I first saw with some geek dancing to "Material Girl" and she's bored and with me now and I'm bored and I want to get out of here and we finish our drinks and go to my car and get in and I'm sort of drunk and don't turn on the radio and it's silent in the car as she rolls down her window and Ventura is so deserted it's still silent except for the air-conditioning and she doesn't say a word about how nice my car is and so I finally ask this bitch, while uselessly opening the sunroof to impress her, getting closer to Encino, "How many Ethiopians can you fit in a Volkswagen?" and I take a Marlboro out of my jacket, push the lighter in, smiling to myself.

"All of them," she says.

I pull the car over to the side of the road, tires screeching, and turn the engine off. I sit there, waiting. Somehow the radio got turned on and some song is playing but I don't know which song it is and the lighter pops up. My hand is trembling and I'm staring at her, leaning away, cigarette still in my hand. I think she asks what's going on but I don't even hear her and I try to compose myself and I'm about to pull out onto Ventura but then I have to stop and stare at her some more and, bored, she asks what are we doing? and I keep staring and then, very slowly, still holding the cigarette, push the lighter in, wait until it heats up, pops out, light the cigarette, blow the smoke out, looking at her still, leaning away, and then I ask very quietly, suspiciously, maybe a little confused, "Okay"—taking a deep breath—"how many Ethiopians can you fit into a Volkswagen?" I don't breathe until I hear her answer. I watch a tumbleweed come out of nowhere and hear it graze the bumper of the Porsche.

"I told you all of them," she says. "Are we going to your place or, like, what is this?"

I lean back, smoke some of the cigarette, ask, "How old are you?"

"Twenty."

"No. Really," I say. "Come on. It's just the two of us. We're alone now. I'm not a cop. Tell the truth. You won't get in trouble if you tell the truth."

She thinks about it, then asks, "Will you give me a gram?"

"Half."

She lights a joint I mistake for a cigarette and she aims the smoke out the sunroof and says, "Okay, I'm fourteen. I'm fourteen. Can you deal with it? God." She offers me the joint.

"No way," I say, not taking it.

She shrugs. "Yes way." Another drag.

"No way," I say again.

"Yes way. I'm fourteen. I was bas-mitzvahed at the Beverly Hills Hotel and it was hell and I'll be fifteen in October," she says, holding in smoke, then exhaling.

"How did you get into the club?"

"Fake ID." She reaches into her purse.

"Did I actually mistake Hello Kitty for Louis Vuitton?" I murmur aloud, grabbing the purse, smelling it.

She shows me the fake ID. "Guess you did, genius."

"How do I know it's fake?" I ask. "How do I know you're not just teasing me?"

"Study it real carefully. Yeah, I was born twenty years ago in 1964, uh-huh, *right*," she sneers. "Duh."

I hand it back to her. Then I start the car up again and, still looking over at her, pull onto Ventura Boulevard and start heading toward the darkness of Encino.

"All of them." I shudder. "Whew."

"Where's my gram?" she asks, then, "Oh look, a sale at Robinson's."

I light another cigarette.

"I usually don't smoke," I tell her. "But you're doing something weird to me."

"You shouldn't smoke." She yawns. "Those things'll kill you. At least that's what my hideous mother always said."

"Did she die from cigarettes?" I ask.

"No, her throat was slashed by some maniac," she says.

"She didn't smoke." Pause. "Mexicans have basically raised me." Another pause. "Let me tell you, that is no fun."

"Yeah?" I smile grimly. "You think cigarettes will kill me?"

She takes another drag off her joint and then it's gone and I pull into the garage and then we're walking into the bedroom and everything's speeding up, where the night's heading is becoming clearer, and she checks out the house and asks for a large vodka on the rocks. I tell her beer is in the fridge and that she can get it the fuck herself. She pulls some kind of demented hissy fit and slouches into the kitchen, muttering, "Jesus, my father has better manners."

"You can't be fourteen," I'm saying. "No way." I'm taking off my tie and jacket, kicking my loafers off.

She walks back in with a Corona in one hand, a fresh j in the other. She's wearing too much makeup, these ugly white Guess jeans but she looks like most girls, waxy and artificial.

"You poor pitiful bitch," I murmur.

I lie down on the bed, kick back, my head resting on some bunched-up pillows, stare at her, reach down, adjust myself.

"You don't have any furniture?" she asks.

"I've got a fridge. I got this bed," I tell her, running my hand across designer sheets.

"Yeah. That's true. Boy, you sure have a point." She walks around the room, then over to the door near the end of the room, tries it, locked. "What's in there?" she asks, looking at the sunrise/sunset chart I clipped from the L.A. *Herald-Examiner* for this week, Scotch-taped to the door.

"Just another room," I tell her.

"Oh." She looks at me, finally a little scared.

I pull my pants off, fold them, throw them on the floor.

"Why do you have so much, like . . ." She stops. She's not drinking the beer. She's looking over at me, confused.

"So much what?" I ask, unbuttoning my shirt.

"Well . . . so much meat," she says meekly. "I mean, there's so much meat in your refrigerator."

"I don't know," I say. "Because I get hungry? Because red snapper appalls me?" I put the shirt down, next to the pants. "Christ."

"Oh." She just stands there.

I don't say anything else, prop my head back up on the pillows. I ease my underwear off slowly and motion for her to come over here, to me, and she slowly walks over, helpless, with a full beer, a sliver of lime in its top, a joint that has gone out. Bracelets circling her wrist look like they are made from fur.

"Uh, listen, this is—this is gonna sound like totally bizarre," she stammers. "But are you . . ."

She's coming nearer now, toward me, floating, unaware that her feet aren't even touching the floor. I rise up, a huge erection on the verge of bursting jutting out in front of me.

"Are you, like . . ." She stops smiling. "Like, a . . ." She doesn't finish.

"A vampire?" I suggest, grinning.

"No—an agent," she asks seriously.

I clear my throat.

When I say no, I'm not an agent, she moans and I have her by the shoulders now and I'm taking her very slowly, calmly, to the bathroom and while I'm stripping her, throwing the ESPRIT T-shirt aside, into the bidet, she keeps giggling, wasted, and asking, "Doesn't that sound weird to you?" and then finally her young perfect body is naked and she looks up into eyes that cloud over completely, black and bottomless, and she reaches up, weeping with disbelief, and touches my face and I smile and touch her smooth, hairless pussy and she says, "Just don't give me a hickey," and then I scream and jump on her and rip her throat out and then I fuck her and then I play with her blood and after that basically everything's okay.

* * *

I'm driving down Ventura tonight toward my psychiatrist's office, over the hill. I did a couple of lines earlier and "Boys of Summer" is blasting from the tape deck and I'm singing along with it, air-jamming at stoplights, passing the Galleria, passing Tower Records and the Factory and the La Reina theater, which will close soon, and past the new Fatburger and the giant Nautilus that just opened. I got a call from Marsha earlier, inviting me to a party in Malibu. Dirk sent me these ZZ Top stickers to put on the lid of my coffin and I think that's pretty tacky but I'll keep them anyway. I'm watching all these people in their cars tonight and I've been thinking a lot about nuclear bombs since I've seen a couple of bumper stickers complaining about them.

In Dr. Nova's office I'm having a hard time.

"What's going on tonight, Jamie?" Dr. Nova asks. "You seem . . . agitated."

"I have these images, man, no, these *visions*," I'm telling him. "Visions of nuclear missiles blowing this place away."

"What place, Jamie?"

"Melting the Valley, the whole Valley. All the chicks rotting away. The Galleria just a memory. Everything gone." Pause. "Evaporated." Pause. "Is that a word?"

"Wow," Dr. Nova says.

"Yeah, wow," I say, staring out the window.

"What will happen to you?" he asks.

"Why? You think that would stop me?" I ask back.

"What do you think?"

"You think a fucking nuclear bomb is gonna end all this?" I'm saying. "No way, dude."

"End all what?" Dr. Nova asks.

"We'll survive that."

"Who is we?"

"*We* have been here forever and *we* will probably be around forever too." I check my nails.

"What will *we* be doing?" Dr. Nova asks, barely paying attention.

"Roaming." I shrug. "Flying around. Looming over you like a fucking raven. Picture the biggest raven you've ever seen. Picture it looming."

"How are your parents, Jamie?"

"I don't know," I say and then, my voice rising toward a scream, "But I live the cool life and if you do not refill my prescription of Darvocet—"

"What will you do, Jamie?"

I consider my options, then calmly explain.

"I'll be waiting," I tell him. "I'll be waiting in your bedroom one night. Or under the table of your favorite restaurant, mutilating your wittle foot."

"Is . . . this a threat?" Dr. Nova asks.

"Or when you take your daughter to McDonald's," I say, "I'll be dressed as Ronald McDonald or the Grimace and I'll eat her in the parking lot while you watch and quickly get fucked up."

"We've talked about this before, Jamie."

"I'll be waiting in the parking lot or in your daughter's schoolyard or in a bathroom. I'll be crouching in your bathroom. I'll follow your daughter home from school and after I play fucky with her I'll be crouching in your bathroom."

Dr. Nova just looks at me, bored, as if my behavior is explainable.

"I was in the hospital room when your father died of cancer," I tell him.

"You've mentioned this before," he says idly.

"He was rotting away, Dr. Nova," I say. "I saw him. I saw your father rotting away. I told all my friends your father died of toxic shock. That he stuck a tampon up his ass and left it there too long. He died screaming, Dr. Nova."

"Have you . . . killed anyone else recently, Jamie?" Dr. Nova asks, not too visibly shaken.

"In a movie," I say. "In my mind." I giggle.

Dr. Nova sighs, studies me, largely unassured. "What do you want?"

"I want to be in the backseat of your car, waiting, drooling—"

"I hear you, Jamie." Dr. Nova sighs.

"I want my Darvocet refilled or else I'm gonna be waiting beneath that lovely black-bottom pool of yours one night while you're out for a little midnight swim, Dr. Nova, and I'll pull veins and tendons out of your well-muscled thigh." I'm standing now, pacing.

"I'll give you the Darvocet, Jamie," Dr. Nova says. "But I want you here on a less irregular basis."

"I'm totally psyched," I say. "You're as cool as they come."

He fills out a prescription and then, while handing it to me, asks, "Why should I fear you?"

"Because I'm a tan burly motherfucker and my teeth are so sharp they make a straight razor seem like a butter knife." I pause. "Need a better reason?"

"Why do you threaten me?" he asks. "Why should I fear you?"

"Because I'm going to be that last image you ever see," I tell him. "Count on it."

I head toward the door, then turn back around.

"Where's the place you feel safest?" I ask.

"In an empty movie theater," Dr. Nova says.

"What's your favorite movie?" I ask.

"*Vacation,* with Chevy Chase and Christie Brinkley."

"What's your favorite cereal?"

"Frosted Mini Wheats or something with bran in it."

"What's your favorite TV commercial for?"

"Bayer Aspirin."

"Who did you vote for last election?"

"Reagan."

"Define the vanishing point."

"You"—he's crying—"define it."

"We've already been there," I tell him. "We've already seen it."

"Who's . . . we?" He chokes.

"Legion."

11

THE FIFTH WHEEL

"Are we gonna kill the kid?" Peter asks, looking jumpy and nervous, rubbing his arms, his eyes wide, a huge belly sticking out beneath a BRYAN METRO T-shirt and he's sitting in a ripped-up green armchair in front of the TV, watching cartoons.

Mary lays on the mattress in the other room, strung out, wasted, listening to Rick Springfield or some other asshole on the radio, and I'm feeling pretty sick and trying to roll this joint and I try to pretend that Peter didn't say anything, but he asks it again.

"I don't know if you're asking me or Mary or one of the fucking Flintstones on the fucking TV, man, but don't ask it again," I say.

"We gonna kill the kid?" he asks.

I stop trying to roll the joint—the rolling papers are too wet and dissolving all over my fingers—and Mary moans some name. The kid has been tied up in the bathtub for something like four days now and everyone's a little nervous.

"I'm getting itchy," Peter says.

"You said it was going to be really easy," I say. "You said everything was going to be cool. That it was all working out, man."

"I fucked up." He shrugs. "I know it." He looks away from the cartoons. "And I know you know it."

"You get a medal, m-man."

"Mary doesn't know anything." Peter sighs. "That girl never knew a damn thing."

"So you know that I know that you fucked up in, like, a real big way?" I'm asking. "Huh—is that it?"

He starts laughing. "We gonna kill the kid?" and Mary starts laughing with him and I'm wiping my hands listening to them.

Peter gets hold of me from some dealer I used to work for and he calls for me from Barstow. Peter is in Barstow with an Indian he picked up near a slot machine in Reno. The dealer gives me the number of a hotel out in the desert and I call Peter up and he tells me that he's coming down to L.A. and that he and the Indian need a place to hang out for a couple of days. I have not seen Peter in three years, since a fire we both started got out of control. I whisper to him, over the phone, "I know you're fucked up, dude," and he says, back over the line, "Yeah, sure, let me come on down."

"I don't want you to do what I fucking think you're going to do," I say, my face in my hands. "I want you to stay a night and move on."

"You want to know something?" he asks.

I can't say anything.

"It's not going to happen like that," he says.

Peter and Mary, who isn't even an Indian, come out to L.A. and they find me in a place out in Van Nuys around midnight and Peter comes in and grabs me and says, "Tommy, dude, how's it hanging, buddy?" and I stand there shaking and say, "Hi, Peter," and he's fat, three hundred, four hundred pounds, and his hair is long and blond and greasy and he's wearing a green T-shirt, sauce all over his face, marks all up and down his arms, and I get pissed.

"Peter?" I ask. "What the fuck are you doing?"

"Oh, man," he says. "So what? It's cool." His eyes are wide and weird and he's creeping me out.

"Where's the chick?" I ask.

"Out in the van," he says.

I wait and Peter just stands there.

"Out in the van? Is that right?" I ask.

"Yeah," Peter says. "Out in the van."

"I guess I'm expecting you to move or something," I say. "Like, maybe, get the girl?"

He doesn't. He just stands there.

"The girl's in the van?" I say.

"That's right," he says.

I'm getting pissed. "Why don't you bring the cunt out here, you fat fuck?"

But he doesn't.

"Well, man." I sigh. "Let's see her."

"Who?" he asks. "Who, man?"

"Who do you think I mean?"

He finally says, "Oh yeah. Mary. Sure."

This girl is all passed out in the back of the van and she's tan and dark with long blond hair, skinny because of drugs but in a good way and cute. She sleeps on the mattress the first night in my room and I sleep on the couch and Peter sits in the armchair watching late-night TV shows and I think he goes out once or twice for some food but I'm tired and pissed off and ignoring the situation.

The next morning Peter asks me for money.

"That's a lot of money," I say.

"What's that mean?" he asks.

"That you're out of your fucking mind," I say. "That I don't have any money."

"Nothing?" he asks. He starts to giggle.

"You're taking this pretty good," I point out.

"I need to pay off some guy out here."

"Sorry, dude," I say. "I just don't have it."

He doesn't say too much, just goes back into the dark room with Mary, and I go to the car wash in Reseda that I work at when I'm not doing anything else.

I come home after a fairly crappy day and Peter is in the armchair and Mary is still in the back room listening to the radio and I notice these two little shoes on the table next to the TV and I ask Peter, "Where did you get those two little shoes, man?"

Peter is wasted, out of it, a dumb scary grin on his balloon face, staring at cartoons, and I'm staring at the shoes and I hear something far off crying, bumping around somewhere, a humming from behind the bathroom door.

"Is this a . . . joke?" I ask him. "I mean, because I know what a fucked-up guy you are, dude, and I know that this isn't a joke and, man, oh shit."

I open the door to the bathroom and see the kid, young, white, blond, maybe ten or eleven, wearing a shirt with a tiny horse on it, faded designer jeans, his hands tied up behind his back with a cord and his feet bound by rope and Peter has stuck something in the kid's mouth and put duct tape over it and the kid's eyes are wide and he's crying, kicking at the sides of the bathtub that Peter stuck him in and I slam the door to the bathroom and run over to Peter and grab his shoulders and start shouting into his face, "What the fuck you think you're doing shithead what the fuck have you done you fucking shithead?"

Peter is staring calmly into the TV screen.

"He'll bring us money," he mumbles, trying to brush me away.

I'm squeezing his fat beefy shoulders harder and keep

shouting "Why?" and I panic and it causes me to swing a fist at him, hitting Peter hard across the head and he doesn't move. He starts laughing, the sounds coming out of his mouth don't make sense, can't be connected to anything else I've ever heard.

I punch his head harder and sometime after the sixth blow he grabs my arm, twisting it so hard I think it will snap in two, and I fall slowly to the floor, one knee at a time, and Peter keeps twisting harder and he's not smiling anymore and he growls, low and slowly, four words: "Shut—the—fuck—up."

He yanks my arm up, giving it one more hard twist, and I fall back, holding my arm, and just sit there for a long time until I finally get up and try to drink a beer and lay on the couch and my arm is sore and the kid stops making noises after a while.

I find out that the kid is skateboarding at the parking lot of the Galleria that Peter and Mary scoped out all morning long and Peter says they "made sure no one was looking" and Mary (this is the part I have the hardest time picturing, because I cannot imagine her in motion) drives up to the kid as he's tying a shoelace and Peter opens the back door of the van and very simply, without any effort, lifts the kid up and calmly shoves him into the back of the van and Mary drives back here and Peter tells me that even though he was going to sell the kid to a vampire he knows who lives over in West Hollywood, he'd rather deal with the kid's parents instead and that the money we receive will go to paying off a fag named Spin and then we'll head for Las Vegas or Wyoming and I am so freaked out that I cannot say anything and I have no idea where Wyoming is and Peter has to show me in a book, on a map, a purple state that seems far away.

"Things do not work out like that," I tell him.

"Man, your problem, the thing that screws you up, is that you don't relax, man, you don't lay back."

"Is that right, man?"

"It's bad for you. It'll be bad for you, dude," Peter says. "You've got to learn to flow, to float. To mellow out."

Three days will pass and Peter will watch cartoons and he will forget about the kid laying in the bathtub and he will pretend, along with Mary, that there never was a kid and I will try to keep cool, pretending to know what they are going to do, what will be accomplished, even though I have no idea what will happen.

I go to the car wash because I wake up and Peter will be heating a spoon in front of the TV and Mary will stagger in, thin and tan, and Peter will make jokes while shooting her up and then he will do himself and before the car wash I smoke pot and watch cartoons with Peter and Mary goes back to the mattress and sometimes I can hear the kid kicking against the tub, freaking out in there. We play the radio loud, praying the kid will stop, and I piss in the sink in the kitchen or go to the Mobil station across the street to shit and I don't ask Peter or Mary if they feed the kid. I will come home from the car wash and see empty Winchell boxes and McDonald bags but don't know if they ate the food or if they gave it to the kid and the kid moves around in the tub late at night and even with the TV on and the radio playing you can hear him, driving you to hope that someone outside will hear, but when I go outside you can't hear anything.

"Just to you," Peter says. "Just to you, man."

"Just to me fucking what?"

"I can't hear anything," Peter says.

"You're . . . lying," I say.

"Hey, Mary," he calls out. "You hear anything?"

"Don't ask her, man," I say. "She's . . . fucked up, man."

"That's why you're going to do something about it," he says.

"Oh shit, man," I groan. "This is all your fault, man."

"Coming to L.A. is my fault?" he asks.

"Just getting the kid like that."

"That's why you're going to do something about it."

On the fourth day Peter realizes something.

"I don't know what you mean when you say that," I tell him, near tears, after he explains a plan.

"We gonna kill the kid?" he repeats, but it's really no longer a question.

I get up late the next morning and Peter and Mary are in the back room passed out on the mattress and the TV is on and animated balls, blue and fuzzy and with faces, chase each other around with big hammers and pickaxes and the sound is turned down low so you can imagine what they are saying to each other and when I'm in the kitchen I open a beer and piss in the sink and actually put part of what's left of an old Big Mac laying on the counter into my mouth, chewing, swallowing, and I put on a pair of new overalls and am about to leave when I see that the bathroom door is open a little and I walk over, carefully, afraid that maybe Peter did something to the kid again, last night, but finally I can't even check, so I just close the door quickly and drive my car out to Reseda, to the car wash, because two nights ago I went in, high, and the kid was on his stomach, his pants bunched up around his bound ankles, and his backside was dirty with blood and I left and the next time I see the kid he's cleaned up, dressed, someone even brushed his hair, still tied up with a sock in his mouth, freaked out, his eyes redder than mine.

I get to the car wash late and someone Jewish yells at me and I don't say anything back, just walk into a long dark tunnel and out the other end, where I dry a car with a guy named Asylum who thinks of himself as a "real goof" and everyone in the Valley wants their car washed today and I keep drying the cars, not caring how hot it is, not looking at anybody or talking to anyone, except Asylum.

"I'm not even, like, worried anymore," I tell him. "You know? Or suspicious or anything."

"You, like, just don't give a shit anymore?" Asylum asks. "Is that it? Am I clear on this?"

"Yeah," I say. "I just do not care."

I finish drying a car and I'm waiting for the next one to come out of the tunnel and I notice a little kid standing next to me. He's in a school uniform, watching the cars coming out of the tunnel, and I'm slowly aching with paranoia. A car comes off the belt and Asylum steers it over to me.

"That's my mom's car," the kid says.

"Yeah?" I say. "So fucking what?"

I start drying a Volvo station wagon with the kid still standing there.

"I'm getting angry," I tell the kid. "I don't like you looking at me."

"Why?" he asks.

"Because I want to kick you in the head or something, y'know?" I say, squinting up at smog.

"Why?" he asks.

"I'm pretending that I don't notice you talking to me," I say, hoping he will go away.

"Why?"

"You're a little fucker who is asking me a stupid question like it's important," I point out.

"Don't you think it's important?" the kid asks.

"You talking to me?" I ask the kid.

He nods his head proudly.

"I don't know why you need to ask me this, man, I just don't know." I sigh. "It's a stupid question."

"What's 'need'?" the kid asks.

"Stupid, stupid, stupid," I mutter.

"Why is it stupid?"

"It's needless, you fuckin' little retard."

"What's needless?"

Fed up, I make a move toward the kid. "Get outta here, you little fuck." The kid laughs and walks over to a woman drinking Tab and staring at a Gucci purse and I dry the Volvo fast and Asylum tells me about a girl he fucked last night who looked like a combination bat and large spider and I finally open the door for the woman with the Tab and the kid and suddenly it's so hot I have to wipe sweat from my face with a smelly hand and the kid keeps looking at me as she drives off.

Peter goes out around ten because he has to do some business and says he'll be back at midnight. I try watching some TV but the kid starts moving around and I get freaked out so I go into my room where Mary is laying on the mattress, the lights off, the room dark, with the windows open but still hot and I look over at her and ask if she wants to split a joint.

She doesn't say anything, just moves her head real slowly.

I start to leave, when Mary says, "Hey, man . . . stay . . . why don't you . . . stay?"

I look at her. "Do you want to know what I'm thinking?"

Her mouth moves, eyes rolled up. ". . . No."

"I'm thinking, man, this girl is so fucked up," I tell her. "I'm thinking any girl who hangs out with Peter is so fucked up."

"What else are you thinking?" she whispers.

"I don't know." I shrug. "I'm . . . horny." Pause. "Peter won't be home until—when? Midnight?"

"And . . . what else?"

"Shit, why not stick around and see what happens."

"You . . ." she swallows. "Don't . . . want to see that."

I sit down on the mattress next to her and she tries to sit up but settles for leaning against the wall and asks me about my day at work.

"What are you talking about?" I ask. "You want to know about my day at the *car wash?*"

"What . . . happened?" She breathes in.

"There's a car wash," I tell her. "There was a freaky little kid. It was all really interesting. Maybe the most interesting day of my life." I'm tired and the joint I light goes out too soon and I reach over her and take matches that are next to a spoon and a dirty plastic bag on the other side of the mattress and light the joint and ask her how she met up with Peter.

She doesn't say anything for a long time and I can't say I'm surprised. When she does it's in a low soft voice that I can barely hear and I lean in closer and she mumbles something and I have to ask her what she's saying, her breath smelling like something almost dead. From the radio the Eagles are singing "Take It Easy" and I'm trying to hum along.

"Peter did some . . . bad stuff out . . . in the desert . . ."

"Yeah?" I ask. "I, like, don't fucking doubt it." Another toke and then, "Like what?"

She nods like she's grateful I've asked.

"We met a guy in Carson . . . and he turned us on to some real heavy . . . shit." She starts licking her lips and I'm getting sad. "And . . . we hung out with him . . . for a little while . . . and the guy was real nice and once when Peter went out to get some donuts . . . he went out to get some donuts . . . and this guy and I started fooling around. It was nice. . . ." She's so far off, so druggy, that I get turned on and she stops and looks at me to make sure I'm here, listening to this. "Peter walked in . . ."

My hand is on her knee and it looks like she doesn't care and I nod again.

"You know what he did?" she asks.

"Who? Peter?" I ask. "What?"

"Guess." She giggles.

I pause a long time before guessing, "He ate . . . the donuts?"

"He took the guy out to the desert."

"Yeah?" I move my hand up to her thigh, which is bony and hard and covered with dust, and I'm moving my hand across it, wiping flakes off.

"Yeah . . . and he shot him in the eye."

"Wow," I say. "I know Peter's done shit like that. So I'm not too surprised or anything."

"Then he starts screaming at me and he pulled the guy's pants down and he got out this knife and cut the guy's . . . thing off and . . ." Mary stops, starts giggling, and I start to giggle too. "And he threw it at me and said, Is that what you want, whore, is that it?" She's laughing hysterically and I'm laughing too and we keep laughing for what seems like a long time and once she stops she starts crying, real hard, choking and coughing up stuff, and I take my hand off her leg. "This is all we will ever talk about," she sobs.

I try to fuck her anyway but she's so tight and dry and high that I get sore so I give up for a little while. But I'm still pretty horny so I try to make her blow me but she falls asleep and I try to pick her up, lean her back against the wall and fuck her in the mouth but that doesn't work and I end up jerking off but I can't even come.

I wake up because someone is banging on the door. It's late and the sun is high and coming through the window, hitting me full in the face, and I get up and look around and don't see Peter or Mary anywhere and I get up thinking maybe it's them at the door and I walk over and open it up, tired, groggy, and it's a young tan guy with blond hair, blow-dried, in pretty good shape, a tank top, boat shoes, baggy shorts, Vuarnets, and he's standing there looking at me like he's all the things I want.

"What do you want, man?" I ask.

"I'm looking for someone," he says, adding *"man."*

"Someone's not here," I say, about to close the door. "I don't care anymore."

"Dude," the guy says.

"I just want you to go away," I say.

The guy pushes his hand against the door and walks past me.

"Oh, man," I say. "What the fuck do you want?"

"Where's Peter?" he asks me. "I'm looking for Peter."

"He's . . . not here."

The guy looks around the apartment, checking everything out. He finally leans against the back of the couch and after looking me over asks, "What in the fuck are you looking at?"

"I'm not even too mad," I say. "I'm just really tired. I just want everything to be over because I can't deal with it anymore."

"Just tell me where the fuck Peter is," the dude asks.

"How the fuck should I know?"

"Well, dude"—he laughs—"you better find out." He looks at me and says, "You know why?"

"No. Why?"

"Do you really want to know?"

"Yeah, I just said I wanna know why," I say. "Come on, man, don't be a prick. It's been a harsh week. We can be friends if—"

"I'll tell you why." He stops and dramatically, in a low voice I've become accustomed to, says, "Because he is in deep"—he stops, then—"deep"—and another pause, then—"deep shit."

"Is that right? Yeah?" I ask casually.

"Yeah, that's right," the tan guy says. "Señor."

"Yeah, well, I'll tell him you showed up and all." I open the door for this guy and he moves near it. "And I'm not a Mexican."

"It's a simple message," the guy says. "I'll be back and if Peter doesn't have it you are all dead." He stares at me for a long time, this guy, eighteen, nineteen, thick lips and blank handsome features that are so indistinct I will not be able to remember them, give Peter any particular characteristics, in five minutes.

"Yeah?" I gulp, closing the door. "What are you gonna do? *Tan* us to death?"

He smiles in a sweet way as the door slams shut.

I stay home from the car wash waiting for Peter or Mary to show up and I don't even know if they are going to show up and I'm not even sure what "it" is, what the surfer was talking about, and I just sit on a couch staring out of a window onto a street not looking at anything. I cannot even think about how Peter came and fucked everything up, because everything was fucked up to begin with and if Peter didn't come this week it would have been the one after that or one next year and in the end it's hard to think it makes a difference because you always knew this would happen and you just sit there staring out the window waiting for Peter and Mary to roll back in so you can surrender.

I tell them about the surfer who came over.

Peter walks around. "I think I'm gonna shit or something."

Mary starts saying, "I told you I told you."

"Get your shit together," Peter tells us. "We're getting out of here real fast."

Mary is crying.

"I don't have anything to bring with me," I tell Peter. I watch him walking around nervously. Mary moves into the back room, flings herself onto the mattress, stuffs a hand into her mouth, gnaws on it.

"What the fuck are you doing?" Peter shouts.

"I'm getting my shit together," she sobs, writhing on the mattress.

While she's back there Peter comes up to me and reaches into his back pocket and hands me a switchblade and I ask, "What's this for, dude?"

"The kid."

I've forgotten about the kid and I look over at the bath-room door, feeling tired.

"If we leave the kid," Peter is saying, "somebody will find him and he will talk and we will be in shit."

"Let him starve," I whisper, staring at the knife.

"No, man, no," Peter says, forcing the knife into my hand.

I squeeze it and it pops open with a click and it's mean-looking, long, heavy.

"It's so fucking sharp," I say, looking at the blade, and then I look at Peter for directions and he looks back.

"This is all it comes down to, man," he says.

We stand there for I don't know how long and when I start to say something, Peter says, "Do it."

I grab him and, straining, tell him, "But I'm not protesting, see?"

I walk over to the bathroom door and Mary sees me and runs, limping toward me, but Peter hits her a couple of times, knocking her back, and I go into the bathroom.

The kid is pale and pretty and looks weak and he sees the knife and starts crying, moving his body around, trying to escape, and I don't want to do it with the light on so I turn it off and try to stab the kid in the dark but I get freaked out thinking about stabbing him in the dark so I turn the light on and get on my knees and bring the knife down into his stomach but not hard enough so I stab him again, harder, and he arches his back way up and I stick it in again, trying to cut up but the kid keeps bringing his stomach up like he can't help it and I keep stabbing him in the stomach then in the chest but the knife gets stuck on bones and the kid isn't dying so I try to cut his throat but he brings his chin down and I end up stabbing his chin, slicing it open and I finally grab his hair and pull his head back with it and he's crying, still arching his back up, trying to twist free, bleeding all over the tub from shallow wounds, and Mary is screaming in the living room and I ram the knife deep into his throat, hacking it open, and his eyes go wide with realization and a huge geyser of hot blood hits me in the face and I can taste it and I'm wiping it out of my eyes with the hand that still has the knife in it and blood is basically spurting everywhere and it takes a long time for the kid to stop moving and I'm on my knees, covered with blood, some of it purple, darker than the rest and the kid moves into more quiet spasms and there aren't any more sounds from the living room, just the sound of blood running down a drain in the tub, and sometime later Peter comes in and dries me off and whispers, "It'll be okay, man, we're going to the desert, man, it'll be okay, man, shhh," and somehow we get into the van and drive away from the apartment, out of Van Nuys, and I've got to convince Peter that I'm all right.

Peter stops the van in the parking lot of a Taco Bell way out in the Valley and Mary stays in the back of the van because she has the shakes and Peter is hoarse from telling her to shut up and she's rolled up like a baby, clawing at her face.

"She is freaking out," Peter says, while he hits her a couple of times to shut her up.

"You could say that," I tell him.

Now we're sitting at a little table beneath a broken umbrella and it's hot and my overalls are drenched with blood, making cracking noises every time I move my arms, get up, sit down.

"Do you feel anything?" Peter asks.

"Like what?"

Peter looks at me, figures something out, shrugs.

"We really didn't need to off that kid," I mumble.

"No. You didn't need to do it," Peter says.

"I hear you did some bad stuff out in the desert, man."

Peter's eating a burrito and says, "I'm thinking Las Vegas." He shrugs. "What's bad?"

I stare at the taco he brought me.

"No one'll find you there," he says, mouth full.

"You did some bad stuff out there," I say. "Mary told me."

"Bad stuff?" he asks, confused, not faking it.

"That's what Mary told me, man." I shiver.

"Define 'bad,' " he says, finishing the burrito off too fast, and then, once more, "Vegas."

I pick up the taco and am going to eat it when I notice blood on my hand and I put the taco down and wipe it away and Peter eats part of my taco and I eat some of it too and he finishes it and we get into the van and head out to the desert.

12

ON THE BEACH

"Imagine a blind person dreaming," she says. I'm sitting next to her, on the beach in Malibu, and even though it's getting totally late we both have our Wayfarers on and even though I've been lying in the sun, on the beach, next to her, since noon (she's been on the beach since eight), I'm still kind of hungover from that party we went to last night. I can't remember the party too well but I think it was in Santa Monica, though it could have been down farther, maybe Venice. Only things that pass through my brain are three tanks of nitrous oxide on a veranda, sitting on the floor next to the stereo, Wang Chung playing, holding a bottle of Cuervo Gold, a sea of tan hairy legs, someone screeching "Let's do Spago, let's do Spago" in a fake high voice, over and over again.

I sigh, don't say anything, shiver a little and turn the Cars tape over. I can see Mona and Griffin down the beach, walking slowly along the shore. It's getting too dark to wear sunglasses. I take them off. Look back over at her. The wig isn't crooked anymore—she straightened it while my eyes were closed. Then I look back up at the house, then back at Mona and Griffin, who seem to be getting closer but maybe not. I bet myself ten dollars that they will avoid walking over here. She's not moving. "You can't understand, you can't comprehend the pain," she says, but her lips barely move. Stare back at the beach, at the drifting pink sunset. Try and imagine a blind person dreaming.

She first told me about it at the prom.

I went with her and with Andrew, who was going with Mona, and we had this weird limo driver who looked like Anthony Geary, and me and Andrew had rented tuxes that came with bow ties that were way too big and we had to stop at the Beverly Center to buy new ones and we had about six grams that me and Andrew went in on and a couple tins of Djarum cigarettes and she looked so thin as I pinned the corsage to her dress and her hands, bony, shook as she pinned a rose onto my sleeve. High, I stopped myself from suggesting it should be pinned somewhere else. The prom was held at the Beverly Hills Hotel. I flirted with Mona. Andrew flirted with me. Snuck into the Polo Lounge, did coke in the bathroom. She didn't say anything there. It was later, at the party after the prom, on Michael Landon's yacht, after the coke had run out, while we were making out in the cabin below, that she broke away, said there was this problem. We walked up to the top deck and I lit a clove cigarette and she didn't say anything else and I didn't ask because I really didn't want to know. The morning was cold and everything looked gray and bleak and I went home horny, tired, had dry mouth.

She asks me, actually whispers, to turn the Cars off and put the Madonna tape in. We have been on the beach every day for the last three weeks now. It's all she wants to do. Lie on the beach, in the sun, outside her mother's house. Mother is on location in Italy, then New York, then Burbank. I have spent the last three weeks in Malibu with her and Mona and one of Mona's boyfriends. Today it's Griffin, a beach bum with a lot of money and friendly and who owns a gay club in West L.A. Mona and her boyfriends sometimes hang out on the beach with us too but not a whole lot. Not as much as she does. "But she's not even getting a tan," I had to point out one night. Mona waved a hand in front of my face, lit candles, offered to read my palms, passed out. She often looks even more pale when me or Mona run suntan oil over her body, which is beginning to look totally wasted—a tiny bikini already looks baggy, is draped around flesh that has the same color as milk. She stopped shaving her legs because she doesn't have the strength and everyone refuses to do it for her and the dark stubble is too noticeable, greasy due to the oil and sticking up on her legs. "She used to be totally hot," I shouted at Mona when I was packing a bag, ready to leave last Sunday. Tall (she still looks tall but more like a tall skeleton) and blond (for some freaky reason she bought a black wig when she started losing it all) and her body was supple, carefully muscled, aerobicized, and now she basically looks like shit. And everyone knows too. A friend of mine and hers, Derf, from USC, who was over here on Wednesday to screw Mona, said to me while waxing his board, nodding over at her, alone, in the same position, an overcast sky, no sun, "She's looking pretty shitty, dude."

"But she's dying," I said, understanding where he was coming from.

"Yeah, but she still looks pretty shitty," Derf said, waxing the board while I looked over at her, nodding.

I wave over at Mona and Griffin as they pass by on their way up to the house, then I look over at the pack of Benson & Hedges menthol by her side, next to an ashtray from La Scala and the tape player. She started smoking when she found out. I'd lie on her bed watching MTV or something on the VCR and she'd keep lighting cigarettes, trying to inhale, gagging or closing her eyes. Sometimes she couldn't even do it. Sometimes she'd put the cigarette out in the ashtray, which usually already had five or six crushed, unsmoked cigarettes lying in it, and light another one. She couldn't stand it, the smell, the first inhale, the lighting of it, but she wanted to smoke. Reservations made at Trumps or the Ivy or Morton's would inevitably end with me asking, "Smoking section, please," and she'd say it didn't make any difference now, looking over at me, like hoping that I'd say it would but I'd just say yeah, cool, I guess. So she'd light, inhale, cough, close her eyes, take a sip of the diet Coke ("No problem there," she'd groan. "Fuck NutraSweet") that would be sitting warm on her makeup table. Sometimes she'd sit there for two hours and watch cigarettes turn to ash and then she'd light another one and she told me that sooner or later she would get it right, and it would all kind of bum me out and I'd just watch her open a new pack and Mona would watch too and sometimes she would wear her sunglasses so that nobody could see that she had been crying and she'd mention that the sun bothered her or at night she'd say the lights in the house did it, made her put the Wayfarers on, or the glare from the large-screen TV, which she would watch anyway, made her eyes sore, but I knew that she was bummed out, crying a lot.

There's nothing to do but sit here in the sun, on the beach. She doesn't say anything, barely moves. I want a cigarette but hate menthol. I wonder if Mona has any pot left. The sun is low now, the ocean's getting dark. One night last week, while she was getting treatments at Cedars, Mona and I went to the Beverly Center, saw a bad movie and had frozen margaritas at the Hard Rock and then came back to the house in Malibu and had sex in the living room, stared at the tendrils of steam rising up from the Jacuzzi for what could have been hours. A horse rides past us and someone waves but the sun's setting behind the rider and I have to squint to see who it is and I still can't tell. I'm starting to get a major migraine, which will only be helped by pot.

I stand up. "I'm going up to the house."

I look down at her. The sun, sinking, reflected in her sun-glasses, burns orange, is fading. "I'm thinking about leaving tonight," I say. "Heading back into town."

She doesn't move. The wig still doesn't look as natural as it first did and even then it looked plastic and hard and too big.

"Want anything?"

I think she shakes her head no.

"Okay," I say and move up toward the house.

Mona's in the kitchen, staring out the window, cleaning a bong, watching Griffin on the deck. He takes his bathing suit off and, nude, washes sand from his feet. Mona knows I'm in the room and mentions that it's too bad the sushi we had for lunch didn't cheer her up. Mona doesn't know she dreams of melting rocks, meeting Greg Kihn in the lobby of the Chateau Marmont, conversations with water and dust and air, the sound track an Eagles medley, "Peaceful Easy Feeling" playing loud, booming, sprays of turquoise napalm illuminate the lyrics to "Love Her Madly" scrawled on a cement wall, a tomb.

"Yeah," I say, opening the refrigerator. "Too bad."

Mona sighs, keeps cleaning the bong.

"Did Griffin drink the rest of the Corona?" I ask.

"Maybe," she murmurs.

"Shit." I stand there staring into the refrigerator, my breath steaming.

"She's really sick," Mona says.

"Yeah?" I say. "And I'm pissed off. I wanted a Corona. Badly."

Griffin walks in, towel wrapped around his waist. "What's for dinner?" he asks.

"Did you drink the rest of the Corona?" I ask him.

"Hey, dude," he says, sitting down at the table. "Like, mellow out, lighten up."

"Mexican?" Mona suggests, turning the faucet off. Nobody says anything.

Griffin hums a song, in a trance, his hair wet, slicked back.

"What do you want, Griffin?" she asks again, sighing, drying her hands. "Do you want Mexican, Griffin?"

Griffin looks up, startled. "Mexican? Yeah, babes. Salsa? Some chips? Fine with me."

I open the door, move out onto the patio.

"Hey, dude, close the fridge," Griffin says.

"You do it," I tell him.

"Your dealer called," Mona says to me.

I nod, don't bother shutting the door, walk down the steps back onto sand, thinking of where I'd rather be. Mona is following me. I stop, turn around.

"I'm going to split tonight," I tell her. "I've been hanging out here too long."

"Why?" Mona asks, staring off.

"It's like a movie I've seen before and I know what's going to happen," I tell her. "How the whole thing's gonna end."

Mona sighs, just stands there. "What are you doing here, then?"

"I don't know."

"Do you love her?"

"No, but so what?" I ask. "What would that fix?" I ask. "If I did—that's going to help?"

"It's just that everything feels like it's on the periphery," Mona says.

I walk away from Mona. I know what the word gone means. I know what the word dead means. You deal with it, you mellow out, you head back to town. I'm looking at her now. Madonna's still playing but the batteries are running low and her voice is all wobbly and far off, spacey, and she's not moving, doesn't even acknowledge my presence.

"We'd better go," I say. "The tide's coming in."

"I want to stay," she says.

"But it's getting cold."

"I want to stay," and then, more weakly, "Need some more sun."

A fly from a batch of seaweed lands on a white, bony thigh. She doesn't slap at it. It doesn't go away.

"But there's no sun, dude," I tell her.

I start to walk away. So what, I mutter under my breath. When she wants to come in, she will. Imagine a blind person dreaming. I head back up toward the house. Wonder if Griffin will stick around, if Mona made reservations for dinner, if Spin will call back. "I know what the word dead means," I whisper to myself as softly as I can because it sounds like an omen.

13

AT THE ZOO WITH BRUCE

I'm at the zoo with Bruce today and right now we are
staring at dirty-pink flamingos, some standing on one leg
beneath a hot November sun. Last night I drove past his
house in Studio City and saw the silhouette of Grace glide by
the giant video screen that is placed in front of the futon in
the upstairs bedroom. Bruce's car was not in the driveway,
though I'm not sure what that means since Grace's car wasn't
there either. Bruce and I met at the studio my father is
currently running. Bruce writes for "Miami Vice" and I am
now a fifth-year junior at UCLA. Bruce was supposed to
leave Grace last night and it's obvious today, right now, that
he hasn't made the move. We drove over the hill to the
zoo pretty much in complete silence except for the new
salsa band on the tape deck and Bruce's comments about
the quality of the sound accompanying the silence between songs. Bruce is two years older than me. I am twenty-
three.

It's a weekday, late on Thursday morning. Schoolchildren
walk by, forming crooked lines, while we stare at the flamingos. Bruce is chain-smoking. Mexicans with the day off drink
cans of beer concealed in paper bags, stop, stare, mumble
things, giggle drunkenly, point at benches. I pull Bruce closer
to me and tell him I need a diet Coke.

"They sleep like women," Bruce says, about the flamingos. "I can't explain it."

I notice that there are literally hundreds of elementary-school children, holding hands in pairs, passing by us. I nudge Bruce and he turns away from the birds and I'm laughing at the size of the mass of children. Bruce loses interest in the confused, smiling faces and points at a sign: REFRESHMENTS.

Once the children are out of my range of vision the zoo seems deserted. The only person I see on our walk to the refreshment stand is Bruce, up ahead of me. It is so empty in the zoo that someone could get murdered and no one would notice. Bruce is not the kind of man I usually go out with. He's married, not tall, when I reach him he pays for my diet Coke with the change he kept from me for parking. He complains about how we can't find the gibbons, something about how the gibbons have got to be around here somewhere. This means that we aren't talking about Grace but I'm hoping that he will surprise me. I'm not asking anything because of how disappointed he seems about not finding the gibbons. We pass more animals. Hot, miserable-looking penguins. A crocodile moves slowly toward its water, avoiding a large dead tumbleweed.

"That crocodile's looking at you, baby," Bruce says, lighting another cigarette. "That crocodile's thinking: mmmm."

"I bet these animals aren't exactly what you could call happy," I tell him as we watch a polar bear, patches of its fur stained blue from chlorine, drag itself toward a shallow pool, a fake glacier.

"Oh come on," Bruce disagrees. "Sure they're happy."

"I can't see how," I say.

"What do you want them to do? Light sparklers? Tap-dance? Tell you how nice that blouse looks on you?"

A keg is actually floating in the piss-yellow water and the polar bear avoids the water, pacing around it instead. Bruce moves on. I follow. He's now looking for the snow leopard, which is high on his list of must-sees. We find where the snow leopards are supposed to be but they're hiding. Bruce lights another cigarette and stares at me.

"Don't worry," he says.

"I'm not worrying," I say. "Aren't you hot?"

"No," he says. "The jacket's linen."

"What is that?" I ask, staring at a big, strange-looking bird. "Ostrich?"

"No," he sighs. "I don't know."

"Is it an . . . emu?" I ask.

"I've never seen one before," he says. "So how would I know?"

My eye starts twitching and I throw the rest of the drink into a nearby trash can. I find a rest room while Bruce watches the polar bears some more. In the rest room I splash warm water on my face, willing myself out of an anxiety attack. A black woman is helping a little boy sit on the toilet without falling in. It's cooler here, the air sweet, unpleasant. I fix my contacts quickly and leave to rejoin Bruce, who points out to me a huge red scar crisscrossed with massive black stitches that runs across the back of one of the polar bears.

Bruce watches a kangaroo hop worriedly toward a zoo-keeper, but it won't let the zookeeper pick it up. It reaches out a tentative paw and hisses, a horrible sound coming from a kangaroo, and the zookeeper grabs it by its tail and drags the animal away. Another kangaroo watches, backed into a corner, terrified, munching nervously on brown leaves. The remaining kangaroo squeals and hops around in circles, then stops with a sudden jerk. We move on.

I'm still thirsty but all the refreshment stands we pass are closed and I cannot seem to find a water fountain. The last time Bruce and I saw each other had been on Monday. He picked me up in a green Porsche and we went to a screening at the studio of the new teenage sex comedy, then dinner, Tex Mex in Malibu. As he was leaving my apartment that night he discussed with me his plans for leaving Grace, who has become one of my father's favorite young actresses and who Bruce tells me he never really was in love with but married anyway, for reasons "still unknown," a year ago. I know he hasn't left Grace and I am ninety-nine percent sure he will explain it all to me later but I am also hoping he has made the move and that this is the reason why he is so silent right now, because he will offer it as a surprise later, after lunch. He smokes cigarette after cigarette.

Although Bruce is twenty-five he looks younger and this is mostly due to his boyish height, his unblemished, consistently hairless, stubble-free face, his crop of thickish, fashionably cut blond hair, and since he does a lot of drugs he's thinner than he probably should be but in a good way and he has a dignity that most of the men I know don't have, will never have. He disappears up ahead. I follow him into some new world now: cactus, elephants, more strange birds, huge reptiles, rocks, Africa. A gang of Hispanic boys roams aimlessly, following us, playing hooky but probably not and I check my watch to verify that I will be missing my one o'clock class.

We met at a wrap party at the studio. Bruce came up to where I was standing, offered me a glass of ice and said, "You look like Nastassja Kinski." I stood there, mute, made a concentrated effort that lasted nine seconds to decode this gesture. Three weeks into the affair I found out he was married and I cursed myself miserably that whole afternoon and night after he told me this at Trumps one Friday before he had to fly to Florida for the weekend. I didn't recognize the signs that accompany an affair with a married man since basically in L.A. there aren't any. After I found out, it made sense and things totally came together but by then it was "too late." A gorilla is lying on its back, playing with a branch. We are standing far away yet I can smell it. Bruce moves on to a rhinoceros.

"They like to be here," he says, staring at a rhinoceros that lies immobile, on its side, and that I'm pretty sure is not alive. "Why wouldn't they like it?"

"They were captured," I say. "They were put into cages."

By the giraffes, lighting another cigarette, making a wise-crack about Michael Jackson, Bruce says, "Don't leave me."

This is what he said when British *Vogue* offered me a ridiculously well-paying job that I was not capable of doing and that my stepmother arranged and that, in retrospect, I should have taken and he said it again before he left me that weekend for Florida, he said "Don't leave me" and if he hadn't made the request I would have left but since he did, I stayed, both times.

"Well," I murmur, carefully rubbing an eye.

All the animals look sad to me, especially the monkeys, who mill around unenthusiastically, and Bruce makes a comparison between the gorillas and Patti LaBelle and we find another refreshment stand. I pay for his hamburger because he doesn't carry cash. We got into the zoo today because of a friend's membership Bruce had borrowed. When I asked him what kind of person would have a membership to the zoo, Bruce silenced me with a soft kiss, a touch, a small squeeze on the back of my neck, offered me a Marlboro Light. Bruce hands me a receipt. I pocket it. A newly married couple with an infant sit at a table next to ours. The couple make me nervous because my parents never took me to a zoo. The baby grabs at a french fry. I shudder.

Bruce takes the meat patty off the bun and eats it, ignoring the bread since he considers it unhealthy, "bad for me."

Bruce never eats breakfast, not even on days he works out, and he's hungry now and he chews loudly, gratefully. I nibble on an onion ring, giggling to myself, and he will not talk about us today. It crosses my mind, stays, starts melting, that there is no impending divorce from Grace.

"Let's go," I say. "See more animals."

"Mellow out," he says.

We move past uselessly proud llamas, a tiger we can't see, an elephant that looks as if it has been beaten. This is a description hanging by the side of the cage of something called a bongo: "They are seldom seen because of their extreme shyness and the markings on their sides and back make them blend into the shadows." Baboons strut around, acting macho, scratching themselves brazenly. Females pick pathetically at the males' fur, cleaning them.

"What are we doing here?" I ask. "Bruce?"

At some point Bruce says, "Are we as far back as we can get?"

I'm staring at what I think are ostriches. "I don't know if we are," I say. "Yes."

"No, we're not," he calls out, walking ahead.

I follow him to where he stops, staring at a zebra.

" 'The zebra is truly a magnificent-looking animal,' " he reads from a description hanging next to the habitat.

"It looks very . . . Melrose," I say.

"I get the feeling an adjective just escaped you, baby," he says.

A child suddenly appears at my side and waves at the zebra.

"Bruce," I start. "Did you tell her?"

We move to a bench. It has become overcast but it's still hot and windy and Bruce smokes another cigarette and says nothing.

"I want to talk to you," I say, grabbing his hands, squeezing them, but they lie there limply, lifeless in his lap.

"Why do they give some animals big cages and some not?" he wonders.

"Bruce. Please." I start crying. The bench has suddenly become the center of the universe.

"The animals remind me of things I can't explain," he says.

"Bruce." I choke.

I swiftly move a hand up to his face, touching his cheek gently, pressing.

He takes my hand and pulls it away from him and holds it between us on the bench and he quickly tells me, "Listen— my name is Yocnor and I am from the planet Arachanoid and it is located in a galaxy that Earth has not yet discovered and probably never will. I have been on your planet according to your time for the past four hundred thousand years and I was sent here to collect behavioral data which will enable us to eventually take over and destroy all other existing galaxies, including yours. It will be a horrible month, since Earth will be destroyed in increments and there will be suffering and pain on a level your mind will never be able to understand. But you will not experience this demise firsthand because it will occur in Earth's twenty-fourth century and you will be dead long before that. I know you will find this hard to believe but for once I am telling you the truth. We will never speak of this again." He kisses my hand, then looks back at the zebra and at the child wearing a CALIFOR-NIA T-shirt, still standing there, waving at the animal.

On the way out we find the gibbons. It's as if they appear from nowhere, materializing for Bruce only. I have never seen a gibbon before and I don't particularly want to see one now, so it's basically a rather unilluminating experience. I sit on another bench and wait for Bruce, the sun beating down through haze, breaking it up, swirling it around, and it dawns on me that Bruce might not leave Grace and it also dawns on me that I might fall in love with someone else and I might even leave college and head for England or at least the East Coast. A lot of things might keep me away from Bruce. In fact, the odds look pretty good that something will. But I can't help it, I think to myself as we leave the zoo and get back into my red BMW and he starts it up, I have faith in this man.

VINTAGE CONTEMPORARIES

WHERE I'M CALLING FROM
by Raymond Carver

The summation of a triumphant career from "one of the great short-story writers of our time—of any time" (*Philadelphia Inquirer*).   0-679-72231-9

THE HOUSE ON MANGO STREET
by Sandra Cisneros

Told in a series of vignettes stunning for their eloquence—the story of a young girl growing up in the Latino quarter of Chicago.

"Cisneros is one of the most brilliant of today's young writers. Her work is sensitive, alert, nunceful . . . rich with music and picture."—Gwendolyn Brooks
0-679-73477-5

ELLEN FOSTER
by Kaye Gibbons

The story of a young girl who overcomes adversity with a combination of charm, humor, and ferocity.

"Ellen Foster is a southern Holden Caulfield, tougher perhaps, as funny . . . a breathtaking first novel."   —Walker Percy
0-679-72866-X

NOTHING BUT BLUE SKIES
by Thomas McGuane

This high-spirited novel, chronicling the fall and rise of Frank Copenhaver, is set in a Montana where cowboys slug it out with speculators, a cattleman's best friend may be his insurance broker, and love and fishing are the only consolations that last.

"So sizable in vision and execution, so funny, so tragically and truly about America . . . that one is moved to stand and applaud."   —*Boston Globe*
0-679-74778-8

THE JOY LUCK CLUB
by Amy Tan

"Vivid . . . wondrous . . . what it is to be American, and a woman, mother, daughter, lover, wife, sister and friend—these are the troubling, loving alliances and affiliations that Tan molds into this remarkable novel." —*San Francisco Chronicle*

"A jewel of a book."   —*The New York Times Book Review*
0-679-72768-X

VINTAGE CONTEMPORARIES